THE CHRONICLE KEEPER

EARTH'S GUARDIAN SERIES ~ BOOK ONE

WREN KINGSLEY

First Published May 2023
ISBN 979-8-9883102-0-4 (paperback)
ISBN 979-8-9883102-1-1 (ebook)
ASIN: B0C43VHST5 (Amazon)

Book cover and formatting by
Uniquely Tailored Publishing
Editing by Lynn Post

Published by Wren Kingsley
32577 Co. Rd. 3
Crosslake, MN 56442

authorwrenkingsley.com

PRAISE FOR THE CHRONICLE KEEPER

Wren Kingsley is a talented writer whose debut novel, The Chronicle Keeper— an adventure-filled story with lots of clever plot twists and an intriguing story line— will leave readers wanting more. Don't miss the first book of her Earth's Guardian series; you won't be disappointed!

– Lynn Post, Editor

The Chronicle Keeper is the beginning of Aislin's epic journey to find a woman called Destiny and to discover her own true identity. The Chronicle Keeper is an intriguing book that promises the Earth's Guardian Series will be a captivating adventure. Highly recommended!

– Pax Sinclair, Author

I loved it! The descriptions are fantastic and the book will have you turning the page until the very end. I can't wait to read the second book!

– Mary Dye, Beta-Reader

I normally find myself reading heavy fantasy novels, but The Chronicle Keeper, with a moderate element of fantasy, sparked my interest. I liked the characters, especially Aislin's organic character, and never found myself bored with the story. I look forward to reading the second book.

– Nemo Lockeheart, Author

"I found Wren to be a very engaging author. She did a great job of telling the story through two sets of eyes one chapter at a time."

– Tim Kulseth, Reader

CONTENTS

CONTENTS

. CONTENTS .

. Chapter Fifteen .

. Chapter Sixteen .

. Chapter Seventeen .

. Chapter Eighteen .

. Chapter Nineteen .

. Chapter Twenty .

. Chapter Twenty-One .

. CONTENTS .

. *Chapter Twenty-Two* .

CHAPTER ONE

. ESCAPE .
AISLIN

Curled beneath a ratty blanket, frigid wisps of damp air seep through and grip my body. In the stillness, I clamp my jaw, keeping my teeth from rattling, but it only causes the pounding in my head to become more violent. As I lay half-awake, where reality and dreams blur together, I hear the faint echo of footsteps and smell the homie aroma of the Croatian Iris.

"Shhh...you don't want to wake her."

Darkness swallows me as I slowly open my eyes. The moonlight filtering in through the tiny, carved out hole in the wall makes it difficult to focus on my surroundings. One thing is certain; I wasn't home.

"I don't understand what the big fuss is about. I mean, compared to everyone else *she* drags here, she seems pretty normal."

My breathing hitches, and I cover my mouth, slightly choking on my saliva. The whispering and quiet shuffling of feet continue outside the room. I remain silent, hoping whoever they are, leave.

"Amelia, quiet! We can get in trouble for being here."

"Nonsense. Who comes down here, anyway?"

"*She* does."

Goosebumps prick my arms at the eerie, soft-spoken words. I try to push myself into a sitting position. Instead, my fingers slip through the holes in the mattress, and my arms buckle beneath my weight. A searing jolt of pain shoots across my side, and I collapse against the bed.

"Ahhhmmmph!" I bite my lip to keep from screaming.

"Did you hear that?"

My facial muscles tighten, creasing my forehead, and my gut twists. The warm liquid slides down my cheek as I pinch my eyes shut.

"Hear what?"

"It sounded like it came from her room."

"Oh, don't be such a sissy, Clarice."

"Hmph."

In the sudden silence, cold, musty air infiltrates my nose while I take a moment to look around. The creamy white walls and floor soak in the moonlight from the makeshift window as I slide my fingers over the granular texture of stone.

No wonder why it's so cold and damp in here. I'm in a cave.

Pulling the blanket under my chin, I spy a hidden chair in the room's corner. A form takes shape on the chair as light creeps in. It takes a moment, but within those moments, my hand reaches to scratch my arm and legs and I realize I'm in my underwear. The heat rises in my cheeks and my pulse is on fire.

Oh, this isn't good. Those are my clothes!

I purse my lips with determination, eyeing the distance to the chair. It can't be more than twenty steps. Careful to roll onto my good side, I attempt to sit up when the sharp clicking of heels against the stone floor steals my attention. My muscles stiffen and any communication between my body and my brain freeze. My side pulses as I try to remain still and listen.

"What do you two think you're doing? Hmmm?" A woman's voice cuts through the silence, rendering Amelia and Clarice speechless. "Get back to your rooms before I have you thrown into the chamber. Hurry, before I change my mind."

I imagine the woman looking down her nose at the two younger girls, with her piercing gaze and aristocratic posture. I hear Amelia and Clarice's footfalls scurrying down the hallway, leaving me to wonder what my fate will be.

What if she opens the door and finds me awake?

The wait is torturous. Butterflies swirl around in my stomach as I wait for the door to fly open. The weight on my chest makes it hard to breathe.

How long does she plan on standing outside my door? What is she waiting for?

Then, just as she came, the echo of her heels fade, ricocheting off the corridor walls. That was too close for comfort. In the stillness that follows, I take a deep breath, and my shoulders relax as I exhale. The beating against my chest steadies, and I feel anxiety leave my body. I look at my clothes on the chair and a new challenge presents itself. Retrieving my clothes will not be easy.

Come on, Aislin. You got this.

I take one last breath and grit my teeth, rolling onto my side. I brace my elbow against the flimsy mattress and push myself into a sitting position. My face scrunches as a single tear slides down my cheek, but my pain is no longer a shock.

I push the ratty blanket aside and stare at the blood-stained gauze wrapped around my abdomen, unsure if I should scream or cry. Or maybe both. With trembling fingers, I reach down to touch the dressing as the room begins to spin. My hand snaps back and I close my eyes, swallowing hard against the acid threatening to burn my throat.

What happened? Where am I?

I inhale a heavy breath and place my feet on the cold stone floor. A shiver runs up my spine and already I am feeling defeated. Arms shaking, I'm not sure I trust my strength as I push myself up onto legs of jelly. With each step, I grapevine around the room, bracing myself against the wall and biting my lip to muffle my agony induced cries. I finally reach the chair and take a minute to rest. The unrelenting pulse in my head and side refuse to stop, and I cringe as I slip on my top. The piney and earthy aroma, with a hint of citrus, tickles my nose.

Hops.

I remember the smell but can't place where from.

Strange.

Frustrated, I pull on my pants and hiking boots. It's like someone erased almost every memory from the past couple of days.

My messenger bag leans against the back of the chair, and I reach out to brush my fingertips over the coarse burlap. A twine and lace rose embellishment adorn the front flap. The nostalgia of the day I finished weaving it is bitter.

The fifth anniversary after losing my parents to the war.

The back of my hand becomes wet as I wipe it across my cheek. I reach out and snatch the bag, searching for an old ornate locket. It was the last thing my mother gave me before everything changed.

Where is it? It has to be here. Where else would I have left it?

In a last attempt, I flip my bag upside down, sending its contents scattering across the floor. The clattering of miscellaneous things makes me cringe.

Perfect.

I bite my lip and hold my breath, squeezing my eyes shut. Anxiously, I wait for the wooden door to slam against the cavernous wall. But when it doesn't, I let go of a heavy sigh and kneel. The locket had to be here somewhere.

Among the scattered items, my gaze lands on a picture of my eighth birthday. We're looking at the cake, laughing at something my dad said. The picture reminds me of simpler times when life wasn't dictated by one government.

A crooked half-smile pokes at the corners of my mouth as I flip the photo over. My mother was notorious for leaving me messages on the back of photos. But unfortunately, I had only recovered a handful of them. This photo mum dated September twenty-first, two-thousand-and-eighteen. Her scribbled message read:

With a rose come thorns,
like life comes death,
but even in death,
there is life.

I stare at the note, trying to understand what she meant. She was always writing in riddles and sometimes spoke in riddles, too. But this riddle is personal, like she's warning me of things to come. I hold the picture as I continue looking for my locket, but it's not here among the scattered items.

Where is it? It has to be here; it just has to be.

The locket had been a special gift from my mother. And now it's gone. I rub my eyes, feeling my chest swell and compress simultaneously. My heart aches as I open my bag to clean up the mess. But at the bottom, snagged in the corner, is my locket. Stifling a squeal of delight, a neatly folded piece of paper attached to my locket catches my attention. Addressed to me, I stare at it, leery.

Who is it from? How do they know I'm here? Where is here anyway?

Curiosity wins out, and I hesitantly reach for the note. It crinkles against the deafening silence as I unfold it. The message is brief.

If you want answers, come and find me.
—Destiny

Heavy footfalls accompany the echo of heels on stone. Then her voice and a male's steal my attention. I shove the note into my pocket and quickly sweep the rest of my things back into the bag.

The moonlight illuminates one escape route and my body shutters at the thought of squeezing through the tiny hole in the wall. The other option is through the door.

"Her surgery went well. She can start her training within the next couple of days." The male's voice, although authoritative, sounds distant and impartial, like he really doesn't care about his patients.

"Glad to hear that, doctor. We have confirmed she is the chosen one, and need her in prime condition." Her voice is hard to mistake; she is the lady from earlier.

A gut-wrenching feeling claws at me. Suddenly, I feel nauseous and more petrified than when she first stood outside my door. I grab the rickety wicker chair and place it beneath the hole, knowing what I have to do. The clang of metal-on-metal snaps my attention toward the door. I say a quick prayer; it's now or never.

I take a tight hold of the shoulder strap and breathe deep before carefully climbing onto the chair, avoiding the worn center. Unsure of how high up I am from the ground; I slip my bag through the hole and hold on tight. My jaw clenches as I pull myself up through the tiny opening.

"We have waited too long already for anything to happen to her." The door unlocks and swings open. My throat constricts with panic, and I feel my wound split open as I wiggle through the hole. A shattering cry escapes my lips.

"Don't let her escape!" Her sharp words are like ice, and I feel myself freeze in terror. Spindly fingers slip around my ankle and quickly tighten, pulling me back into the room.

"Ahhh!" My side scrapes against the stone, staining it with my blood. My vision blurs, but I can't give up. Not now. Not when I am close to escaping and finding answers to my questions. I kick with newfound strength and feel my foot connect with my assailant's head. A grunt echoes behind me, and his grip slackens. I make a dire push through the hole, taking the only opportunity I may have.

"No!" The women's shriek follows me out the tiny opening as I fall and land hard in a patch of thorny bushes. I feel my lungs deflate as I gasp for air, while millions of tiny thorns stab my side.

"Well, don't just stand there, you imbecile! Call for the

hounds!"

The vibration of the door slamming shut shakes the earth beneath me and then the howl of her hounds split the night silence. Salty tears saturate my face and tease my tongue. I close my eyes and count to three as I slowly get to my knees before standing on shaky legs. I place my hand over my wound, and the sticky feeling of blood on my fingers leaves me dizzy. Trying to get my bearings, I look for a safe place to hide. Beyond the field, a dense forest looms ahead.

That's my destination.

The baying of hounds drowns all hope I have. Adrenaline pumps through my veins. Slinging my bag over my head, I make a mad dash for the forest. My ears are ringing with nothing but howls of terror. My lungs are burning hot, and my heart is about to burst from my chest.

What if I don't make it? What will happen to me?

Don't think that. You can do it!

The ground rumbles beneath me. Terrified, I go against my better judgment and glance behind me.

What the hell are those!?

With each stride, the four-legged beasts gain ground, the earth trembling in their wake. Weak and tired, the tall grass ensnares my feet, and my face plants into the ground. The bitter taste of grass permeates my taste buds. Getting up is useless, even though I am so close. My side throbs and I feel fresh blood trickle down my side.

What is going to happen to me?

I can almost feel the hot breath of the monstrous hounds on my neck as a wave of darkness passes over. I close my eyes and shiver against the warmth of the night, while blades of grass stick to my skin and earth's gravity pulls me harder into the ground.

Suddenly, a yelp from one hound pierces the night. Scared and confused, I open my eyes in time to see an ungodly beast crumple next to me. I watch his snarling maw go limp in one gust of air before his menacing eyes go void. His mangy fur dances in the light breeze, and it all seems a bit too poetic. I want to scream, but I can't. Any energy I had is gone.

Its companion snarls, sharp white fangs under the moonlight. Evil silver eyes lock on something behind me, hidden in the forest. Then, within two shakes of its head, the hound reluctantly retreats.

I can't fight off the dark void of unconsciousness, but before it takes me, I promise myself one thing; I will find this Destiny person if it is the last thing I do.

Then everything goes black.

. RESCUE .

NOLAN

He sneers, "Yer mum is no bedder than the rest of 'em."

"Take it back, Harvey." I level my eyes at him. No one talks about my mum that way. Not even a drunk Harvey.

"Wha? It's da truth! Didn't ya know?"

My fist rattles on the bar counter on contact and I imagine it's his face. The pint glass rattles against the wooden countertop, and his eyes narrow at me. "I paid for that der drink!" He cradles the pint glass as if to protect it from spilling. I wish it had.

"Ya, she slept with…." But he doesn't get another word in before I jump over the counter, and his stout body thumps against the tavern floor.

"Nolan!" Greyson's warning echoes across the bar, but I only see red.

Before I can pummel him into his grave, fingers dig into my side, prying me off a laboring Harvey. His bloodied face taunts me, warping into a gleeful sneer. I wrench myself free, seething. Knuckles white; he's lucky I don't take a cheap shot at him. Instead, I snatch my hunting gear behind the bar counter before storming out of the tavern.

Red clouds my vision as I weave boldly against the flow of traffic, slipping through a narrow passage between the farrier's and welder's shop and into the forest. Only there will I find sanctum from the tavern's gossip and venison for the tavern's dinner special tomorrow, per Greyson's request.

Within the refuge of the forest, I take a deep inhale and sigh. My shoulders sag, and my lungs no longer burn from laboring breaths. The solitude of the forest brings me peace and sanity.

No longer stiff, my easy-going stride takes me down a worn game trail. It's the only safe passage through the dense vegetation of the forest and leads me to a small clearing. Amiable water laps at some boulders protruding from the surface of a nearby brook. An old sycamore maple branches out across the brook at the edge of the clearing, providing a nice shady spot to rest and quench my thirst. My weight shifts and I make my way over to the tree, hoisting my pack, bow, and quiver from my shoulder. I kneel beside the bank and splash a few handfuls of the cool liquid on my face, extinguishing the burning in my cheeks.

As the sun sets, I estimate about four hours of daylight left. I take a few refreshing swigs of water before hefting my things over my shoulder and setting out on the deer trail again.

Each step is deliberate as the trail winds through a large thicket area. It takes some time, but I reach a small glade hidden within the forest's walls. Resting my things against the closet tree, I grasp my bow with steady hands and wait amidst the serenity of the forest.

It doesn't take long before a roar like sound emits from

the forest's depths, breaking the stillness. Although a familiar sound, I'm always left feeling humbled by his presence. My gaze lands upon the magnificent stag emerging from the trees. His reddish hide glistens, and his omniscient gaze holds mine. I almost lay aside my bow as we both share an understanding. But with feather-like precision, my instincts kick in, and in one swift motion, I nock the arrow and aim the sight pin. I hold my position and exhale against the fletching before letting the arrow sail across the glade, striking him true.

Branches snap as he bounds out of sight while I wait for him to bleed out. The grass rustles beneath my boots, and at first, the trail is cold. I follow broken twigs directing my path for a while before pools of bright red blood lead me to his lifeless form. Resting in a small clearing, the last of the sun's rays blanket him in a heavenly light.

I work efficiently to peel the hide, remove the organs, and then quarter the meat. My muscles twitch as I try not to dwell on the village folklore of ghosthounds roaming these parts. A monstrous black dog-like creature conjures up in my mind and I fumble with the meat, working a little quicker to pack it up.

A howl echoes through the forest as I slip the last of the meat into my pack. The leaves flutter with the nightly breeze, and I feel my blood run cold. The cry of the hunt sends a chill down my spine, and the hair on my arms stands on end.

Ghosthounds.

I find myself rooted and attentive to the next cry. I am about to leave quickly and quietly when curiosity strikes. With little known about ghosthounds, and their presence in Korana becoming more prevalent, the village can benefit from my investigation. But at what cost? If I involve myself, I will be their next target.

Do I want that?

I am about to continue on my way when I feel a tug on my conscious. The next howl reverberates through the forest and down my bones.

A tiny prickle of guilt enters my subconscious, and I run a hand over my face. I find a secure place to leave the deer meat, and take my bow and quiver, following the ghosthounds' cry against my better judgment. Deeper into the forest I head, which becomes unknown territory to me. *Private Property* and *No Trespassing* signs litter the trees. I hesitate as a vast field with a massive complex off in the distance becomes somewhat visible. A heavy breath fills my lungs as I make my way to where the forest meets the meadow when I see her.

The moonlight illuminates her fragile body. But her wild movements look jerky, like she's favoring her right side. I can't quite make out her expression, but the rumble of the Earth beneath my feet terrifies even me. It's then that I lock eyes on the two ghosthounds making chase. They are enormous, nothing like the bedtime stories we are told as children. Is it even possible to have such a monster look hideous and terrifyingly captivating?

I watch the girl take a sudden dive, eating a mouthful of grass and dirt. Mere seconds pass as I draw a silver arrow and aim it at the nearing ghosthounds. A piercing howl of pain rings in my ears as the arrow strikes true, and I watch the massive beast crash, sliding to a halt beside the girl. Its companion slides to a halt, its ebony fur ripples in the breeze, and he shakes his massive head, glaring at me with fiery blue eyes. My spine straightens and becomes rigid as I stand my ground, terrified he will charge me. But his weight shifts imperceptibly to his hind paws before he pivots, turning back to the compound.

Throwing aside my bow and quiver, I sprint toward the girl, leaping over field mounds and pocket holes. I kneel beside her, stroking a piece of hair from her face. Underneath the dirt, I see her fair complexion.

"Don't worry. You're safe now. Let's get you out of here."

Careful not to disturb any potential wound she may have; I slip my arms beneath her limp body and stand. I take one last look at the fallen beast. He is almost triple my size. There is no telling the damage those ghosthounds can do.

Questions swarm through my head as I hurry back to the safety of the forest, where I retrieve my bow, quiver, and the meat. It's going to be a long night with no sleep.

Great.

What did I get myself into?

CHAPTER TWO

. FIRST IMPRESSIONS .
AISLIN

I wake to songbirds and a strange rustling nearby. Fog clouds my head, and my body aches terribly, but I don't dare move. A small groan escapes my lips before I pry my eyes open. Then the rustling stops and a blurry figure fills my vision.

"Good morning." His voice is smooth and sweet.

I nod in reply, afraid to speak. In response, the figure disappears, and the rustling resumes. It feels like a boulder plowed me over. I bet I look worse than I feel. Although, I don't know how that is possible. Then, fragments of last night fill my head and the ominous void of the hound's eyes startles me. I throw myself back against a tree trunk, but a familiar sharp pain shoots across my right side, stopping any further effort to sit up. My hand wanders to my side, where I feel the soft fabric of a fresh bandage. The heat in my cheeks flares up.

Did he change it?

Was I naked and unconscious when he did?

"Here, let me help." I watch his blurry figure come closer and try to shrink back.

"Who the hell are you? And what do you want with me?" My voice squeaks with uncertainty and anger.

Slowly, my vision comes to, and I can focus on my surroundings. The green treetops overhead billow lightly in the breeze. To my left, steady wisps of smoke waft toward the sky, and the smell of meat cooking tickles my nose. Finally, the blurry figure takes shape.

I grab the nearest thing I can reach and point a scrawny stick in his direction. He stops and holds his hands up in peace.

"I'm Nolan." The deep but light raspiness of his voice makes my heart flutter. "I saved you from those ghosthounds last night."

Nolan. The name fits him. But I am still suspicious and watch his steady and confident stride slowly close the distance between us. As he kneels beside me, I flinch. But he gently lends his hand, bracing me with his other. I slowly feel my muscles relax, and he has me comfortably leaning against the tree in no time.

"It was *you. You're* the reason that hound is dead." The memory of the beast's fur ruffling in the night air floods my memory. Cringing, I intake a sharp breath and cry out, holding my side.

"Here, let me get you something for the pain." A few strands of dark chestnut hair fall over his eyes as he moves to retrieve his bag. It's hard not to stare at his athletic physique and blush when he turns to look at me.

"What are you getting?" I avoid his gaze and look at some wildflowers.

"It's homemade turmeric and ginger tea. It should help with the pain and if there is any inflammation." I turn my gaze back to him with a raised brow, and he gives a soft chuckle. "I dabble in herbs and keep an emergency supply on hand."

"What for?" I lean forward, despite the searing pain in my side.

"Among many things, I hunt alone. And it's nice to be prepared for uncertainties." He nods in my direction. I'm not sure exactly how to respond, but I'm sure my heated cheeks speak volumes.

I watch him, with practiced care, boil the tea and tend to the sizzling meat. I almost forget how hungry I am until I feel drool slide down the corner of my mouth. The potent fragrance coming from the cooking causes my stomach to grumble in protest, but if Nolan heard it, he doesn't let on. He looks peaceful and right at home here out in the woods. He finishes the tea and pours it into a thermos, then dishes up some meat.

"Here you go. I can't promise it tastes good, but it will help with the pain." He hands me the thermos and I take a sip, sputtering out the hot liquid. His attempt at holding back a laugh causes him to snort and I have to bite my lower lip to keep from making a snide comment.

The mixture of earthy bitterness and spicy sweetness churns my stomach. I plug my nose with my free hand, resolving to drink what I can of the tea. Momentary bursts of muffled laughter reach my ears and I wish I could pummel him.

I set down the empty thermos and can feel the warm tingling sensation of the tea course through me. Out of the corner of my eye, I see him wiping his eyes with his shirt and feel steam leave my ears.

"Are you crying because you're laughing at me?"

He hesitates before he looks up at me, guilty.

"Sorry, that's insensitive of me. But…it's just…" He bites the inside of his mouth to keep quiet.

"Fine, laugh for all I care. But karma will come back to bite you." I cross my arms over my chest and all I feel is a dull ache.

At least the tea is working.

With my pain sedated, I want to launch an attack on him. But I think better of it, not wanting to risk splitting open my cut again.

He reaches for the plate of meat and hands it to me. "I hope you like venison." I eye it and him with suspicion. "Consider it a peace offering. Please?"

I reach over and grab a few pieces, popping them into my mouth before snatching the plate from his hand. The tea scorched my mouth, so I don't feel the burning sensation from the venison on my tongue. A gamey and semi-sweet earthy smell mixes with the tangy, sweet, resinous aroma of the juniper berries. I just wish I could taste it.

As I shove another piece in my mouth, I sneak a peek at him. He has a strong jawline, and his facial expression is a mixture of what, I can't say. We are silent as we finish our breakfast. The birds and the rest of the critters continue their chatter, filling the silence. It's a pleasantly surprising relaxant. Something I don't remember enjoying for quite a while.

"So…"

I look up from my plate and squirm uncomfortably under his silver gaze. My stomach does a little nervous flip-flop as I try to act normal.

So...what? I wonder.

"Do you have a name?"

I hesitate for a moment. Although Nolan helped me, I'm still wary of him and his intentions. Why is he out here, anyway? We had to be miles from the nearest town or village. But he had saved my life, so I owe him at least my name, right?

"Ais..." My voice croaks. Embarrassed, I clear my throat and try again. "My name is Aislin." There, that's better.

"Well, Aislin, I am happy to see you have an appetite for my cooking." I feel a smile twitch at the corner of my mouth and watch his smile turn into a humorous one.

"Well, the tea did burn my taste buds..." I throw a half smirk his way.

"Hey now, it's not my fault you chugged the hot tea." He raises his hands in defense and lightly chuckles. I snort, but grab my side and, gasping for air, pinch my eyes shut.

Gosh, that hurts.

"Hey now, take it easy." His tone is soft as he sits down next to me. "I don't want to have to change that bandage again." Half-smiling, I keep my eyes closed, focusing on ridding the pain and keeping the tears at bay. I sense him wanting to ask what happened, but he doesn't push for answers, and I relax a little.

"Thanks," I mutter under my breath.

"You're welcome." Instead of a very awkward moment, two cute dimples form at the corner of his mouth and his eyes twinkle before he attends to packing up the campsite.

Despite the dull ache, I stand up using the log beside me. I smile to myself from the awkward accomplishment and lean over to pick up his sleeping bag, but stop midway. I hate feeling so helpless.

"Don't worry. I got it."

He's beside me before I can blink away the stray tear that slides down my cheek. But he's too focused on his sleeping bag and doesn't see it. Thankful for the distraction, I don't want to appear any weaker than I already feel.

"Do you know where my bag is?" I glance around the campsite, suddenly panicking. My locket was in my bag, along with all my other belongings, and if I lost them...I didn't even want to think about it.

"Oh, let me get it. I put it with my stuff."

I follow him to the pile he has created and pick up his bow. "How long have you been bow hunting?"

I lose him in thought when his eyes fix on the bow. "I remember taking archery lessons as a kid. But it wasn't until the government confiscated all the guns during the war that I started using my bow to hunt for food."

I nod. Everyone has their own story of the Blackout War. A war started by a global EMP that left the world to defend themselves in the dark. Conspiracy theorists went crazy with new ideas about a one world order coming into power. But even those who lived off the grid had been affected.

The blackout lasted years before the one world government came into power. It was a false sense of security everyone needed and everyone clung to. Even I fell for it. We were all looking for that silver lining. A ray of hope that things would and could get better.

It didn't take the government long before they gained control over every continent, turning Antarctica into the new Alcatraz. Fear was their mode of control, and it worked.

Anyone found resisting the government disappeared and word soon got out about the New Alcatraz. The missing persons list got shorter and shorter until the names of the people missing were just a whisper on your lips.

"I remember my parents using their cell phones to take pictures and videos of our family vacations. But now, all I have left are a couple of pictures of us and the locket my mother gave me before she disappeared." I avoid mentioning the note from Destiny. I don't know how much I can trust him. Even if he saved my life from the hounds.

"Thank you for getting my bag," I add, slipping the locket around my neck.

He nods before gesturing towards the worn path. "We should get going. It's a good hike from here and Greyson needs this meat by lunch."

"Where are we headed?" I fall in step behind him, enjoying the cool morning.

"The Old Tavern. My brother Greyson and I own it." His strides are long, making it challenging to keep up.

"And where exactly is this tavern?" I trip over unsecure twigs and thank my lucky stars he doesn't look back.

"In a small village on the Korana River."

"I've heard of it, but never been there." I step over a large fallen tree and feel my pants snag on a broken branch. "Ouch."

"Are you okay?" He stops and turns to me. Grimacing, I rub my thigh but nod.

That means I am close to home. Hope fills me for the first time in a while, but when I turn back to follow Nolan, he is nowhere in sight.

"Nolan!" I turn around in circles, feeling lightheaded, fighting the urge to dart off the beaten path. The potent fragrance of resin sticks to my tongue as I desperately seek him out.

"There you are," I scream as a hand reaches out and grips my shoulder. Spinning around, I come face-to-face with Nolan.

"Don't ever sneak up on me like that again." My heart is racing, and I can feel my blood pulse through my veins.

He lifts my chin to meet his gaze. "Sorry." I nod, finding it near impossible not to accept his apology. He pulls back his hand, smiling, and turns back to the trail. I bring my fingers to my chin, where it has grown cold without the warmth from his hand.

Come on, Aislin. Pull yourself together.

"So...does this tavern of yours have showers?" I fall back in line, trying to pay better attention this time.

A soft chuckle floats back to me. "Yes, I suppose you will need one. Maybe some clothes and a place to stay, too?" My nose scrunches with uncertainty at his mockery or seriousness.

"That would be nice." I hold my breath and watch Nolan's head bob, exhaling with relief. I feel grimy and probably look like a bum. But that shouldn't warrant him the right to make fun of my situation, either.

"We will stop by a little clothing boutique before heading home."

"Home?" My face wrinkles in confusion. I thought he needed to get to the tavern... Instead, he chuckles softly, shaking his head.

"Home is The Old Tavern. It also acts as an inn. We have

some spare rooms if you need a place to stay awhile."

"Oh," I didn't expect his home to be the tavern.

"Isn't that weird?"

"Isn't what weird?"

"Living at the tavern with all your guests?"

There's a slight pause, "no, not really. Watch out!" I look up just in time to duck under an oncoming branch. My brows knead together, and my jaw tightens. Was that done on purpose? I decided to not call him out on it. Not worth wasting my energy over.

"Well, maybe one night."

"Huh?"

I shake my head and repeat, "I'm taking you up on your offer to stay at the tavern. Only one night, though," I keep my plans to find Destiny to myself. I don't need him thinking I am crazy. Because I am not. And because I don't care what others think of me.

"Oh!? Okay, great." His tone rises a bit in surprise, but other than that, he plows on ahead.

The corner of my lip twitches upward, and I watch him for a moment, debating if I should dig out the note or not. But when he doesn't look back, I reach deep into my bag and dig the note out. I pay extra attention this time as I follow Nolan through the forest.

Despite hauling his backpack, bow, and quiver, he moves gracefully and almost without a sound. Maybe that is a trait you learn as a hunter? I wonder as I try to keep up while mulling over Destiny's note at the same time.

If you want answers, come and find me.
-Destiny

Finally, with the note committed to memory, I focus more on following Nolan and not getting lost this time. The drumming of a woodpecker echoes through the forest, occasionally giving off a long *kweek*. At other times, the sweet warble of a Woodlark sings his song. I would have joined in if circumstances had been different, mimicking the soft lullaby. But I am too self-aware of my company and stay quiet, enjoying the forest music instead.

"Do you have other obligations?"

"Not exactly…" I fidget, not knowing the intent of his question.

Not exactly…What kind of response is that?

"Well, either way, you should have dinner at the tavern. Greyson is making his special venison dish. You won't be disappointed."

Even though I can't see him, I can hear the pride in his voice, the way he talked about his brother. It made me smile for a brief moment, wishing for a sibling of my own. Born the only child, life got pretty boring at times. Although, my parents tried to make me happy and spent every waking moment with me they could.

"It sounds wonderful. Thank you for the invitation." I am careful to step over a root as high as my knee. I hear a "you're welcome" as he maneuvers through a thick patch of brush.

The sunlight persistently penetrates the dense canopy, making for a fairytale-like feel. Flowers in all varieties sporadically cover the ground as we continue on the path. I can't help but feel my luck changing.

. SECRETS .

NOLAN

"So, what brings you all the way out here? Do you live around here or something?"

Last night's events still plague me. What did she get herself into? And what was that compound all about? Seeing it for myself, I had to report it to the townsfolk. Extra precautions will now have to be put in place.

"No. Just passing through to visit a friend." Her nonchalant tone doesn't sit well with me, but I nod in acknowledgment.

"Does your friend live around here?" I try to keep my tone light, so it doesn't seem like I'm prying. But I've never been good at conversations with girls.

I don't think she hears me when she responds flatly, "that's none of your business."

Wow, a bit touchy?

I sigh, reining in my emotions. With everything that has happened within the past twenty-four hours, the last thing I want to do is pick a fight with her. At the moment, it didn't seem very wise.

"You're right; it's not. I just thought maybe talking would keep us from getting bored. We still have a long hike." I can't see her, but the tension that had been as thick as smoke lifted. As I breathe in and exhale, my shoulders relax, and my legs don't feel as stiff.

"Sorry, just not in the mood to spill my life story to a stranger yet." There's a hint of sadness in her undertone, so I try to lighten the mood.

"You mean a cute stranger who saved your life?" I jest, keeping my eyes forward to avoid any unwanted stares and to keep from tripping over vines and tree roots.

She snorts, "arrogance and flattery won't get you anywhere."

"Ouch!" I feign rejection, but knowing full well she is right once again. "I'll have you know; it works wonders with the ladies back home."

"The tavern?" She questions incredulously. I scratch my head, wondering if keeping my mouth shut is the better option to keeping my dignity intact.

It's clear that Aislin isn't like the tavern girls. She is sweet, mysterious, down-to-earth, and confident in her own skin. She's not afraid to speak her mind; from what I see, there is no drama.

I'm building up the courage to ask another question when I hear an exaggerated sigh behind me.

"Actually, I'm not sure where they live."

Taken aback by her comment and not sure how to respond, my lengthy pause must have been an invitation to continue on.

"They're not really my friend."

"Not your friend? How is that?" Distracted, a twig snaps under my foot, startling her and me.

Another long pause, but I patiently wait this time.

"I received a note addressed to me. It said if I wanted answers to find Destiny." Reluctant annoyance fills the silence. Internally, my stomach twists at the mention of her name. I hope she is looking for a different Destiny for both our sakes. But, if she is looking for who I think she is, I don't even want to consider the consequences.

I can't stand the awkward lull between us. Stopping to check if she is alright, I'm shoved forward a few steps. I turn and look at her, and she looks away, flushed with fidgeting hands.

Combing my fingers through my tousled hair, I keep my eyes on her, "look, when we get back to the tavern, you can take a nice hot shower, and then you can have dinner and ask around to see if anyone knows this...Destiny person, you are trying to find. Okay?" She nods, but avoids my gaze.

It would be easier to ignore my infatuation if she weren't so attractive. Like the way her silver blonde hair falls against her back or how she stares at me with her ocean gaze. I'm not sure I like this unsettling feeling she gives me.

Not waiting for her to change her mind, I start back down the path towards the road that leads to the village. She remains quiet for the rest of our travels, and I am left to my thoughts. Thoughts that involve a certain person known as Destiny.

I sigh with relief when we break through the grove of trees and step onto the stone-paved road. I take a peek behind me, noting a smile and a sparkle in her eyes. Tomorrow, she would be on her way, and what difference would it be if I never told her where she might find Destiny? Nope, best to keep what I know to myself. For her sake, anyway.

CHAPTER THREE

. THE BOUTIQUE .
AISLIN

As we enter the village, people crowd the streets, and the excitement drowns out my pulsating side. It was a strenuous hike, and my legs wobble like jelly as I follow Nolan. My heart skips a beat as I watch the surrounding activity starry-eyed.

"Fresh fruit! Get your fresh fruit here!" A gravelly voice shouts as we pass by. I'm staring at all the wonderful fruit he has on display but can't look away quick enough, "Miss! How about some freshly picked nectarines? Or maybe a juicy peach to enjoy as you shop?"

Before I can answer, Nolan stops at the old man's, "We'll take two peaches."

"Yes, sir," the man smiles and hands Nolan the fruit and pockets the coins given in exchange.

"Here you go. The best peaches around," Nolan smiles and hands me one. I take a bite, and its juicy liquid slides down my chin. The peach's syrupy nectar is sweet against my taste buds, and I close my eyes with enjoyment.

"Mmmm. This is delicious." I open my eyes in time to see Nolan smile.

"Come on, we still need to find you some clothes, and I have a boutique in mind," his light-hearted enthusiasm was a bit peculiar, but I'm not about to complain. So I follow him down a narrow alleyway.

Flower pots line the stone buildings, while English Ivy drapes from hanging pots, clinging to the building's stone walls. I can't contain my giddiness at the village boutiques. So charming with their colored doors and window planter boxes.

"The clothing boutique is just around the corner." He gestures at the next building and takes a left. I round the corner and stop next to him in front of the third shop. A juliet balcony sits over a turquoise store, and a large window chime made of seashells hangs to the right of the door. Potted Casablanca lilies frame the entryway, and beautiful ornate jewelry is displayed in the window.

"You coming?"

The shop store has a cute circular window, giving the customer a sneak peek into the boutique. He opens the door, gesturing for me to go in first. Smiling my thanks, I head inside.

The shop is overwhelmingly busy with lamps lining the top shelves, an assortment of clothing and shoe racks, and antique tables of various heights arranged with jewelry, perfume, and other miscellaneous female items.

"Hello, can I help you find anything?" A middle-aged brunette woman appears from behind one of the clothing racks. Her hair is busy with blonde streaks, loosely woven braids, and feathers. "Do you like it?" She catches me looking at her hair and I blush with embarrassment.

"Miranda, this is Aislin. Aislin, this is Miranda, a friend of the family."

"Nice to meet you, Aislin. How can I help?" Her voice is rich and smooth. A mellow tone that is pleasant to listen to.

"Well, I'll be doing a lot of traveling and need clothes that will hold up." *Not like yours*. I add, keeping my comment to myself.

Miranda's eccentric Bohemian clothing choice is bold, bright, and colorful with teals, mustard yellows, and burnt reds. Her jeans are torn just above her knees and hug her long, lean legs. To top it off is a gaudy beaded necklace that caresses her neck.

"Oh! I used to travel. Well, that was before the war," she pauses for a moment, the corners of her mouth upturning slightly. But as subtly as her smile comes, it's gone. Miranda looks at me and nods, "follow me."

As I follow her around, weaving through furniture and down narrow aisles, I notice a patchwork area rug. "That's a gorgeous rug. Where did you get it?" There's an uncomfortable silence for a few minutes as she continues draping clothes over her arm.

"During the war, I moved around a lot. There was this gentleman and lady with a handful of soldiers that would ransack every home I settled down in." Miranda cuts off, picking out a couple of hiking boots for me to try. Sighing, she continues toward the back of the boutique, "the patches in the rug you see are remnants of houses I lived in."

The patches are ornate, colored deep red wine, midnight blue, creamy white, and soft black. There is one patch that reminds me of home, but I shake off the feeling.

"Do you know why they ransacked the houses you lived in? Was it just the houses you stayed in?" I stop a few times and marvel at the jewelry displayed on some end tables.

"I was hiding when they came through. But I heard them mention something about looking for a child, whom they called the *chosen one*." Miranda pulls back a curtain to reveal a changing room. But I'm frozen in place. I need to remain alert. I am becoming too comfortable with Nolan letting personal information slip.

"Well, here you go. Let me know if I can grab you anything else." Miranda leaves me in the changing room. Closing the curtain, I'm on autopilot as I change clothes.

The changing room is cozy, with a generous area to move about. There is hanger space for clothes and shelving space to hold anything else. An elaborate wine bottle hangs from its neck by a thick silver chain, illuminating the changing room in a soft amber glow.

What a cute idea.

I slip on a pair of charcoal cargo pants, grimacing as I shift my weight. Slowly peeling off my shirt, I look at my bandaged side. The dressing needs to be changed again.

I hope this doesn't prevent me from looking for Destiny.

I stare at the shirt draped over the chair's back, shivering at the thought of shimmying into it. Although the thermal undershirt is stretchy, I still make painful facial expressions. Finally, I pull down the hem and look at myself in the mirror. A stoic expression reflects back at me with perfect porcelain doll facial features. My chest tightens, and I look away. Every day it gets harder to look at my reflection without seeing my mum in me.

There are a few more clothes, but I find I don't have the strength, physical or mental, to try them on. So, I carefully change back into my old clothes and gather what Miranda has picked for me.

I exit the changing room and catch Miranda and Nolan conversing awfully close. She smiles and leans closer to Nolan, and suddenly I feel hot as I walk up to them. I keep my cool, forcing a smile as I clear my throat.

"I'm ready, Miranda," I say more forcefully than I plan to.

"Oh! Okay, great. Follow me and I'll ring you up," she sends what she thinks is an inconspicuous smile toward Nolan. But Nolan blushes and shrugs his shoulders at me, like he has no clue what is going on.

As if. I roll my eyes and follow Miranda up front; laying the clothes and boots I want on the counter. Suddenly, I remember having no money, and my cheeks flush with warmth. But before I can explain my predicament, she has me all rung in. Nolan appears beside me, handing over some bills to cover the cost. I bite my lip, holding back my tongue.

"Thanks, Miranda," Nolan says, grabbing my bag of clothes.

"It's not a problem." She reaches across the counter and touches Nolan's hand. Then, remembering I'm there, she pulls back and smiles at me. "It was a pleasure meeting you, Aislin. I hope we see each other again."

Over my dead body.

I plaster a smile on my lips, "It was a pleasure to meet you too, Miranda." But I don't return the sentiment of seeing her again.

I'm not jealous. I'm not jealous. But who am I fooling? Of course, I am jealous.

I can't get out of the boutique quick enough and nearly trip over Nolan. I squeeze my eyes shut and clutch my side.

"Easy there. Are you okay?" He asks, resting his hand on

my shoulder.

"I'll be fine. Just give me a moment," I grit under my breath.

"So, is she your girlfriend or something?" I mumble, trying to catch my breath. Nolan's loud snort and monologue chuckle answer my question, but I would still like to hear him say it.

"No. We had a fling for a while. But it ended a few years ago. Why? Are you jealous?" Now it was my turn to snort.

"You wish," I retort, gesturing for him to continue back to the tavern.

"Maybe I do," he answers with a twinkle in his eye. It only infuriates me more, and I refuse to talk the rest of the way. My focus on reaching the tavern is taking a long, hot shower.

Three minutes later, Nolan leads me up to a wooden gate. The tavern is a picturesque view of serenity and beauty. Like the rest of the village, the historical heritage is in its architecture. A white picket fence with its gate set between the rose-covered arbor welcomes us. Little teardrop lights embellish the arbor and glow like tiny stars.

Past the gate is a beautiful garden with paved paths, fountains, and an area designated for fruits, vegetables, herbs, and spices.

They must provide a lot of food to the townspeople.

I follow Nolan as he climbs the wooden steps up to the porch. The porch has a couple of candlelit tables and chairs. He waits for me with a smile before he swings open the door. "Here we are. Home sweet home."

. HOME SWEET HOME .
NOLAN

The door slams open, and the tavern roars with life. Girls with drink trays are squeezing through the throng of people, and Greyson is behind the bar counter filling shot glasses for a group of guys. He looks up for a split second, eyes me, and grins, "Nolan!"

"Grayson!" I shout back over the loud chatter.

I rest my hand against the small of Aislin's back and guide her through the crowd. The tavern aroma is a mix of men's stench, women's perfume, and the smell of alcohol. She tenses beneath my hand, and I give her a gentle squeeze.

"I wasn't expecting it to be so...crowded," Aislin's voice carries over the noise.

"Oh, this is typical. Wait until happy hour comes. Then, you won't even be able to move," I grimace immediately, regretting my response, and keep pushing forward.

Laughter echoes from an alcove booth in the back, separated by a tall wooden slat divider. To the left, centered between two massive windows, is the grandeur of the handcrafted, floor-to-ceiling stone fireplace. A roaring fire blazes hot with sunset flames licking at the dry, thickly chopped logs. For a moment, I watch the flames dance, leaping higher and higher until disappearing into the chimney's height.

"Where are we headed?" She tilts her head back in my direction, and I can't help it as my eyes trace down her neck to her chest. She stares expectantly at me, and I gulp down a load of nerves.

"I have to drop off the deer meat for tonight's dinner special with Robert. Then, I want you to meet Greyson before I show you where you'll be staying." I pull my gaze away from her and focus on where I am going.

We round the other side of the fireplace and slip through a set of swinging aluminum doors into the kitchen. Robert, our chef, is barking out orders as he stands at the range.

"Robert! I have something for you." I weave around the kitchen staff and hand off the heavy bag of deer meat to him.

"Everyone is in for a special treat," he smiles, patting my shoulder and handing the bag to a prep cook.

"Oh, yeah? And what's that?" I ask casually, trying to coax an answer out of him.

He laughs, "Nice try, Nolan. But it looks like your lady friend is getting antsy."

Aislin. Shoot, I forgot. A sheepish smile plasters my face as I turn to see Aislin ready to bolt out the kitchen doors.

"Thanks, Robert. We'll talk later." He is already focusing on the food as I move closer to Aislin. "Sorry about that. I just want to introduce you to my brother, and then I will show you your room. Promise." She rolls her eyes in disbelief.

Suppose I deserve that. Reconnecting my hand on the small of her back, I guide her up to the bar where Greyson is in the middle of taking drink orders.

I pound on the counter. "What does a guy have to do to get some service over here?" My voice carries down the length of the counter, and Grayson looks up.

"Nolan! Be right there," he hands the drink order off to the other bartender on duty, then shuffles over to where Aislin and I are waiting.

"Greyson, I'd like you to meet Aislin. Aislin, this is my brother Greyson," a sense of pride swells in my chest. I don't know why, but Aislin is making me feel emotions I didn't know were possible.

"Why didn't you tell me you were bringing such a beautiful girl home with you, Nolan." Greyson leans over the counter and takes Aislin's hand, bringing it up to his lips; he kisses the back of it gently. And just like that, he pokes my balloon of pride, and my chest deflates. My cheeks burn under his mischievous gaze. He won't get any more of a rise from me.

"It's a pleasure to meet you, Greyson. Nolan speaks highly of you," I watch her naturally blush cheeks darken, "and, of course, he talked about the tavern too." She quickly swallows, drumming her fingers against the counter.

"The pleasure is all mine, Aislin." He smiles before turning his attention to me. "And my venison?"

I roll my eyes, "already with Robert." Grayson nods.

"Well, what can I get you two to drink?" He raises a brow, smirking, "maybe a tequila shot?" Before he can reach for the liquor and a couple glasses, I cut him off.

"No, just give me the key to the suite." I wait patiently

but swallow hard as Greyson's eyes light up, handing me the keys to a room called *Lover's Lane*. Then, tightening my fist around the keys so Aislin can't see, I gently pull her away from the bar and toward the stairs leading to the second floor.

"Wow, talk about a grand staircase." Her hand gently sweeps up the wooden banister.

"Yeah, it's the original staircase." I marvel at the ornate, hand-carved balusters.

"So, how did you and your brother end up with the tavern?" By her tone, I sense her thoughts are elsewhere because she is attempting small talk. I know because I do the same thing. At least, that is what Greyson tells me.

On the surface, it is a harmless question. But the answer to that question digs deep and opens a wound to a past life I don't want to relive. I pull at my shirt collar and wipe my hands repeatedly on my pants. I'm relieved to be behind Aislin, so she doesn't see my reaction.

"When Greyson and I were young, our mother left without saying goodbye and with no goodbye letter. Our dad wasn't exactly the greatest, so the previous owner of the tavern took Greyson and me in under his wing. He taught us everything we know." I watch her nod, and then she turns to face me as we reach the landing.

"Sorry to hear that," our eyes meet, and my chest constricts. I rub the left side of my chest and she asks, "Are you okay?" Her brows knit together as she looks at me, but I wasn't about to tell her she is making my insides twist and churn with want.

"Yeah, I'm fine," I brush past her and stop outside *Lover's Lane* door, "Well, here's the room you can use for the night... or for however long you want," my face scrunches, "I mean, however long you need."

She takes the key I hand her, and if she is aware of the room's name, she doesn't show it. Relieved, I continue, "If you need me and I'm not downstairs, my room is the last room on the left." She nods again but says nothing. "I'll come by just before dinner."

She turns around, and her eyes look glassy. "Sounds good," she says before shutting the door.

I stare at the door longer than I should, too dumbfounded to know what to do next. I am used to girls always craving my attention, but now I am vying for hers. This is a new development that I am not sure I am comfortable with.

I take a few steps back and rest against the corridor wall, contemplating what I did wrong when something jabs me in the back. *Ugh*. Scowling, I feel my bow stab me in the back. I glance one more time at the door, half expecting Aislin to open it. But after a moment, my head droops, shoulders sag, and my lungs expel a breath. I walk to my room and drop off my hunting gear next to my closet. I head downstairs to meet up with Greyson, but hesitate outside Aislin's room for a moment before moving on.

"You're pretty into this Aislin chic, aren't you?"

Greyson and I grab a booth in the back. A server drops off our beers and heads back into the sea of people. I'm silent for a moment, debating how much to share with him. We share everything, but this was different. At least it felt different.

"She isn't like the others I've been with," I start out.

"You mean she isn't like Miranda?" I flinch at the mention

of her name. I hear Greyson sigh and feel the quiver of the table as he sets down his glass. "Look, Nolan, just go for it. It's been what, three years since you and Miranda broke it off. So what's holding you back?" He takes another swig, waiting, staring at me for an answer.

"I don't know," I pause, racking my brain for an answer, "She's just different. Plus, she's leaving in the morning." I throw my head into my hands, breathing deep, trying to calm my racing heart and thoughts.

"That's what you said about Miranda."

"You don't get it," I grit.

"Then tell me, Nolan. What don't I get?" He leans back in the booth and throws his hands up.

I rake my hands through my hair and pull hard. My thoughts won't quit racing, and my heart pounds against my chest harder and harder.

"She's leaving tomorrow in search of...*her*." I can't even bring myself to say Destiny's name. My chest constricts, and I do all I can to just breathe. Greyson is silent, making it feel like we are the only two in the tavern.

"Well, that changes things a bit, doesn't it?" He mumbles, mystified.

I take another breath and rub my temples. "If Aeneas were here, he would know what to do." I chug the last of my beer and leave Greyson to his thoughts. I need to cool off.

CHAPTER FOUR

. LOVER'S LANE .

AISLIN

I feel Nolan's gaze penetrate the door and into my back. My body slides to the floor, knees press against my chest and my head rests against the door as I wait for him to leave. After a few minutes, I hear him shuffle down the hallway and breathe a sigh of relief. Walking into the tavern had been like walking into a brick wall. The feeling of déjà vu left me vulnerable and unable to think. I had clung to Nolan's side for comfort as he led me through the tavern. But now...

I shake my head, trying to free myself of her voice, the clicking of her heels, and the cold, damp room. But closing my eyes only intensifies my memory.

"Her surgery went well. She can start her training within the next couple of days."

"Glad to hear that, doctor. We have confirmed she is the chosen one."

The chosen one. What did that mean?

A laughing couple startles me from my thoughts, and I

wipe the salty liquid from my face. I look around the room, feeling a little more comfortable here. The huge bed is inviting, with fluffy pillows and soft blankets. And although the wooden floor is smooth beneath my hand, the rug separating the bed from the floor looks barefoot-worthy.

I gather my things and set them down on the bed, then enter the bathroom. It is pretty simple, with a full-length mirror stretching the width of the double white vanity, and a separate water closet sits off to the right. A smile brightens my face when I stare at the reflection in the mirror. My eyes trail the detail of the clawfoot tub and the gorgeous floor-to-ceiling shower curtains.

Talk about dramatic.

I turn around to face the tub and trace my fingers along the rim until they reach the chrome faucet handle. Before I turn on the hot water, I double check the drain plug. I busy myself while I wait for the water to fill the tub, combing through the mats in my hair and gingerly stepping out of my soiled clothes.

I step into the tub, shut off the water and submerge myself beneath the surface, letting all my worries and stress dissolve. My side doesn't throb as much, and with a clear conscience, my thoughts run wild...

The aroma of hops infuses my senses as I enter the tavern. I scan the crowds for Anna, but eventually give up and head to the bar, slipping onto an empty stool. I wave the bartender down and smile when he waves back, moving past the other bartender to stand in front of me.

"Hey Ivan, I'll have my usual."

He nods and smiles, "a rum manhattan coming right up." He

mixes my drink but keeps his green eyes on me. "Anything special happening tonight?"

"No, nothing special. Just waiting on Anna so we can have our girl's night." He nods, his blonde hair frozen in place with so much gel that it glistens under the bar lights.

"Hey, is this seat taken?" I am about to answer yes when I see a man with dark features leaning against the bar counter. His espresso eyes slowly draw me in, and I feel myself leaning closer. Anna won't mind.

"It's yours now," I say. He smiles, nodding to the drink Ivan sets in front of me. "That looks interesting," he turns his attention to Ivan, "I'll take one of those." Ivan raises a brow in my direction, and I feel my cheeks flush.

Taking a sip of my drink, I quickly glance sideways and notice a slight scar on his jaw. I'm curious, but ask instead, "so, what brings you to this small-town bar?"

He gives me a mischievous, haunting look before he answers, "I'm looking for the chosen one..."

Coming up for air, I gasp, flailing my arms as I feel for something sturdy to grasp. Water sloshes onto the floor as I try to recollect and calm myself. My heart pounds against my chest, and my veins pulsate as blood races through my body.

What is going on? I don't want to acknowledge that this *chosen one* could be me. I mean, no one has directly told me. But then why chase after me?

I drain the water from the tub and take a quick, cold shower. Too many thoughts run through my head as I step onto the soaked bath mat. Exhausted, I throw some extra towels on the floor to soak up the spilled water and drag myself into the bedroom, flopping onto the bed.

I don't know how much time has passed, but frankly, I don't care. Still overloaded with questions, I keep breathing, but roll over onto my good side and push myself into a sitting position. At this point, I feel hopeless.

Who is Destiny? Who is the chosen one? Why is this happening to me?

Ha! I sarcastically laughed to myself.

"Anything special happening tonight?" Ivan had asked me.

I roll my eyes. *Nope. Nothing.* Except for everything. Before I can start rehashing what has happened, I hear a knock on the door.

"Aislin?"

Shoot.

"Give me a few minutes." When I don't hear an answer, I dart up off the bed and dump my clothes over the comforter. An intricate tulle and lace dress gracefully lands on top of the pile. I brush my fingers over the dress and smile.

Perfect.

Gently, I slip the rose beige dress over my head and let it fall softly, so the thick straps rest against my shoulders. I throw my hair into a loose braid and hesitate a moment before looking at my reflection in the mirror. Afraid things I don't want to remember might come flooding back. But the girl staring back at me seems scared and uncertain.

"Aislin, are you okay?"

I shake my head but answer, "I'm fine. Be out in a minute." Then, taking a deep breath, I apply a light coat of mascara to my lashes and dab a few drops of my favorite fragrance to the nape of my neck. I take one last look at myself in the mirror before walking to the door and opening it to find Nolan resting against the frame.

"I'm ready."

. MEMORIES .
NOLAN

I climb the stairs and walk past Aislin's room. My head pulses and my chest burns from breathing too hard. Too many emotions and thoughts jostle for my attention. Mostly memories I spent half my life trying to forget. And then she shows up and threatens to undo it all.

In the confines of my room, I walk into the bathroom and start the shower. I throw my clothes aside and hope to wash away every memory down the drain. But at the moment, I'm not feeling too confident it will work.

I reach to retrieve my body wash off the sink counter and glimpse my mum's parting gift to me. My thumb hesitates, hovering over the cross-like symbol on my chest. The pull to graze my thumb over the mark is strong. What would happen this time? Would I see her again? Or would I see him? Too weak to resist, I brush my thumb over it and immediately feel a familiar pinch. An unworldly separation of my body leaves my physical form in a frozen like state and my spiritual state drifting. The bathroom becomes distant until I am standing in an entryway.

"Don't leave. What about the boys? What about us?" He reaches for her, but she whips her arm from his grasp.

"My time has come." Her eyes are cold as she stares at him. But when she turns to Greyson and me, her face softens. She hesitates for a moment before kneeling and opening her arms. Greyson and I run to her and wrap her in a big hug. I feel a few warm tears slide against my cheek and I don't know if they belong to her or me.

"My boys," she whispers in our ears. "I will always be with you."

Greyson doesn't know it, but I feel his body tremble as he tries to stay strong for me.

"Please, mum, don't go. Stay," I plead with her.

"Nolan," she pauses, pulling back and pushes my shaggy bangs aside. "My handsome little noble defender of men," she brings her lips to my forehead and kisses me. "Any time you need to see me, just brush your thumb over your chest like this," she says, taking my right thumb and gently guides it over my heart. I flinch at the sudden pinch to my chest and a soft glow lights up the area. But it's gone as quickly as I blink. When I look up to see her, to see if she just experienced the same thing, her face is solemn. But I notice a slight twinkle in her eye. This was our little secret.

I watch her lean over and whisper something in Greyson's ear. He looks at me, but nods at her, promising her whatever she had asked of him. Then she stands up and walks out the door. Never to be heard from again.

I lean against the counter as the vision abruptly ends. There is a sheer film of water droplets covering the mirror and I wonder how much of the hot water I wasted. My skin is clammy and at this point, a cold shower might be better.

The cold water pelts my skin like pin needles. It's a nice distraction from my vision and I finish my shower clean and refreshed. The smell of fresh mountain air fills my nose as I slip on a pair of clean jeans and a blue polo shirt.

Eager to meet up with Aislin, I keep my pace controlled as I exit my room and walk down the hallway toward her's. I shouldn't be this excited, especially since she is leaving tomorrow. I know I am setting myself up for disappointment, but somehow, I don't care.

The staccato beating of my heart thrums heavy against my chest as I reach up to knock on her door. I could have slapped Greyson silly for handing me the key to Lover's Lane. But I knew why he did it; because it's the only girly room in the tavern.

I knock on the door a few times and wait.

There is some rustling and then, "Give me a few minutes," she responds. Half smiling to myself, I lean up against the door and wait patiently.

Twiddling my thumbs, I think back to what Greyson mentioned earlier about just going for it. Maybe I can convince her to stay. I picture her asking me to give her one good reason to stay and I would answer; me.

I'm pretty sure a few minutes have gone by and I throw a couple of light taps on the door. "Aislin, are you okay?"

"I'm fine. Be out in a minute."

I sigh and fold my arms over my chest. I forgot how long Miranda used to take to get ready and wonder if it's in the girl's code book to always keep a guy waiting. Can't this be considered rude? I know Miranda would always complain if I was late.

The door clicks open before I gain my balance and I nearly fall into her. I brace myself against the door frame, turning to meet her gaze, and my breath catches in my throat.

"I'm ready," she says. Stepping out into the hallway.

The light pink sleeveless dress hugs her lean body. My eyes trace the lace flower pattern over her torso to her hips, where the ballerina skirt stops short of her knees. Her braided hair rests over her shoulder and the smell of a spring garden radiates off her.

"Wow, you look...beautiful," I say, wishing I had the guts to tell her how ravishing she looks instead. She smiles and blushes, but doesn't shy away from my compliment.

"Thank you," she smiles, eyeing my choice of clothing. "You clean up nicely yourself," she adds, surprising me with her response. Then I notice a slight tremble in her legs and reach out to help steady her.

"Are you sure you're okay?" I ask, taking a quick glance at her side. She nods, but leans into me. I give her my outstretched arm and she takes it as we move to the staircase.

As we reach ground level, a mixture of tobacco, alcohol, and sweat fills the air. Her arm tightens around mine, taking in the crowded tavern. Smiling to myself, I puff my chest out a tiny bit and stand straighter as I guide her to our table.

"I had Greyson put in an order for both of his specials tonight. They tend to be a big thing, and so I didn't want you to miss out." I pull out a chair for her and wait for her to sit before scooting the chair closer to the table.

"I hope you're hungry," I add.

"I'm starving," she replies. As if on cue, her stomach

rumbles in protest and I watch her cheeks heat up.

"Here you two are."

Aislin subtly jerks at Greyson's sudden appearance. He smiles, setting down our plates in front of us.

"For Miss Aislin, I have the Divljana, also known as Wilderness. It is a grilled tenderloin venison steak, in a creamy champignon sauce, over risotto, paired with creamed spinach and caramelized carrots."

I take a sip of my beer to hide my amusement. She licks her lips a few times, eyeing her dish. I surely thought she would devour the meal before her, but am surprised as she waits to hear Greyson's description of my meal.

"And for my dear brother, I have prepared for you what I call Zmaj, or Dragon. It's a lightly seared, grilled tenderloin venison steak, topped with a spicy pepper sauce, and a side of fresh vegetables."

"Thank you, Greyson."

He nods, "Uzivati. Enjoy," and leaves.

"Don't worry if you can't finish it all. Greyson tends to give hearty portions." She nods, taking the first bite.

CHAPTER FIVE

. GREYSON .

AISLIN

I dip a small piece of venison in the champignon sauce and place it in my mouth. Mmm. The distinct taste of Armagnac brandy teases my tongue. It's mixed with some cream and other spices, enhancing the overall flavor of the sauce. The smell of chocolate and caramel, with a hint of cinnamon, brings me back in time, like it was just yesterday.

"Papa! Let me have a taste," I beg him.

He just returned home from work and is pouring himself a glass of his favorite golden drink. He thinks he hides it from mum, but I watch her constantly replace his empty bottles with new ones.

"My little Aislin, this is for adults, not a young angel."

"But Papa! Please," I plead, running up to him. I tug on his untucked shirt and bat my eyes at him. His hearty laugh is warm, causing my smile to stretch across my face. I am consumed with giddiness, knowing he is going to let me try the forbidden liquid.

"Alright, my precious Aislin. Buy you must promise not to tell your mum. She will punish me if she finds out I let you have a drink."

A sly smile tugs at the corners of my mouth, for he doesn't see mum peek her head from around the kitchen door. She winks at me, letting Papa give me a taste and never mentions a word of it.

As the liquid enters my mouth, I try to swallow it, but spit it all over papa instead. His laugh roars through the house and that is the last time I try any of his drinks.

The Armagnac that my papa let me try that day now delights my senses. It is an aroma of flavors. Everything from toasted almonds to sweet caramel and vanilla, with a bit of spice but is bitterly pungent. The silky rich texture of the champignon sauce lingers on my tongue. I glance up to see Nolan show a lot of self-control while eating his meal. Savoring and chewing every bite. I look down at my half-eaten plate and suddenly feel like a pig, scarfing down my meal like it is the last thing I will eat. To my astonishment, he keeps the steady pace until the very last bite.

We were both so hungry that we forget to have a dinner conversation. Nolan looks up and smiles when he sees my plate is also empty. His eyes sparkle as he wipes his mouth.

"Now for dessert." As he stands up, I am about to protest, but Greyson appears at the table.

"Mind if I steal Aislin for a bit?"

"Have a seat. I am going to get desert." He winks at me and then disappears toward the kitchen.

Underneath the table, my hands fidget with my dress. I watch Greyson take Nolan's seat and stare at the table for a few seconds. The awkward tension between us is almost too much and I am about to excuse myself to find Nolan when Greyson clears his throat.

"When Nolan was twelve, our mum left. She never wrote or tried to contact us. Our father wasn't around much and when he was..." Greyson's subtle shiver did not go unnoticed. I stay quiet, waiting for him to continue.

"Nolan and our mum were close," he says, heavily. "And since her leaving, Nolan has had trouble trusting girls. The one serious relationship he had..."

"With Miranda?" I can't help but blurt out her name. Greyson's eyes narrow and stare at me. Probably trying to figure out how much I know.

"Nolan took me to her boutique. Hence the dress." His face softens as he nods.

"That makes sense. And yes, it was with Miranda. Those two were serious for a time." He stops to take a sip of his brother's beer. His beard is a little longer and scruffier than Nolan's trimmed appearance, with darker, sexier eyes compared to Nolan's lighter, hazel eyes. Greyson's hair, although a milk chocolate brown like his younger brother's, is an inch or two longer. Perfect for combing your finger through.

"I guess what I am trying to say is, don't play games with him. If you like him, then fine. We'll discuss that later. But don't lead him into thinking you're interested if you're not." I open my mouth to respond, but he holds up his hand to stop me.

"The truth is, I can tell he is already falling for you. So just be honest with him."

I'm stunned into silence but find the strength to nod, agreeing to his terms.

"Hey, how did your talk go?" Nolan appears behind Greyson, sliding two plates of Croatian apple pita onto the table before slapping his brother's shoulder. I can only muster a half smile as Greyson and I lock eyes.

"Great. I'll leave you two to talk about whatever it is you need to discuss." He doesn't bother to glance back, but heads straight for the bar.

"Well, I hope he didn't intimidate you too much. He can be a bit overbearing at times." Smiling, Nolan pushes one of the Croatian apple pitas in my direction. I pick up my fork and poke the dessert, totally distracted by the conversation Greyson and I shared.

His fork clatters against the plate, followed by a long, heavy sigh. I look up against my better judgement to see Nolan staring very intently at me. I can't read his facial expression, but I sense a question coming on.

"Okay, what did he say? Did he mention anything about Miranda?" He rubs his temples with eyes closed and head down.

I am not sure exactly what I am supposed to say, but answer, "well, I technically brought up Miranda." Admitting that she still bothers me has my cheeks burning with embarrassment.

"You know I'm over her, right? That relationship ended a couple of years ago. We're just friends." Nolan looks at me with his blue-ish green and amber speckled eyes, searching for something.

"And what are we?" I ask, trying to catch him off guard. I tried to test Greyson's theory, but I am not getting the sign that Nolan is interested in me like he said.

"I don't know, we just met this morning," he shrugs.

"Correction, you saved me last night and bandaged my wound. And then invited me to stay at your brother's tavern."

"I was - am - trying to be nice."

I want to push him more, but his brows suddenly furrow as he stares past me. Twisting in my seat, I look in the same direction and watch a tall, cloaked figure rise from the shadows of a dark corner booth. The lithe shadow slips through the crowd, toward our table. My pulse quickens and I wonder how bad can it be? Nolan is with me, his brother is tending the bar, and the tavern is full of people. But as the stranger looms closer, I might be more intimidated if the familiar aroma of cinnamon and vanilla, with a woody undercurrent, didn't invoke pleasant nostalgia.

The cloaked figure stops a few paces from the table. "Aislin Camille Burd, I knew your mother and your father. I am here to warn you about the long journey ahead of you."

. THE STRANGER .
NOLAN

"How do you know my parents, and what journey are you talking about?" Aislin demands.

For a brief moment, the tall shadow stops and a rush of goosebumps prick my arms. I watch bewildered as the surrounding chaos slows to a standstill. I'm not sure Aislin is aware of the situation, but I'm not fooled. This stranger is more than he or she is pretending to be.

The stranger's cloak sways lightly as their stance alters. Under the hood, a pair of blue eyes stare at me. I am not sure if they can be trusted or not. I open my mouth to say something, but am silenced by the smallest gesture of the stranger's hand, as their attention remains on Aislin.

"All your questions will be answered within time, but today I come to help you find Destiny."

"Destiny?! You're going to help her find Destiny?" I scoff, "are you insane?"

Aislin glares at me with her icy stare and the stranger just stands there. The black void under the hood just stares at me. I turn my gaze to Aislin and shrug. If she only knew the consequences of finding Destiny.

"Actually, you will be helping Aislin find Destiny."

I let out a roar of laughter. The tavern remains frozen in time, but my laughter fills up the space. The stranger ignores my outburst and continues to talk with Aislin.

"Your journey, Aislin Camille Burd, begins with finding the Chronicle Keeper, also known as Aeneas." The voice is deep and solemn.

I inhale a sharp breath, but Aislin is too laser focused on the stranger to hear me. My head throbs with a million thoughts. The years I spent building walls around my life are now crumbling, and this stranger is forcing my hand to face a past I'm not ready to face. And for what? To help a girl I just met on her journey. I don't think so.

"Absolutely not. I refuse to help." I refrain from the urge to cross my arms over my chest. Instead, I keep my gaze level with the hidden face under the hood.

There is a deep rumble, a chuckle, that escapes from underneath the hood. "As for your friend here, Aislin, he should know how to find Aeneas. Right, Nolan?"

A lump suddenly forms in my throat and it takes everything I've got to swallow it. My name is said with such ease and familiarity, it causes my chest to tingle, right where my mark is. I subconsciously reach up to rub it, but quickly catch myself. If I act on this calling, just like what happened in the bathroom, what will I see this time? Not wanting to find out, I force my hand back on the table. The internal tearing sensation as the distance between my hand and my chest increases is almost unbearable. But I can't risk Aislin finding out my secret.

Instead, Aislin turns to me and intently watches as I nod

my head, agreeing to help her with her journey and find Aeneas. For all I know, this will be the death of me.

Just when I think the cloaked figure is about to leave, they step forward. "Do you know what your name even means, child?"

Aislin shakes her head. Apparently smart enough not to talk, because look how well it worked for me, or because she is too scared.

"It means A Vision of a Noble Girl. You would do best to live up to the name your mother gave you, Aislin."

Yep, no pressure there.

And just like that, within a blink of an eye, the tavern is chaotic once again, and the stranger is gone.

Aislin and I stare at each other for a while, trying to comprehend what had just happened. It's like a tornado came through, stripping us of our security and leaving us to face our raw emotions and memories meant to be left in the past.

"Who's Aeneas?" Her voice is almost a whisper, but I hear her. Her question catches me off guard and I continue to stare at her like an idiot.

"Who?"

She rolls her eyes but then hesitantly looks around the room before leaning in closer, resting her arms on the table.

"Aeneas? The Chronicle Keeper. Who is he?"

My heart skips more beats than I can count and suddenly I feel a bit lightheaded. I close my eyes and lean back in my chair. I sigh heavily, rubbing my temples, trying to prolong this discussion.

"Can we not discuss this here, please?" I avoid eye

contact, but try to be nice.

"Why?" Her voice is becoming testy.

"Because this discussion needs to happen in private. Away from unknown eavesdroppers."

Aislin slowly sits taller in her seat, finally understanding our situation.

"You know, I didn't ask for this. Any of this. Especially you, being my tour guide." She folds her arms over her chest and slumps against her chair.

I run my hand over my face and growl under my breath. Why? Why me? Why now? What did I do to get stuck with this whole mess? Oh ya, I remember. I rescued her from certain death by two ghosthounds.

"Are you done with your dessert?" We both look at our plates, hardly touched. I don't need to wait for her answer to know what she is going to say. "Come on, let's go for a walk." I get up and pull out her chair so she can follow me through the crowd and out the back door.

Under the starry night, Aislin and I walk in silence for a bit. A heavy weight burdens my shoulders as I gauge how much to tell her and how much to keep a secret.

"My mother left when Greyson and I were young. My father wasn't around much and when he was around, he was drunk and physical." I pause for a moment to calm my breathing. I'm thankful she remains quiet as she waits for me to continue.

"It was Greyson's idea to leave and one night when our father didn't return home, we left and never looked back. It was Aeneas who found us wondering around the woods, hiding, starving. And he took us in. Taught us everything we know and helped us with getting the tavern started."

We walk in silence again, but this time I stop by a bench and take a seat. I tilt my head back and glance up at the stars.

"Aeneas taught Greyson and I how to read the stars, so that when the time came for him to leave, we would have the skills necessary to find him."

"Why would you need to use the stars to find him?"

I take a moment and breathe in the crisp night air. The breeze lightly rustles the leaves on the tees and I can hear the frogs and crickets in the background.

"Because he is a nomad and doesn't believe in technology. Not that technology is readily available anymore." I add under my breath.

"So how do we find Aeneas?"

"Leave that to me. To find the old man will take more than reading a few stars in the sky."

I'm still in disbelief as I stand and help Aislin up. I never agreed to help her on her journey. In fact, I had half a mind to try and convince her to stay here with me. But that isn't going to happen now.

"Come on. We have a long road ahead of us. We leave tomorrow morning."

CHAPTER SIX

. THE PLAN .

AISLIN

"What aren't you telling me, Nolan?" I ask as I follow him up the stairs. Within the past hour, the tavern became quieter and less crowded. There are a few stragglers spread out over a couple of tables and a few at the bar finishing their drinks.

"What do you mean?" His pace quickens slightly and the veins in his neck bulge a little.

"Don't play dumb with me. I'm not stupid. How do you know Destiny?" Maybe I should have eased into that question a little more gracefully.

Nolan spins around quickly, bumping into me. I feel my feet try to gain traction, but slip off the stairs' ledge. I'm falling backwards, arms flailing as I try to grab on to something, but I can't reach anything. Just as I close my eyes, I feel muscular arms beneath my back, holding me safely. Slowly, I open my eyes to stare into Nolan's.

"Sorry, I didn't mean to knock you off your feet." Surprisingly, I'm not mad, but more perplexed about how he was able to catch me before I hit the stairs.

With a quizzical look, I start to ask, "how…" but Nolan gently presses a finger to my lips and shakes his head.

"Let's get you up to bed. We have a big day tomorrow and you need sleep." As he picks me up to carry me the rest of the way, I suck in a sharp breath and bite my lip. My side pulses and I scrunch my face at the sudden pain.

"Is everything okay?"

I shake my head no and tightly squeeze his arm.

He grimaces but replies, "I'll need to look at your wound and possibly change the bandage again."

The muscle in his arms tense as he tightens his hold on me. I rest my head against his chest and close my eyes, listening to the beating sound of his heart. With that, and the drumming of his boots against the stairs, I almost fall asleep.

"Where are we going?" I ask as he passes my room.

"My room. It'll be easier to treat your wound there. I have all my herbs, bandages, and some sedatives to help ease the pain." I just nod and close my eyes until I hear him open the door.

"Here we are. Nothing special," he says, laying me down carefully on the bed. He helps me adjust the pillows to I am comfortable before heading over to his wall of shelves and cabinets, gathering the supplies he needs.

I feel a sense of déjà vu as I look around the room. Once again, I'm stuck on a bed in a room unfamiliar to me. But this time, the room has a distinct aroma of wood and smoke, giving it a cozy and inviting atmosphere. Floor-to-ceiling drapes frame the large windows and an animal rug sprawls over the floor. A large leather armchair adorns the rug and faces an old stone fireplace.

"You have a cozy bedroom," I say, admiring the simple rustic decor.

"Thanks. A lot of the furniture Aeneas and I built together." He retrieves one more vial and then crosses the room back to me. The wooden floors creak beneath his boots and his shadow dances on the wall from the mounted sconces.

Grabbing a side table and a simple chair, he positions everything next to the bed and then gestures to my dress, "may I?"

I forgot about my dress and blush. This is going to be a bit more awkward than I thought. But I nod because I don't know anyone else who can help me. I turn my head to look the other way, so I don't have to look at my bandaged side.

Nolan's fingertips are warm against my skin as he slowly and carefully lifts one side of my dress. Just enough to expose the bandage.

"How does it look, doctor?" I half jest.

I hear his smile as he replies, "not bad. But I think I should give you a fresh bandage and put some more ointment on it. To help fight infection and help your wound heal faster." I nod and continue to stare at the animal rug.

"What kind of animal is that?" I ask, trying to keep my focus on something other than Nolan cleaning and dressing my side.

"Hmm? Oh, the rug? That was my first stag. Shot him with my bow. His head is mounted above the fireplace."

I shift my gaze above the mantle and gaze at the deer's serene expression. There is no doubt he had been a big boy by the size of his head and antlers.

"He's beautiful," I mention under my breath.

"Mm-hmm…There. All done. Hopefully, this should hold until tomorrow evening. At this rate, I don't know how much time we will have in the morning before we have to leave."

"What time is that?" I ask, holding back a yawn.

Nolan reaches for a thick fur blanket resting on a bench at the foot of the bed. He unfolds it and lays it on top of me.

"You'll need to get some sleep. I need to discuss our plans with Greyson."

"Where will you sleep?"

A huge yawn escapes and I fight the urge to close my eyes. The second I do; I'll be fast asleep. I watch him walk over to one of the kerosene sconces and turn the dial. The flame flickers once before it burns out. The fireplace and moon are the only sources of light in the room, but it feels cozy and secure.

"Probably your room."

"No," my reply is instantaneous, stopping Nolan at the door.

"Oh, then where do you propose I sleep?" His tone is clipped, probably tiredness taking over.

"Here?" I suggest. I just can't bear the thought of being alone. Not after what happened two nights ago. I hear him sigh and vaguely see his shoulders droop a little.

"I suppose I can sleep next to the fire." He voices softly, almost like he is talking to himself.

I'm too tired to respond, so I smile and finally close my eyes. The last thing I hear is Nolan exiting the bedroom and the click of the door closing behind him.

"Are you crazy?"

I bolt upright in bed. I hear Greyson's voice carry in from down the hall. Groggy, I rub my eyes until they have adjusted to the low-lit room. Nolan is nowhere in the room. What time is it anyway?

"Shh, keep it down. Aislin is sleeping in my bed."

"She's what?!"

"Keep it down, will you? I changed her bandages."

"Wow, you are really in over your head with her, aren't you?"

"Ugh. How do you propose we find Aeneas?"

"Do you honestly plan on going with her? Helping her on her journey to find Aeneas so she can find *her*?"

Suddenly, I'm wide awake and I need to get closer to wherever Greyson and Nolan are having their little spat. I crawl out from under the blanket with no pain and smile. *Thank you, Nolan, for the sedatives.*

I tiptoe to the bedroom door and listen.

"Yes, I do."

"You know what this means, right?"

No answer. If Nolan gave an answer, I didn't hear it or see it. *Draught.* I have to get closer. Slowly turning the handle, I gently pull the door open and gingerly peek my head around the door frame and into the hallway. A sigh of relief warms my lips as the hallway is vacant.

"Fine. Aeneas and I casually stay in touch. If a situation arises, he has been keeping me informed of his whereabouts."

Greyson's voice carries down the hall and I suddenly notice a pale orange glow coming from under a closed door. Leaving Nolan's door ajar, I quietly make my way toward the two brothers.

"Now you tell me?" I hear the rejection in Nolan's tone. The door is cracked open a little, and I peek through the tiny gap. Greyson is leaning against what looks to be a desk, and Nolan is pacing the room.

"Nothing has ever come up to warrant me telling you this. Not until now." Greyson gets up and moves behind the desk. He pulls open a drawer and retrieves a journal.

"I have been keeping track of Aeneas' whereabouts and how to find him. You can only look at this. It needs to stay here, so it doesn't fall into the wrong hands."

Nolan steps up to the desk and takes the journal. The pages rustle as he impatiently flips through them. Until he stops about midway through and points to what resembles a sketch of a map.

"Firtina Valley?"

"I'm not sure he even…"

I creep away from the door. That is all I need to know. Now, I can leave Nolan here and embark to find Aeneas on my own. I make my way back to Nolan's room because his bed is much more comfortable and already warmed by my body. Now, I just need to wake up and leave before Nolan. I crawl back under the blanket and within seconds, I'm fast asleep.

. CONFESSION .
NOLAN

CLICK!

I stir in my sleep as I hear the door shut. I had spent the better part of last night planning and packing my things, so Aislin and I could leave at the first crack of dawn. But it appears she has other plans. As I roll over from my spot on the rug, the cold air clings to my warm body and an empty bed confirms my suspicions. Now I just need to intercept Aislin before she completely disappears. Getting up off the rug, I climb into the shower and take a moment to fully wake up.

I just finish securing the bags to the saddles when I hear footsteps on the gravel behind me. Despite starting my day extremely early and having little sleep, the birds' songs have already brightened my day. I turn around just in time to watch Aislin try to sneak past me, heading in the wrong direction and away from the route leading to Aeneas. A mischievous grin spreads across my face and I fold my arms in front of me.

"What are you doing here?" Her cheeks blush as she pops her hip to one side, eyeing the horses skeptically.

"Helping you," I say, watching her nibble the inside of her cheek.

"I don't need your help. I heard where I can find Aeneas." She says, adjusting her bag.

"Oh? Eavesdropping now, are we?"

"Well, you and your brother shouldn't argue so loud. You could wake someone."

I nod in agreement and add, "you do know you're heading in the wrong direction and it will be quicker to travel by horse than walk." I gesture to the horses and see her seriously consider her options.

"Plus," I add, "who'll help you with your bandage?" I let that sink in a little. "You need me, Aislin, whether or not you want to admit it."

She reaches up with one hand and rubs her face, expelling an exacerbated sigh. "Fine, Mr. I-Need-You, Nolan. Let's get going before I change my mind. And I am only agreeing to this on one condition." I raise my eyebrows and wait. "This is all business, got it?"

Great. Not sure how I'm going to pull that off.

"Got it," I agree with a smile. I offer to take her bag and secure it to her horse's saddle.

"They're gorgeous. What are their names?" Aislin reaches out to gently stroke her horse's nose.

"Your girl's name is Belle, and this lovely lady over here is, well, Lady." I laugh at how silly that must sound.

"I've never seen an all-black horse with hair, or is that fur, on its legs before," she says, pointing to the cluster of hair on Belle's leg, just above her hoof.

"Belle and Lady are Friesians. And the hair on the lower part of their legs is called feathering. It protects their lower legs from rough terrain elements, such as sharp and pointy objects."

"Oh, wow. That's pretty cool."

I finish checking the saddle, making sure the girth is tight before turning to Aislin. "Have you ridden before?"

"I used to, a long time ago."

I nod and gesture for her to stand by me. "Would you like me to help you up?"

I watch her eyes go up to where the saddle is sitting on Belle's back and see her swallow. "That might be a good idea," she answers.

"You know something else pretty cool about Friesians?" I cup my hands together and instruct Aislin to place her foot in my hands.

"Hmm?" She grabs the reins in one hand and the saddle in the other. I gently vault her up into the saddle.

"Friesians were in high demand back in the Middle Ages."

"Really? What for?"

"Their sturdy build, lightness of foot, and elegance on the battlefield." I move over to Lady and swing into the saddle.

"Fascinating."

"How do you feel? In the saddle in I mean."

"Good, actually." She smiles, hands gentle on the reins.

"Looks like you're a natural."

Her cheeks turn a light pink. "Thanks."

"Okay, let's head out. We're burning daylight and we have a lot of ground to cover today."

We ride in silence most of the morning, trotting through the forest, following game trails. I try multiple times to start a conversation but am lost at what to say. Instead, I've been paying attention to Lady, watching her swiveling ears and picking up on her nervous prance.

"Why is she doing that?" Aislin startles me from my thoughts.

"She's nervous," I answer calmly, not wanting to alarm Aislin any more than need be.

"Nervous? Of what?"

Before I had a chance to answer, a twig snaps in the distance. I hold up my hand to quiet Aislin and pull on the reins, bringing Lady to a halt. I watch Aislin quietly do the same.

"What is it?" She whispers, moving Belle right next to Lady. Lady pins her ears back and stomps her hoof. I put my finger to my lips and nudge Lady sideways a little to give her some space.

I'm just about to give the okay to move forward when a few birds startle from their perch in the trees. Their warning calls echo through the trees and I scan the surrounding area for any imminent danger, but can't see any. On full alert, I motion for Aislin to move ahead of me while I follow behind, waiting a few minutes before I dare say anything.

"Are we being followed?" Aislin's voice is a little shaky, but she looks calm in the saddle. Belle's fidgeting says otherwise, though.

"What makes you ask?" I have my suspicions but keep them to myself for now.

"The snapping twig, the startled birds, Lady acting up, and you telling me to be quiet."

I scratch my head. *She doesn't miss a thing.*

"I suspect as much." I encourage Lady to pick up the pace and pass Aislin to continue leading the way, since she clearly had no sense of direction, even knowing Aeneas' location.

"Why would someone be following us?" Without giving me a chance to answer, she blurts out, "you didn't steal these horses, did you?"

"What? No! A dear friend of mine and Greyson gave us the horses for our journey. I think whoever was following us was at the tavern last night. There were a lot of unfamiliar faces, and, after our dinner encounter last night, anything is possible."

Aislin falls silent for a minute, taking a deep breath, and I prepare myself for her question. "It just doesn't make sense. I got up before you. How did you manage to pack and get the horses all ready before I even made it outside?"

"Magic," I chuckle, trying to keep my nerves in check.

"No, I'm serious."

"Greyson helped. He picked up the mares from our friend Lanna and then packed us some food. I packed all of my things last night before going to bed." I explain, omitting something she didn't need to know.

There's a moment of peaceful bliss. I almost forget the predicament we're in. The sun has since lost its peak position and as sunlight streams in through the canopy; the shadows are growing longer and longer.

"We should make camp soon. It'll be dark soon and I'd rather work while there is still sunlight." When Aislin doesn't respond, I look back to check on her. Her eyes are glazed over, like she is deep in thought.

"Aislin!" I refrain from yelling and startling the horses, but raise my voice hoping she'll hear me.

"Huh? What?"

"We're going to stop soon and make camp while there is still daylight."

"You mean we're camping out here in the forest?" She glances around with a sudden fear-stricken face.

"What if they followed us here? What if they attack at night? What if..."

"Aislin,"

She looks at me, scared, and my face softens. "We'll cross that bridge if and when it comes. But there is not a town within another day's travel from here. We need to rest."

She reluctantly nods her head and joins me in search of a place to stay for the night.

"This should do just fine," I say as we come to a tiny opening in the woods. There are a couple of fallen logs we can use for a lean-to and dry wood lying around to start a fire. We dismount and secure the horses to a nearby tree.

"I'll take care of building a lean-to for shelter, if you can gather some tinder and firewood. Nothing too heavy. I don't need you straining yourself. I'll look at your wound as soon as we have a fire going."

She nods and heads off to get started.

The light is fading fast as I finish bandaging Aislin's wound back up. "It's healing nicely. As long as you don't tear it open, I'd say it should be fully healed within another week or so."

"Thanks." She's been relatively quiet all evening and I get the feeling she isn't telling me the entire story. Or at least what she knows.

"Is there something you'd like to share? You've been awfully quiet the past couple of hours." I watch her fidget with her hands. "Is there something I should know about why we are being followed?"

"Possibly," she squeaks, avoiding my gaze.

I wait patiently, but it's like she's gone mute. "Well, spit it out, Aislin. I can't help if I don't know what I'm up against."

"I'm remembering bits and pieces of what happened to me." She admits, looking at her hands.

I can't imagine what she's feeling right now. All I want to do is tell her it will all work out and let her know I'm here for her. But she made it clear this is just business.

"What do you remember? Anything at all can help." I prod gently.

"Well, I don't know any names, but the night I escaped, there was a woman in charge. She was the one who instructed to release the hounds,"

"You mean ghosthounds," I interrupt.

"What are those?"

"What? Ghosthounds? Those monsters that were hunting you down. Those are ghosthounds. They are mythical creatures…" I stop short and grimace. I've said too much and I rack my brain about how I'm going to fix this.

Aislin eyes me suspiciously, "mythical creatures? Ghosthounds? Are you feeling okay?"

"I'm completely fine," I say, trying my best to sound reassuring. But it doesn't seem to work. So, I try another tactic, the art of distraction. "What else were you going to say before I interrupted you?"

She pauses briefly, remembering our conversation. I can see she is attempting to recall as she taps her chin and closes her eyes. "Oh! Yesterday, when you left me to take a shower, a memory surfaced." Her eyes light up for a split second and then darken.

"What is it?" I want to reach out and rest my hand on her's, but don't. Instead, I swallow down my desire and stay put. It's taking everything I have to respect her wishes. But one of these days, I may not be able to hold myself back.

"I had a flashback. It happened before I ended up in that compound." She bites her lip and wrings her top between her hands. "I was at this bar in Rastoke, waiting for my friend, when this dark, handsome and foreboding man asks to sit next me."

"Do you think he could have been the stranger at dinner last night?" I ask.

"I don't know, maybe?" Aislin stops to think some more and then shakes her head. "No. He couldn't be."

"Are you sure?" I ask again, this time holding her gaze with mine.

"Argh, I don't know. All I know is he was tall, dark, ruggedly handsome, with a scar along his jawline and mentioned he was looking for..." She gulps, shaking her head, trying to keep her whole body from shaking. "He said he was looking for the chosen one."

Now things are starting to make more sense.

CHAPTER SEVEN

. THE OLD MILL .
AISLIN

*M*orning came too quick. I try to get up, but I am stiff from head to foot. Groaning, I roll onto my good side and look for Nolan. The corners of my lips unintentionally curve into a soft smile as I lay eyes on him. Hunched over the campfire with a pot, I make out a slight five o'clock shadow that stirs butterflies in my stomach. Trying to keep this entire journey to find Destiny just as business will not be easy. I see that now.

"It's time to get up. We have a long day ahead of us." He says, standing up. Within two strides, he is standing over me with an outstretched hand, ready to help me up.

I ready myself as Nolan busies himself with making us breakfast. After yesterday's travels, I was so tired; I fell asleep before dinner. Today, I am going to make it a priority to eat enough and stay energized. As breakfast heats up, I help by packing up our things and saddling the horses.

"Hey, you hungry?" Nolan calls from the fire.

"I'm starving," I reply.

"Well, the oatmeal is ready. I know it isn't much, but we don't exactly have a lot of room for food." His attempt at an apology makes me smile.

"I love oatmeal. It's one of my favorite breakfast groups." I grin and make my way over to sit next to him. He hands me a bowl and a small sugar dispenser.

"Oh! What a happy surprise! I wasn't sure if we were going to have to eat bland food or not." I sprinkle some over my oatmeal and dig in.

"Well, don't get too excited. I don't want to disappoint when that may be our only option." He half smiles, like he is joking, but I can't tell if he is or not.

"So, where are we headed today?" I ask, swallowing a spoonful of oatmeal.

"We'll continue to head east," he says, chewing a bite.

"And then where to?"

"I don't know yet. Aeneas is tricky to find. He is always moving. Never staying in one spot." He says, but I am concentrating on the note from Destiny with laser focus.

"Don't burn a hole in that. We might need it." I feel him glance over my shoulder and I quickly fold up the note.

We finish eating, packing up the remains of the camp and covering up our campfire. Nolan gives me another boost onto Belle's back, and I wince as my butt hits the saddle.

"Sore?" Nolan chuckles and pats my knee. "Your muscles will eventually get used to it."

"Is that supposed to help ease my sore butt? Because it's not helping." He just smiles and swings up onto Lady's back.

"Come on, we have a long way to travel again today."

He turns Lady around and heads back into the overgrown forest. I nudge Belle and follow behind.

We encounter the same scenery for the next two days, eat the same food for breakfast, lunch, and dinner, and have the same sleeping arrangements. The terrain is a mix of mountainous forest and flat land, marshy swampland, and dry ground. It isn't until the fifth day of our journey that we stumble upon an old watermill hidden within the overgrown forest.

"Oh, wow! How cool is this?" I squeal in delight, urging Belle past Lady to get a closer look.

Moss and lichen cover the old stone building, a relic of times past. The surrounding ground is thick with undergrowth and ivy, inundated by tall skinny trees and the wildlife of the forest.

"Can we stay here and rest for the night, please?" I turn to face Nolan, who is behind me, and slightly flinch. Despite Nolan's efforts to treat and bandage my wound, it isn't healing as fast as I had hoped. I watch his face soften, seeing the slight pain I'm in.

"Sure. Plus, I see there is a little swimming hole. It'll give us a chance to wash up."

Boys. So practical. Not wanting to spoil my surprise, I nod in agreement and dismount, finding a two-stall stable behind the watermill.

"Nolan, it even has a place for Belle and Lady." I call out. Nolan finds me and smiles.

"Great. Let's get these girls situated and then take a look around."

After unpacking and hanging up the saddles and bridles, we trek through thigh high ferns and brush to the mill's front door. Or what is left of it. The wooden door has since fallen off its hinges, but remains intact because of the vines. I push the door open, stepping into the dark, musty, old building, when a loud clatter echoes inside.

So much for having a door.

"Wow, look at all this machinery. It's like everyone just left midday and never came back." I move to check out the worn-down millstones and wooden-gears, confirming how ancient the technology is.

"This building must be hundreds of years old." Nolan says as he walks around.

I follow his movements with my gaze and note the damp, grey stone walls and the hard packed dirt floor now sprouting plants. Cobwebs hang from the ceiling and the sound of running water fills the silence. The smell of wet wood and musty air is unmistakable.

"Where do you suggest we sleep?" Nolan asks, gesturing to the inadequate space.

I glance around and then notice a hidden door in the back corner. "What do you think is behind door number two?" I skip to the door, which isn't in much better shape than the front door. But at least the hinges were still attached.

"Well, let's find out." He says, right behind me.

"On the count of three," and we both place our hands on the door.

"One…two…three." Together, we push the door open and stumble into a small room.

A wood-burning fireplace is up against the far wall, with an attached kitchen to the right and a broken-down bed frame to the left. The mattress is so tattered the springs are poking through. Stone walls and floors make up the room with a thatched roof that has stood the test of time. A large wooden table sits in the center of the room with two chairs. One with a broken leg and the other a broken seat.

"Well, isn't this homey?" I try to stay optimistic, but I guess I didn't know what I was expecting to find.

"It's better than the alternative," he says, motioning to the other room.

There is an old, dusty fur rug in front of the fireplace. I pick it up and am just about to shake it when Nolan stops me.

"What are you doing?"

"What does it look like? I'm getting rid of all the dust. It's the only warm thing in this room." I argue.

"Maybe. Maybe not." I watch Nolan walk over to a wooden ladder camouflaged into the kitchen shelving.

"I think there might be a small storage loft above this room."

I gently lay the rug back down and move closer to Nolan, who is halfway up the ladder. By the time I reach him, he has already pushed the trapdoor open and climbed up inside the storage loft.

"Wow, there are some neat things up here. Watch out, I'm going to throw down a box full of bedding."

I jump out of the way just in time to avoid being clobbered in the head.

"I wonder when the last time these were used." I take the box and bring it over to the bed.

"Do you suppose the bottom of the mattress is better than the top?" I call up to Nolan.

"It won't hurt to check it out." He calls back. After rummaging around for a few more minutes, he finally comes down with one more box of kitchen stuff.

Nolan helps me flip the mattress and make the bed, and then we unpack the box of kitchen stuff. Finding some dishes and silverware and mugs. We are putting away the last of the dishes when I get a glimpse of the swimming hole out the window. Smiling, I grab Nolan's hand and pull him with me outside.

"Hold on a minute. Where are we going?"

"Swimming!"

"Oh, no. I don't swim." He says, definitively, wrenching his arm from my grasp.

"Don't want to, or can't swim?" I narrow my eyes at him, seeing him subtly flinch. I smile inwardly.

"Both." He admits, brushing off invisible dust from his clothes.

"I don't believe you." I smirk, pushing him closer to the water's edge. "Watch this," I bait him, kicking off my boots and tucking my sock inside, gearing up for a cannonball.

"Don't you dare," he warns, but I charge past him and jump right in.

As I hit the crisp water, a fountain of water rains down on Nolan, drenching him from head to boots. The cool water is refreshing against my skin, and I can feel the stress of the day melting away. Nolan sputters as water droplets drip from his nose and it takes everything I have not to laugh out loud.

"Oh, now it's on." His lips curl into a devilish grin as he strips down to his boxers and charges towards me. I scream and laugh, trying to swim out of the way, but he lands about a meter from me, sending a small tidal wave to douse me.

We continue to splash each other for a few more minutes until the moonlight hits the water's surface, reflecting off the rippling current. The watermill creaks softly in the background, its large wooden wheel slowly turning as the water from upstream pushes from behind. A faint mist rolls in, giving the air a mysterious and romantic feel.

Subconsciously, Nolan and I close the distance between us. Our eyes lock on one another. I can feel his warm breath on my lips and I know I need to pull away, but his presence is so intoxicating. He pulls his hand from under the water and reaches out to cup my face. The sound of water dripping from his hand echoes in my ear and, for a moment, it feels like time is standing still.

"Aislin…"

But before Nolan can finish, I feel something slimy wrap around my ankle and pull me under.

. FOLLOWED .
NOLAN

"islin!"

I dive under the cool, hostile water. My heart pounds against my chest, my lungs burn, and my eyes strain against the murky water. *I can't lose her. I won't.* I promise, swimming harder against the current. Suddenly, I vaguely make out her struggling form. Propelling my body harder towards Aislin, there is an immediate temperature shock, and I am reminded of how little time there is to save her.

For a split second, I hesitate, treading water beneath the surface and watching her fade from my sight. It feels like eternity as I try to decide what to do. If I save her, I risk exposing myself. All the possibilities flash before me. But in the end, all that matters is Aislin stays alive.

I stop treading water and feel icy tentacles wrap around my legs, slowly dragging me closer to the bottom. I focus on my hands, hastily working my fingers to thread Aislin a new lifeline. My lungs are ready to burst and my heart pummels my chest cavity with such force, the surrounding water vibrates. I watch with anxious relief as the thread begins to glow.

I finish the thread and let go. It snakes through the water towards where Aislin disappeared. I am about to follow, but the thread becomes blinding to look at and then it explodes. The disturbance in the water shifts into a vortex, sucking me in and spitting me out next to an unconscious Aislin.

I swim over to her and notice algae infested rope tangled around her ankle. I carefully tug on the rope to see where it leads and see the water wheel try to rotate. With the wheel stuck, I frantically use the opportunity to free Aislin's ankle. Time isn't on our side and I'm afraid of what that might mean.

Come on, Aislin. Don't give up. Hold on. I'm...almost...done... There!

I let the rope sink as the water wheel starts back up. I wrap my arms around her and swim to the surface. As I break free from the water's clutches, I gasp for air and quickly make a beeline for shore. I drag Aislin onto the grass and begin to give mouth-to-mouth CPR.

My whole body feels limp, but I push past it, focusing on saving her life. Suddenly, she spits water and coughs, gasping for air.

"You're alive!" I breathe into her slimy, putrid hair.

Thank you. Thank you. Thank you. I repeat in my head. I would be lying if I didn't admit I'm terrified of losing her. There is more at stake now than just our lives.

"It's okay, I got you." I whisper, stroking her hair over and over again. "You're going to be alright. I got you." I say reassuringly.

She manages to sit up and we both wrap each other in

hugs. In the still of the night, it grows colder. Aislin trembles against me and I tighten my grip around her. Only seven days ago I saved her from ghosthounds, but it feels longer. I am starting to enjoy our time together.

"Can you stand?" I ask, pulling away to look at her. She nods, but struggles even with my help.

"Wrap your arm around my neck." I instruct, sweeping her into my arms.

"What about your clothes? You'll get cold." She mumbles under her breath.

"Don't worry. I'll get them later. They aren't going anywhere." I smile and feel her tension dissolve as she goes limp, snuggling into me.

I carry Aislin back to the mill keeper's quarters; her clothes drip a water trail onto the floor. I go against my better judgement and change her out of her smelly, wet clothes and into something dry before laying her down on the bed. Dinner is out of the question, so I get a fire started and watch the flames lick at the dry wood. For a moment, I'm mesmerized by the flickering flames, watching them dance, leaping from log to log, disappearing and reappearing, fading out and then burning brightly with each new spout of oxygen the fire consumes.

I move the bed closer to the fire, gritting my teeth a few times as the bed posts catch uneven spots in the flooring. All too soon, I join Aislin in a deep sleep.

"Mmm."

I shoot up to a sitting position and look over to find Aislin batting her eyes open.

"Morning," I greet her quietly. I leave out the 'good', not sure if it is a good morning yet or not.

She smiles, "morning."

"How are you feeling?" I feel like I'm prying, but I need to know what to expect for the day ahead of us.

She stares at me for a second, apparently not sure how to respond.

"Do you remember anything from last night?"

Aislin starts to shake her head, and then her crystal blue eyes turn frigid and widen in terror.

"That wasn't a nightmare?" I can see her pleading with me to tell her just that; that it was just a terrible and horrific nightmare. But I can't pretend it didn't happen.

"No, it wasn't a nightmare," I sadly confirm.

She nods, turning her body away from me. I sigh and get up to stoke the fire. It's what I did all night long, that and checking to make sure Aislin didn't break into a cold sweat. But she slept peacefully through the night.

The morning light streams in through the grimy windows and casts warm rays on the furniture. Memories of last night flood back—the shock, the adrenaline, and the relief as I pulled Aislin out of the water. I still feel the remaining remnants of the night shivering along my spine, but shake it off at the thought of Aislin safe and sleeping a few feet away.

Changing into my extra pair of clothes, I trudge over to the wood-burning stove and get that setup. I dig into our food bag for some packets of instant oatmeal and grab a pan to fill with water. I glance at the ancient sink and rusty faucet with a frown. There is no way clean water is coming out of that old thing.

"I will be back. I am going to try to find some clean water around here." I go to slip on my boots, but I can't find them anywhere.

"You don't know where my boots are, do you?" I ask, not really expecting Aislin to answer.

"They are probably with your clothes outside, where you left them."

I turn to look at Aislin, who is now looking at me with tired eyes. Last night really drained the life out of her.

"Thanks," I smile and open the door to head outside.

"Check by the stable. I thought I saw an old water well with a bucket."

"I'll do that and check on the girls. I'll be back." I close the door behind me and head to the swimming hole first to grab my boots and clothes. As I get closer, thoughts of last night's events keep drifting back. Somewhere between the panic and saving Aislin, I realize just how much she means to me. My breath seizes at the thought of not having her in my life.

Picking up my boots, I do a careful check to make sure no snakes or spiders or any other creepy crawly thing has made its home in my boots. When I am satisfied, I slip them on and throw my clothes from last night over my shoulder. Now to go in search of that water well.

I round the old stone building and see Belle and Lady with both beautiful black heads hanging over their stall doors, lazily twitching their ears to the side.

"Hey girls," I say with a cheerful spirit, glad to see they were still in their stalls. I unlatch the doors and let them stretch their legs and graze a bit while I look for the well. I scratch behind their ears and under the chin for a bit, while

I decide which direction to search for the well.

My boots snag some roots hidden in the ferns and undergrowth and I catch myself a few times as I walk further behind the two stalls. The lush green canopy above me forms a natural cathedral, where sunlight pierces through the leaves, casting a myriad of dappled patterns on the forest floor. A mustiness of decomposing foliage with the sweetness of rain-soaked soil fills my nostrils, while the symphony of bird songs, rustling branches, and the occasional snap of a twig under my boots accompany me on my search.

"Finally," I murmur as the old water well emerges a few meters behind the old two-stall barn. Its sturdy wooden and stone frame stands strong, but the bucket boasts a few holes, battered and weathered from years of neglect. At least I didn't need much water. I would come back later and fill our canteens.

I lower the old bucket into the well, hearing the creaking of the pulley system as it strains. When it reaches the water, the bucket creates a soft splash that echoes up the well. I crank the pulley system, lifting the now water-filled bucket back up, and the soft trickle of leaking water echoes in the well. I quickly pour some water into the pan before it's all gone and then dump the rest back into the well, and hang the bucket, locking the level in place.

"Belle! Lady! Come on, girls." I call to the mares. Twigs snap and the brush rustles under hoof as they trot back to the barn. I open the doors and both girls obediently walk right in. I lock their doors and head inside to get breakfast ready.

"Oh good, you're back. I'm starving," Aislin says, clapping her hands. Her hair is slightly disheveled, and her eyes still hold traces of sleep, but there is a soft smile playing on her lips.

I set the table for two while I wait for the oatmeal to cook, placing the brown sugar on the table, along with two bowls and two spoons. I grab our canteens with just enough water to get us through breakfast and set them next to the bowls.

"Nolan," Aislin starts, grabbing my attention. "Thank you," her eyes shimmer with unshed tears, the emotions of the last twelve hours overwhelming her as she approached the table.

"You're welcome," I gently reply, holding her gaze. I walk over to the table with the pan of hot oatmeal and spoon half into Aislin's bowl and half into mine. We eat in silence, enjoying the warmth the food brings and the quiet.

We finish our breakfast and I leave her to clean up the dishes and pack our things, while I head back to the water well to fill our canteens with water. I reach the stables in time to see Belle and Lady pacing their stalls and pawing at the dirt packed floor. Something isn't right.

My brow furrows as I try to pinpoint what's amiss. As I scan the area for anything unusual, my heart pounds against my chest. The horses are clearly agitated, and I instinctively check their stalls, but everything looks okay.

Just then, I hear a faint sound in the distance - perhaps a whispered warning on the wind. Breathing deeply, I attempt to hone in on the noise. The distinct crack of a twig breaking echoes through the forest, causing Belle and Lady to whinny nervously. But it isn't just the breaking twig that sounds an alarm in my head. There is the stench of wet fur and the faint metallic tang of old blood. The same smell from the night I rescued Aislin in the field. I will never forget the awful scent of decay that permeated that field.

Ghosthounds.

Panic-stricken, I am frozen in place, unable to think. Do I grab the horses now and tie them close to the door, or do I take my chances and leave them in their stalls?

I go with my gut, grabbing their bridles and saddles, quickly tacking the girls up and leading them to the door. I thank my lucky stars as Aislin exits the quarters as if on cue with all our things packed.

I place a hand on Aislin's shoulder and move my index finger in front of my mouth, signaling her to keep quiet. I motion for her to hand me our bags, and I quickly and efficiently tie them to our saddles. She guides Belle to the stairs, using them as a step stool, and then mounts her. Belle stands surprisingly calm until Aislin is in the saddle, before she is prancing and throwing her head from side to side. I waste no time and swing into Lady's saddle.

Then I hear the howl of the ghosthounds and twigs snapping behind us.

"RUN!" I yell to Aislin, slapping Belle on the rump with my reins before kicking Lady into a full out run.

CHAPTER EIGHT

. SURPRISE, SURPRISE .

AISLIN

*E*verything happens too quick, with each scrape of a tree branch, I feel a new trickle of blood run down my face. I cling to the saddle with every ounce of muscle I have. One hand grips the front of the saddle, and my other hand holds onto Belle's reins. For a moment, a little freckled pony clouds my vision and my heart races as she barrels towards a cluster of shrubs. I cling on tightly to Belle, as I had clung tightly onto that freckled pony as a little girl.

Behind us, gruff, incoherent voices shout, but I don't dare look behind me for fear of solidifying my worst nightmares. That these men are after me. I know Belle is in tune with my rampant emotions. Her ears constantly swivel back and forth between Nolan and Lady, and then back at me.

The taste for adventure left me the minute Nolan screamed to run. Now, the terror of the chase impedes my ability to use my other senses. As Belle weaves through the tight-knit trees, I find myself blinded by green and brown flashes of color, narrowly evading tree limbs, and mentally incapable of thinking for myself; relying on Belle's instinct to follow Nolan and Lady's lead. The sweet sound of Nolan's voice brings temporary peace. If only I can hear what he is saying.

The shadows cast by the forest canopy create a strobe-like effect as filtered sunlight dapples the ground. I see Nolan and Lady's silhouette sharply veer right. In a split-second, Nolan's incoherent warning and the split-second visual of them veering to the right is a rude awakening. The ground beneath us suddenly angles dangerously, and I watch in horror as the lush foliage gives way to a gaping, deadly chasm. With a snort, Belle veers sharply to the right, barely avoiding the cliff's edge as her hooves scramble for purchase on the unstable terrain.

As I navigate the treacherous path along the cliff face, my breath comes in ragged pants. Whoever is behind us, they're close, and their jeers and threats only fuel my desperation. The forest's oppressive presence looms all around me, a suffocating cloak of shadows and unspoken doom.

I don't know how I stayed in the saddle, but it doesn't matter. My heart pounds in my chest so hard I can barely catch my breath. Froth covers Belle's muzzle as she heaves with exertion. I look back, scanning for any sign of my pursuers, but it's like they vanished.

Tears sting the corners of my eyes. I can hardly believe I escaped. My face presses against Belle's sweat-slicked neck while my trembling hands grip her mane. We made it and we are still alive. But for how long? Would they come back? The thoughts lodge themselves in my head like a burr, refusing to be removed.

Pulling on the reins, Belle comes to a halt, and another bout of panic sets in. Belle and I are completely alone. I was so absorbed trying to stay in the saddle, scared to death, I didn't realize Nolan and I had been separated from one another.

Belle veers from the cliff's edge and back into the overgrown forest. I look over the cliff and am suddenly aware of the natural obstacles that nearly claimed both our lives. My legs feel like jelly and my grip is unsteady. Hesitantly, I loosen my grip on the reins, settling into the saddle and letting Belle choose her way, as I lose myself deep in thought. I feel her muscles bunch and release beneath me as she maneuvers through the tight-knit trees. We walk in silence for what seems like a lifetime before my gaze lands on an object reflecting the sun's light. I urge Belle closer, hastening her walk to a trot, not sure what to expect or find.

When my brain finally recognizes what the object is, my heart leaps into my throat. It is Lady's bridle. I coax Belle up against the tree it is hanging from and scratch my right leg on the trunk. Gritting my teeth and trying to hold back a howl of pain, I look around the area to see if there were any other clues. Belle sniffs Lady's bridle, and I feel her entire body go rigid. What did she sense that I can't see?

I swing my satchel in front of me, taking in my surroundings while slipping the bridle inside my satchel. Belle is still nervous, flickering her ears back and forth and huffing from our mad dash through the forest. I gently pull out my mother's necklace and clasp it around my neck, careful not to spook Belle.

The sun begins to dip below the treetops, casting elongated shadows on the forest floor. Too tired to move and too scared to fall asleep, I didn't know what to do next. There is no way to set up camp, even if I wanted to. So, I let Belle casually weave her way through the trees, trusting she will find Nolan and Lady, because at this point, my internal compass is of no use.

"Well, Belle. It looks like it's just you and me."

I stroke her now sweat-crusted neck, trying to calm my

nerves and fears. She swings her head to gaze at me with her pretty deep chocolate eyes. Her muzzle is soft and spongy as she rubs it against my leg before pulling at the reins.

"Alright already. You can have the reins, but only if you promise not to kill me. It's scary enough being alone, and now I am trusting you to guide me?" And then, as an afterthought, I mumble, "It's not like I have a better idea, I suppose."

We push through our exhaustion in our search to find Nolan and Lady traversing through the thick woods even as dusk rapidly encroaches. My hope dwindles as each moment passes, but then a strong and pungent aroma of burning wood reaches my senses. It carries a pine scent mingled with an enticing touch of spice. I encourage Belle to advance carefully, and soon enough, our ears capture the faint sound of low, rumbling voices in conversation.

As Belle and I draw nearer, I carefully and gracefully slide off Belle's back, silently placing my feet upon solid ground. At first, I lean against Belle. My legs wobble beneath my lightweight frame. Even though my legs and muscles have become acclimated to riding, they have not yet experienced the strenuous involvement it takes to maintain one's balance on a galloping horse, weaving through tightly compacted trees.

Needing Belle to stay out of sight, I remember Nolan mentioning both mares were ground tied trained. I reach up and slip the reins over Belle's head and let the reins rest against the ground. I watch as the black mare dips her head, eyeing the reins and then blowing out a puff of air before she cocks one leg, resting. Convinced she will stay put, I tiptoe over to a congested pile of shrubs, carefully pushing the foliage aside to get a better view. I am greeted by a cloud of smoke traveling downwind and quickly cover my nose and mouth with my shirt.

Two men sit around a crackling bonfire, shadows casting upon their faces. Yet there is no sign of Nolan or Lady nearby. Frowning, I strain my eyes, attempting to discern any clue in the dim light.

Subtly, amidst the various shapes, I notice a considerable mound of fur—the steady rise and fall of the creature's breath betraying its presence. As my gaze wanders beyond the formidable beast, I finally catch sight of Nolan and Lady. Nolan is bound securely to a tree and Lady is tied to a thick tree limb. Nolan's expression is a mix of exhaustion and concern. I start to think of a plan to free them, but the voices of the two men cut into my thoughts.

"... tomorrow morning." A deep, rugged voice comes from the man furthest from me. His baritone vocals sound familiar.

That's strange.

I try to recall why I recognize the man's voice.

"I sure hope so. Chasing these rug rats was not in my job description." His companion complained.

"I hear ya. If it wasn't for the handsome reward, I would have never even bothered."

Bothered? Reward? I glower at the comments. We aren't criminals or outlaws. What were they talking about?

"I hope you were right to take the guy hostage." The man closet to me scratches the back of his head.

"She needs him. She won't be able to find her way out of this forest without him." I can feel smoke billow from my hot ears. How dare they consider me an invalid. I knew more in my pinky than these two put together. The other bloat lets out a full belly laugh and I feel my gaze become ice cold as I glare with dagger-like eyes at their backs. Now, they are going to pay.

Assessing their base camp, there is a dwindling fire surrounded by a company of rocks. Placed on top, playing a risky balancing act is a cooking rack. From the looks of scattered dishes, they must have just gulped down the last of their dinner. Whatever it was, it smells disgusting.

"You know, rumor is, this girl is close to the gods. That's what I heard *her* mention to the General before entering the girl's room." The man farthest away seems in charge of the entire operation. I glare at his back and I get this strange feeling I know the man. But from where?

"You mean to tell me that Lavinia believes stupid stuff like that? Come on, you're pulling my leg here, Adrian." The second man scoffs.

"No, Marko, I'm telling you, Lavinia said something about her mother's past and helping the gods with a task." Adrian's posture is lax, but his voice is passive aggressive.

"Sure. Believe what you want to, Adrian. But the fact is, the gods don't exist."

While the two of them argue, I creep to where Nolan and Lady are being held hostage. I don't get very close before Nolan's eyes spring open and only soften upon seeing me. But as I inch closer, he fiercely shakes his head in warning. I follow his gaze down to where I am standing and immediately understand his concern and caution. There is a huge bushy tail blocking my path.

I swallow several times, trying to calm my nerves. But, flashbacks of those menacing hounds chasing me flood my thoughts. The ground beneath my feet felt like it was going to cave in and swallow me whole. And then that awful image of white, snarling teeth and enormous body coming to a sliding halt right beside me, taking its last breath.

Its black fur rustles in the light breeze and, unfortunately, there is no way around it. I would either run into those monstrous ghosthounds or get caught in a thick clump of thorny bushes. My jaw tightens in frustration. I can't even reach Lady because she is on the other side of Nolan. I only see one option; carefully step over the ghosthound's extremely large and bushy tail. Nervously, I swallow as I make eye contact with Nolan.

His gaze feels like a heavy burden on my shoulders. I keep in mind if I had been paying attention, both Nolan and I would be here, tied to a tree. But another part of me wonders if I had stuck with him, would we have even ended up here? I hate *what ifs* and threw them all out of my head. I have to focus. It is now or never.

Taking a deep and steady breath, I focus on my balance, and successfully making it over the ghosthound's tail. As I move to step over it, it twitches, missing the leg I just lifted and hitting the leg I am balancing on. There is nothing to grab onto to steady myself as I wobble on one leg. Too many things will go wrong if I lose my balance. I just can't let that happen.

Forcing myself to take a deep, steady breath, I carefully and gently do a little leap to clear the tail. A triumphant smile plasters itself on my face as I succeed. I hear Nolan let out a long sigh of relief and swear I see a few beads of sweat on his forehead sparkle in the firelight.

Calmly and quietly, I walk gingerly over to Nolan and begin working on untying his hands. Whoever had tied up Nolan knew their knots, and it took a bit of work to figure out how to undo it. Letting out a low, frustrated huff, I feel Nolan lean in closer to me.

"Don't do that, Nolan!" I hiss through gritted teeth. "It makes my job impossible because you're taking away all the extra slack I need right now."

"Sorry...Sorry for making you come and save me. Sorry, I wasn't better at protecting you. Sorry I..."

"Shut up! You'll draw attention to us!"

That's when I hear the bushes rustle. Freezing what I am doing, I slowly turn my head to see who or what is behind me. But it is just the ghosthound readjusting his sleeping position. I let out the breath I had been holding. I want to slap Nolan so hard it leaves a significant red handprint on that pretty face of his.

"And you didn't make me. I could have continued without you." I mumble under my breath.

"Sorry."

I let his apology disappear into the night. There is a moment of silence. Then, an afterthought strikes me. "What are those large dog-like creatures, anyway? They surely can't be hounds." I ask, looking up at Nolan.

"Those dog-like beasts are ghosthounds. They come from an entirely different world than ours." He answers.

My muscles suddenly tense as I am about a meter away from the mythical creatures Nolan tried to warn me about. I swallow and try to focus back on freeing Nolan.

I am almost done loosening the last of the knots when I hear the leaves rustling against the ground. The smell of wet dog and hot breath on my neck scare me frozen. I snap my head up just in time to see the two guys make their way towards me.

Drat!

Dropping my progress without a second thought, I am up on my feet, jumping over Nolan's legs, trying to place the campfire between the two guys and I.

The crisp night air bites at my cheeks as the campfire crackles and spits embers into the darkness. One of the men towers above me, casting a looming shadow over me as he closes the distance between us, backing me up against the warm stones surrounding the fire. Cracks and pops from the flames should provide a soothing backdrop, but my heart races, as if begging to escape my chest. Adrian's malicious gleam in his eyes sends chills down my spine.

"Well, well, well, looky who we have here. Finally decided to show up, huh?" Adrian taunts me as he steps closer.

The sun disappears behind the horizon, casting eerie shadows among the trees. As darkness drapes the surroundings, I feel an inexplicable chill run down my spine.

"You don't remember, do you?" Adrian asks, his voice dripping with a sickening mix of satisfaction and amusement.

The night at the bar hits me like a ton of bricks. I try hard to focus on the details of that blurry night, sifting through the fog in my head.

"I feel like I've heard your voice somewhere before," I cautiously reply.

Adrian smirks, and in the dim light, I notice a distinct scar running across his jaw. It is the same scar I remember from that night. The man I had been talking to before my world suddenly went dark.

Realization sinks deep within the pit of my stomach; I know him. This man, in front of me, is behind the nightmare I am currently living. He orchestrated everything - from that drugged drink at the bar to my detainment at that compound. My heart-rate picks up as the memories come flooding back.

"You," I can barely conceal the disgust laced in my voice. "You are the one who drugged me, kidnapped me, and brought me to that compound. You're the one responsible for all this."

Adrian lets out a sinister chuckle. "You made it too easy, Aislin," he taunts. My name sounds so twisted coming from his lips, it matches the twisted smile on his face.

The fire inside me burns even brighter, fueled by the boiling rage that surges through my veins. I clench my fists, nails digging into my palms. No matter what, I won't let Adrian see me break. I won't give him that satisfaction.

"That's where you're wrong," I hiss, my voice cold and steely. "You may have managed to drug me, but I'll make sure you pay for what you've done. You have no idea who you're messing with."

The surrounding air grows heavy with tension, and for a brief moment, Adrian's smile falters. He may have succeeded in trapping me here, but he can't extinguish my spirit.

"Now you will finally learn your place," he sneers, his breath hot on my face.

Fear courses through my veins, feeding a fire that has nothing to do with the campfire behind me. I cannot comprehend how this man - this monster - hid such dark intentions from the night at the bar. Every instinct screams at me to run, but I'm rooted to the spot, unable to quell the tsunami of terror washing over me. He reaches out to grab me, but the moment his fingertips graze my arm, something in the blaze behind me stirs.

Adrian's wicked grin falters for a heartbeat as a sudden gust of wind feeds the flames, and they leap eagerly upward, forming tiny, snarling balls of fire. However, instead of dying down with the wind, they gain momentum, hurling across the gap between me and Adrian with an intensity I've never seen.

Adrenaline floods my body, realizing that I am somehow controlling these spitfire balls of fiery hatred. Could this rage actually be causing the fire to exist outside of me?

Brows knitting together in confusion, Adrian recoils as the first ball strikes him full in the chest. He opens his mouth to speak, but the second ball impacts his shoulder. I don't wait long enough for the third ball to connect as I stumble away from the campfire to catch my breath.

The revelation of my new found abilities still has me reeling as I watch Adrian with wide eyes attempt to dodge the inferno of fireballs relentlessly seeking him out. Distracted, Marko blindsides me, grabbing me from behind.

"I've got you now, little freak!" Marko growls, his breath hot on my neck.

Panic surges through me, and just like that, my energy focus shifts to Marko. I don't have time to process what's happening—all I know is that I need to get away. My energy pulsates surrounding me in a crackling glow of sparks.

Marko's eyes widen, realizing what's about to happen. I feel his arms tighten around my waist, and a scream of agony escapes my lips as he digs into my wound. With a sudden burst of power, Marko is thrown into the campfire. All the cooking pots and tools fly in all directions while flames lick at his tender flesh.

I drop to my knees, my breath heaving as I lose control of the energy I unknowingly summoned. The fireballs pursuing Adrian finally lose momentum and fizzle out, the once raging inferno now reduced to smoldering embers.

"You have not seen the last of me, Aislin. I will come for

you." I hear Adrian's voice get swallowed by the forest as he disappears from sight, leaving Marko to fend for himself.

But my fight isn't over. My focus had been on the two men. Now there is one more battle to fight. There is a snarl and then a low, deep, rumbling growl. I look up to see the ghosthound staring me down. Marko's shrieks fill the background noise and I can't see Nolan, Lady, or Belle anywhere. The black creature takes a step forward, saliva dripping from his pearly white fangs. His silver eyes are big and glassy, almost like I can see right into the animal's soul.

Frightening how the past can come back to haunt you. With no more energy to even get up and run. Déjà vu sets in and I collapse to the ground. But this time, the big, terrifying ghosthound takes one last long stride toward me before sinking his teeth into my arm. A searing pain radiates through me before I black out.

. TO THE RESCUE .

NOLAN

I wriggle and pull against the scratchy rope restraints, biting into my wrists and anchoring myself to the tree. The gnarled bark of the tree scrapes against my back with every move I make. The sound of Aislin's battle sounds desperate against Adrian and Marko, fueling my need to aid her. Her newly found telekinesis powers are all that hold Adrian and Marko at bay.

Meanwhile, the ghosthound snarls and paces back and forth, making sure I don't escape. Its insidious, glowing eyes watch Aislin's every move. My heart races in my chest, knowing she cannot take on another opponent without absolute disaster.

Adrian dodges one of Aislin's oncoming fireballs with grace and agility. My eyes widen as the errant fireball, now devoid of its intended target, careens directly toward me, searing the air in its descent. Panic surges through me as the blazing projectile speeds towards me. In a stroke of luck, or perhaps fate, the fireball cuts through the maze of shrubs and bushes before striking the rope binding me to the tree. The rope burns with sudden intensity, snapping and freeing me from its unforgiving grasp. Without a moment's hesitation, I turn my focus to the ghosthound just as it prepares to lunge at Aislin.

I reach out and grab the creature's tail, swinging the beast into the bushes. He leaps from the undergrowth, twigs and dirt clinging to its fur. Eyes blaze as it glares at me; his new found target. I brace myself for the impact as he lunges at me, teeth barred, ready to snap at my neck. My fingers grip his neck fur and hold his snapping muzzle at bay.

Pinned to the ground, my heart races, adrenaline coursing through my veins as I struggle to maintain control over the ferocious beast. Sweat pours down my face, stinging my eyes, but I dare not let go or falter for even a second. I can feel its hot breath on my face, each exhale accompanied by a guttural growl that sends shivers down my spine.

I brace my boots against the ghosthound's stomach and, with all I can muster, fling him backward over my body. The ground trembles beneath his imposing form, and a cloud of dust and debris arises as he crashes into the ground. I scramble to my feet, my breaths rapid and shallow. The adrenaline courses through my veins, sharpening my senses as I prepare for the inevitable counterstrike.

The ghosthound emits an angry roar, shaking off its momentary disorientation. Its diamond white, sharp teeth glisten with hunger and rage as it springs back up on its legs, towering over me once again. He lunges at me again, but I dodge to the side, narrowly missing his snapping jaws. I smirk a little and take the opportunity to attack from behind, but I am too slow. He whips around and, with one large sweep of his paw, his claws slice across my torso and I am sent flying through the air, and crash into a large tree. Out of breath and jolted by the impact, I fight to keep my eyes open, but I can't.

I regain my senses a few minutes later and see the ghosthound prowling towards Aislin, as she kneels in the dirt by the campsite. Desperation surges through me, drowning out any lingering pain from my previous encounter with the monster.

Frantically, I search for my bow and quiver. Those two cads just had to touch what wasn't theirs. Relief floods me as I spot my bow and quiver hanging from a nearby tree. *At least it is still here.* With every ounce of strength and determination that still course through my veins, I use the trunk to propel myself up and grab my things.

Without delay, I nock the arrow with a steady hand. Although I am sweating and terrified for Aislin's safety, I stay calm and collected as I aim the arrow.

The ghosthound snarls, stretching its jaw wide before sinking its razor-sharp teeth into Aislin's arm.

"Aislin!" I scream, my heart lurching in my chest.

Drawing the string back with confidence and precision, I exhale sharply. I release the bowstring, watching the arrow sails through the air, hunting down its target. With a heavy thud, the arrow buries itself deep into the beast's thick flesh. The ghosthound emits a pained, guttural cry before dropping to the ground, lifeless. But my relief is short-lived as I turn my gaze back to Aislin, sprawled out on the ground, unconscious.

Running to her side, I whisper, "Aislin, wakeup." My voice cracks with fear. "Wake up. Can you hear me?" But she doesn't answer. I lean down to see if I can hear her breathing, and a warm breath wraps around my cheek. *Thank you, thank you.* I breathe a sigh of relief.

"I'll be right back. I promise." I get up and sprint to where Adrian threw my bags when he had unsaddled Lady. Digging through my medical bag, I quickly pull-out bandages and medicinal herbs, then beeline it back to Aislin. I dress the bite wound on her arm, then roll her over to check her side wound. I flinch at the discoloration and sigh, seeing the wound slightly torn open.

No.No.No. I punch the ground and hear my knuckles crack. There is one thing I can do to guarantee no internal damage has been done, but it will drain me of all my energy. I rub my temples as I am forced to make a tough decision.

"Aislin, please hang in there. This may hurt, but I can't risk losing you." I plead.

I gently lift her shirt and place my hands over her wound. I feel the pulsating energy flow between her and I.

"Ahhhh!"

For a split second, Aislin's eyes open and she writhes in agony as my healing powers take effect.

"Aislin, it's me. Hold on. It's almost over." I say soothingly, concentrating on reversing the damage done to Aislin's body, repairing torn muscles and mending broken blood vessels. As I continue to heal her, the colors of vivid swirling energy around my hands start to change from a burning red to a soothing green, symbolizing the restoration process.

As the energy within Aislin shifts, I am both amazed and intimidated by her newfound powers. What little I witnessed is staggering, her raw strength unbridled and fierce. Yet, despite her powers, Aislin still lies unconscious and hurt, the intensity of the battle having taken its toll on her weakened body.

I heal the last of the internal damage and can feel her breathing became steady and strong. Gently pulling her shirt back down, I cradle her head in my lap. I can't help but wonder about the consequences of her untrained powers and the danger it poses to her, and even us.

My gaze drifts from Aislin's peaceful face to the destruction left behind in the woods; the deep gouges in the trees, the scorched earth, and the lifeless bodies of Marko and the ghosthound. Adrian somehow managed to get away unscathed. He will be back. And now that he knows what he is up against, he will be prepared next time.

It's clear to me that Aislin needs guidance, protection, and, most importantly, someone who truly understands her and the burden (and blessing) of her abilities.

Although the calm of the woods returns, I can feel the tension in the air. A storm of uncertainty looms, and I know I must stand by Aislin to help her harness her true potential and face the challenges she will inevitably encounter. I make a silent promise that I will always protect her, no matter what may come our way.

Scooping Aislin into my arms, I carry her over to where Lady is waiting patiently. I saddle Lady before gently lifting her unconscious form onto Lady's saddle, making sure she is secure and comfortable. Looking around, I can't find Lady's bridle. Ugh. This is going to make things a little more difficult.

Gently coaxing Lady and holding onto Aislin, we walk over to Belle, who nuzzles my shoulder affectionately. As I grab Belle's reins, I catch site of Aislin's satchel on the ground and pick up, only to see part of a bridle rein and grin. Lady's bridle. I take it out and slip it on over Lady's head. Then, I guide Belle and Lady deeper into the forest, the first light of dawn piercing through the canopy of leaves above.

The ghosthound's scent and Marko's blood still linger in the air, making it obvious that something violent had transpired. I know we can't stay in the area any longer, as the smell is bound to attract more attention from dangerous creatures or other hunters, but we're not safe or far enough away for me to let my guard down.

Exhaustion from healing Aislin nearly renders me useless, and my magic reserves are running low. I need to find us a safe haven soon, where we can recover from our harrowing ordeal.

As we trek further into the woods, the sounds of nature slowly return to replace the ominous silence that clung to us earlier. The serenity of the forest is deceiving, and I remain vigilant, guiding the horses through the winding paths, avoiding areas that hold hidden threats or lead to potential ambushes.

Finally, a small meadow, hidden from sight by a dense growth of trees and foliage, comes into view. A sense of peace and calm fills me and I feel this is a secure location to set up camp. I gingerly lift Aislin down from Lady's back, resting her body on a makeshift bed of leaves, and tie the horses to a nearby tree.

Morning rays of light filter through the protective foliage of our temporary sanctuary. I sit down beside Aislin's still form, gently brushing a few strands of hair away from her pale face, her steady breaths providing some reassurance that she will recover. Despite my fatigue and depleted power, I vow to keep a close eye on Aislin, ensuring her safety and well-being as we regroup.

One thing is certain: our lives have irrevocably changed. But for now, a few hours of rest in this hidden meadow should do us some good before we venture out once more.

CHAPTER NINE

. WHO AM I? WHO ARE YOU? .
AISLIN

s I wake to the sound of birds chirping, the sunlight filters through the dense foliage above, casting a warm golden glow on everything around me. The midmorning air is crisp, with a slight dampness that lingers from the night's dew. My body aches, muscles stiff from sleeping on the forest floor, and my mind is still hazy with the remnants of sleep. My eyes dart over to Nolan, hunched over gathering wood for a fire. Bruises cover his face, and his clothes are torn, but there's a newfound determination shining in his eyes.

As consciousness slowly returns, the events from last night come flooding back like a tidal wave. Sitting up abruptly, the images of Nolan tied to the tree, of Adrian and Marko attacking me, and the ghosthound lunging at me sends a shiver down my spine. But what terrifies me the most is finding I have powers I never knew I had. After last night, I feel it course through my veins, stirring under my skin and waiting to be used again.

I lift my hands and stare at them, torn between amazement and fear.

"What the hell happened last night? How did I end up like this?" I ask, shaking my head in disbelief. "And what are these powers? Where did they come from?" I'm not brave enough to look at Nolan for fear he might think of me as a freak. Or worse, and not want to help me anymore with my quest.

The sound of the forest provides a calming backdrop to my thoughts, but it's not enough to subdue the whirlwind of emotions within me. So many questions run through my head as I wait for Nolan to say something.

Nolan glances over at me with a solemn look. "I don't have all the answers, but I believe there is more to you than we both bargained for."

"What is that supposed to mean?" Confused and irritated, I stare back at my hands, feeling the energy thrum beneath the surface of my skin.

He takes a deep breath, like he is agitated, then replies, "It means you are not fully human, Aislin. You are probably a demi-god. Meaning, one of your parents is a god and the other a human."

"How can you say that!? How the hell would you know?" I rise to my feet, muscles protesting with every move. Suddenly not afraid to look at Nolan, I glare at him, demanding answers.

There is a long pause as Nolan avoids my eyes. He fidgets with the fire as I tap my toe, waiting for an explanation.

"Because I know. If you want answers, Aislin, Destiny is the only one who can give them to you."

Lier. But after spending six days of traveling with him, I know he won't tell me anything.

Shivering from the crisp morning, I walk over to a stump

by the fire and brush it off before sitting down. I hug myself and leaning in toward the warmth of the fire, my fingers rub against my side, looking for comfort in my bandaged side. But the bandage is gone. Panicking, I lift my shirt to see a very subtle scar.

"What the hell did you do?" I scream, jumping up.

"What happened? What did you do? Why does it look like my wound has completely healed?" My ears become hot and my pulse quickens.

"Because your wound is healed." He answers matter-of-fact, infuriating me more.

"Don't you dare weasel your way out of this one, Nolan." I reach out, grabbing his hand and spin him so he is looking at me.

"What. Did. You. Do? And why is my side completely healed? Tell me, Nolan. Now." As I speak and glare intensely at him, I feel a surge of energy transfer from me to Nolan. A little jolt, but Nolan and I both jump backward, surprised by the spark.

"I healed your wound." His voice is almost inaudible and I have to strain against the forest chatter to hear what he has to say.

"You what?" I ask, incredulously.

He sighs, looking at the ground, but speaks a little louder, "Because I healed your wound."

"How?"

"You're not the only one with powers." Nolan replies, his voice resolute.

I stumble backwards, taking in this information.

My eyes widen as I look at him in disbelief. "You... you

have powers, too?" I whisper, my mind racing with the unfamiliar possibility.

Nolan nods, finally lifting his gaze to meet mine. "Yes," he says, a hint of vulnerability in his eyes. "I have the ability to heal others."

The news hits me like running into a brick wall, relief crashing over me as I realize I'm not the only one with powers. I reach for my side, running a finger over the spot where my gash once laid. "Why didn't you tell me earlier?" I ask, curiosity and gratitude wresting for control of my emotions.

Nolan sighs and averts his gaze. "I didn't want to freak you out. But after last night, I figured you can handle it. Besides, it's not something I like to make known."

A few minutes pass as we stare at each other. I try to wrap my head around everything that has happened within the last couple of days, and it's just too much. I sit back down on the stump and rub my temples. Hard.

"So, what do we do now?" I ask, seeking advice from the only person who might have a clue.

"Continue on, just as we were. Last night changes everything, but it changes nothing as to our plan."

The chirping of birds grows louder, accompanied by the soft rustling of leaves as the forest awakens around us. Sunlight filters through the trees, casting a glittering effect of shadows on the forest floor as the leaves rustle. For a brief moment, I'm able to appreciate the simple beauty of it all. However, that peace is short-lived as the weight of our situation settles in.

My powers, unknown and untamed, are both a gift and a burden. I know I can never go back to the life I once knew, but as I gaze at my hands, a spark of determination begins to glow within me.

"How are you holding up there?" Nolan asks me.

"Fine, and you?"

The absent pain in my side has me going stir crazy and is a constant reminder of what or who Nolan was. Is. What I am. I don't know if he is ignoring my question, or didn't hear me. Either way, I suppose I meant it as a rhetorical question.

As the afternoon sun dips lower on the horizon, the shadows grow longer on the forest floor. The winding path seems to stretch on forever, but with each hoofbeat, we know we are one step closer to a town where we can stock up on supplies and hopefully, some well-deserved rest.

"We must be crossing into Bulgaria." Nolan mentions.

"How do you know where we are?" I ask, noticing the change in landscape, from the green fields, to the distant, majestic mountain peaks, and the distinct, far-off view of the occasional quaint village.

"I have traveled a lot and seen pictures."

"So, that makes you an expert?" I question, coming up alongside him and Lady as the path widens.

"How much traveling have you done?" He asks me and I feel my cheeks go hot.

"Not much," I admit. But instead of being snarky, Nolan laughs light-heartedly.

"Then I would say my experience makes me the expert." He throws a wide smile my way before urging Lady forward.

"Why don't we pick up the pace a little? I would still like a decent night's sleep. Wouldn't you?" He asks.

"You're not worried about Belle and Lady tripping over holes or rocks?"

"Lady and Belle are sure-footed. They'll be fine." He says, although I'm still not entirely convinced but move to follow him, anyway. I don't want to be left behind.

"Okay, then. Let's go." I cluck and nudge Belle into a trot.

The sun casts a warm, golden glow on the landscape, and the crisp mountain air fills our lungs as we take in the breathtaking scenery. The rhythmic sound of the horses' hooves sets a steady pace, creating a calming atmosphere.

I glance over at Nolan, his face relaxed and content. He meets my gaze and a small smile spreads across his face, acknowledging the shared happiness in this simple yet perfect moment.

Gentle winds rustle the leaves in the trees around us, and birdsong fills the air, providing a natural soundtrack to our journey. The trail we follow winds through lush forest before opening up to reveal sweeping views of the valley below. The sight leaves us momentarily speechless; the vastness of nature's beauty putting our own problems and worries into perspective.

"Hey, Nolan. Can I ask you a question?" I have been quiet until now, pondering how to ask my question.

"Sure. What's up?" He answers, keeping his eyes focused ahead.

"Why do you avoid talking about your parents?" I pause for a millisecond, not giving him a chance to say a word. "I am not trying to pry into your personal life, just curious.

You don't have to tell me if you don't want to. It won't hurt my feelings." All in one, drawn out breath, the words spill forth from my lips.

"In all honesty, I would rather not talk about my parents. It's a touchy subject. Greyson and Aeneas are really the ones who raised me, and I don't enjoy dwelling on the past." There is a finality in his tone and I pout.

"But it's getting so boring talking about me and my problems. I need something new and interesting to talk about."

"I'm sure we can find something else new and interesting to talk about." He replies, avoiding my gaze.

As the miles pass, each of us lost in our thoughts, the sun shifts its colors to a deepening reddish-orange, signaling that the day is drawing to a close.

"We need to find a place to set up camp for the night." Nolan says, motioning over to a small clearing nestled under the shelter of a grove of trees.

With practiced ease, we unload Belle and Lady and begin the familiar task of setting up camp; breaking twigs and branches to form a small campfire, gathering leaves and moss for beds, and rifling through our saddlebags for any remaining food in need of consuming.

The fire crackles and dances as we warm ourselves near its glow, sharing childhood stories and mulling over the future that lay ahead of us. Only the soft occasional snorts and rustles of the mares broke the calm of the quiet night air.

. THE MARKETPLACE .

NOLAN

Sunlight filters through the dense forest canopy, casting pockets of light and shade across the trampled earth where Lady and Belle proceed dutifully. The light plays with the colors of Aislin's clothes, creating an almost ethereal glow around her. Ever since discovering the truth about her powers five days ago, I feel a sense of responsibility toward her. Another burden I can't share with her. It undoubtedly would stir more questions than I wanted to answer, and I had already told her too much.

As we continue on, the terrain slowly morphs from lush and green to rocky and more arduous. The tree line begins to recede, giving way to a beautiful vista of jagged mountains stretching up to the heavens. The path ahead narrows, forcing Lady and Belle into single file as they continue their downward trek.

"You know," I begin, my voice bouncing off the rocky walls. "We should reach Vratsa by midday if we keep up at this pace. You've never been there, right?"

"No, I haven't," she replies, eyes scanning the landscape

ahead. "What's it like?"

"A lively trading town that's usually well-stocked with supplies," I say. "We'll pick up some food and other essentials. And rumor has it there's an incredible master blacksmith that can forge some great weapons."

Aislin frowns, "you think we'll need them?"

I sigh and take a moment to appreciate the view from horseback.

"I hope we don't. But after what happened, I would like to be better prepared."

She nods and remains quiet as the morning wears on. The sun continues to climb higher into the sky, illuminating the rocky path before us. We delve into silence once more, but it is a comfortable silence.

After a good trek down the mountainside, I move Lady to a sturdy rock overhang that looks out over the picturesque city of Vratsa.

"Come over here," I say, motioning for Aislin to join me. She urges Belle to stand next to Lady, and I watch her features soften into a smile.

It's impossible not to be awed by the view in front of us. The city looks like a painting, nestled perfectly in the valley below the winding mountain ranges, giving the illusion that Vratsa belongs exactly where it is, as if the land had shaped itself around the city.

Old stone buildings blend seamlessly with modern structures, a testament to the resilience and adaptability of the people who call this place home. Cobblestone streets wind their way around the city, their labyrinthine paths leading to bustling markets and quiet parks.

"Wow, this is gorgeous." Aislin sighs deeply, her eyes drinking in the sight of steep terracotta roofs, the shimmering river running along the outskirts, and the colorful markets full of life. I can't help but smile at her enthusiasm; it's infectious.

We stand there for a few more moments, taking in the view, observing the fairy tale like city with a tranquil admiration.

"We should get going if we want to stock up on supplies and find a place to sleep for the night." I say, watching as the sun continues its journey across the sky. I help Aislin up into the saddle and then mount Lady.

The sun blazes overhead as Aislin and I approach the bustling city of Vratsa. Vibrant and alive, the streets and markets are overflowing with traders, travelers, and locals alike. As we reach the city limits, we gracefully dismount Lady and Belle, their hooves clattering against the cobblestone ground. Our eyes scan the area for a temporary place to keep them as we explore the city.

"That older man, in the leather hat looks like he has a couple free stalls." Aislin points out across the road.

"Lead the way," I gesture to her and follow close behind.

"Good afternoon, sir. May we borrow these two stalls for our horses while we do our shopping?" Aislin tactfully inquires, her voice soothing and polite.

"Of course, young lady," replies the man with a warm smile. "That'll be two bronze coins per stall for the day, if that suits you."

Aislin and I exchange glances before collectively nodding in agreement. We each hand him the coins, leaving our horses in his capable care. Now, with our hands free, we eagerly venture into the city's buzzing marketplace.

As we walk through the throngs of busy shoppers, the lively sound of haggling fills the air. A myriad of colors and exotic scents engulf the marketplace as rows of stalls present an enticing display of local and foreign goods. We drift from stall to stall, finding ourselves lost amongst the enticing array of fabrics, spices, and trinkets.

The midday sun blazes above us, casting a warm glow on the cobblestone streets beneath our feet. In the distance, the enticing aroma of various spices and freshly baked treats fills the air, drawing in passersby. The energetic chatter of the townsfolk, the clanging of coins and the rustle of bags adds to the unique symphony of Vratsa's bustling market.

"Let's head over to the food vendors first. I'm starving for some real food. How about you?" I ask, unable to contain my excitement.

"Are you kidding, yes!" Aislin giggles, her eyes lighting up with enthusiasm. She grabs my hand firmly and pulls me toward the food carts.

As soon as her hand wraps around mine, I feel a jolt of energy and stop myself from bulking at the shock. This is the first time, not counting saving her life twice, we have physically touched each other. The feeling is electrifying, and I can't resist being drawn to her even more as we explore the market together, hand-in-hand.

As we approach the food carts, I'm greeted by the heavenly aroma that drew us here. The scene before us is a food lover's paradise: freshly baked pastries topped with sugar crystals, tender strips of seasoned meat sizzling on open grills, and plump, vibrant fruits piled high in woven baskets. The vendors call out their tempting offers, confident in their culinary delights.

"What are you craving?" I ask Aislin, scanning the vast selection of delectable foods.

She slowly releases her grip on my hand and the absence of her touch leaves me feeling naked. But she stays close as she surveys the vast feast laid out before us. Her eyes widen as they land upon a stack of steaming cheese-filled pastries.

"Definitely some of those!" she exclaims, pointing at the pastries. "And maybe some grilled lamb, too. Oh, and roasted vegetables. What about you?"

"I'm thinking I'll take what you're having," I reply, smiling, unable to resist the temptation.

Together, we weave through the crowd, sampling the best that Vratsa's market offers and filling our saddlebags with a selection that would last for several days. Eventually, we find ourselves wandering in front of a humble stall, where an elderly woman is selling various handmade wares. We crouch down to examine her skillful work, which includes everything from intricately embroidered handkerchiefs to colorful beaded jewelry. Aislin picks up a delicate silver bracelet, adorned with tiny sun-shaped charms.

"The design is exquisite," she murmurs, holding it up for me to see.

"It would look pretty on you," I agree, thinking of the sun's gentle rays illuminating the bracelet against her dainty wrist.

Before she can return the bracelet to its place, I take it from her hand and smile at the elderly woman. "Here, let me." I offer some coins to the woman and turn to Aislin. "May I?"

With a slightly surprised look, Aislin nods as I take her wrist gently and fasten the bracelet around it. The sun charms catch the light beautifully, making her eyes shimmer as she glances down at her new adornment.

"Thank you," she whispers, a sincere warmth in her voice that conveys her appreciation for both the bracelet and the moment we share at this little stall.

"You're welcome," I say, as my stomach does flip-flops.

With our arms weighed down from shopping bags, we continue weaving through the bustling market, pausing occasionally to marvel at the wares or enjoy the melodies from a group of street musicians.

As the sun begins to dip lower in the sky, Aislin and I, exhausted yet satisfied with our purchases, return to the stalls to collect our horses. As we prepare for the next portion of our journey, I catch Aislin admiring the bracelet and can't help but let a smile spread across my lips.

During our shopping spree, I failed to find accommodations for the night that had space for Lady and Belle. So irritated with hearing 'no, I am sorry. We are fully booked for the night.' I look to the gentleman who looked after the mares. My last hope before admitting to Aislin we would camp on the ground again tonight.

"Pardon me, sir," I say, grabbing his attention.

"Yes?" He replies, looking at me with kind eyes.

"You wouldn't happen to know of a place where we can spend the night and that is horse friendly?" I cross my fingers behind my back and wait, counting the seconds impatiently. I am drumming up likely scenarios when he quickly responds in a pleasant tone.

"I do." He says cheerfully.

"Where is it?" I ask, hope filling my voice.

"It's a couple hour ride on horseback from here. Just head up the road here. It'll soon taper off to a dirt road and it's at the end. The treehouse is hidden by a lot of trees, but has a gorgeous view looking out over the valley. You can't miss it." He reaches over to a small table and grabs a set of keys and hands them to me. "Go ahead. Take them. Just leave them inside the bench outside the front door when you leave."

"Thank you." I say, accepting the keys.

"Don't worry about it." He smiles and waves goodbye as we head out.

As we mount the horses, Aislin says excitedly, "I've always dreamed of staying in a treehouse that overlooked a beautiful view like this. I can't wait to see it!"

"Well, today is your lucky day," I smile, looking forward to spending the night some place with amenities.

We set off down the road and up the mountainside as directed. Century-old houses line the cobblestone road overlooking the pretty landscape of the valley city below. Oil lanterns line the driveways and light up the doors. With no electricity, burning candles light up the windows. It's just another reminder of the price normal civilians pay every day because of the Blackout War thirteen years ago.

Over the years, the once brightly colored houses faded, and now the muted colors accentuate the lush greenery of the surrounding forests, making it a breathtaking sight to behold. As we continue our ascent, occasionally greeted by smiling locals tending to their gardens or playing with their children, I can't help but feel a sense of serenity.

"You know, there was one year that our father helped us build a treehouse in our backyard." I half smile at the spontaneous thought. I look over at Aislin, as I sway in rhythm to Lady's gait. Aislin's hands are light on Belle's reins as she nods, encouraging me to continue.

"Greyson was about eleven, and I must've been eight," I continue, the memories becoming clearer. "It wasn't grand or anything, but the three of us had built it together. It was more of a platform with a roof and walls, but no windows or electricity. But to us, it was the most magical place." I chuckle and shake my head.

Aislin smiles, her eyes twinkling with intrigue.

"I remember we spent nearly the entire summer up there, playing games, reading books with flashlights, and telling ghost stories—even though we both pretended they never scared us. And there was this rickety old ladder we nailed to the tree trunk, which we thought was the perfect deterrent to keep our parents from ever coming up. But it never worked. Mom would just wait at the bottom, and Dad would assert his right as the builder to climb up whenever he wanted." I laugh to myself. "That is probably the best memory I have."

"Well, at least you have a happy memory. It's something you can hold on to."

I smile at Aislin's words. She's right.

We fall silent as Lady and Belle take us higher up the mountainside. The cobbles soon end, replaced by a dirt path surrounded by a dense yet peaceful forest. The air gradually cools and fills with a crisp, earthy scent of trees and damp soil. I breathe it in deeply, feeling invigorated by nature.

"We're close," Aislin whispers, her eyes shimmering with anticipation.

The sun dips lower in the sky, casting rich golden hues across the landscape as we finally reach the magnificent treehouse, nestled among the branches of several sturdy trees. It stands tall and proud amongst the trees, almost a part of the forest itself, yet still holding the charm of a handcrafted haven.

Aislin and I stop Lady and Belle when we reach a wooden walkway. As promised, I look around for a place for the horses and find a pen a few meters away.

"Let's put the horses away for the night, grab our things, and head inside." I motion for Aislin to follow me.

Aislin nods in agreement, and we lead Lady and Belle to the pen. Aislin opens the gate, and we guide the horses inside. I grab a handful of hay from a nearby stack and give some to each horse as a small treat, patting their heads affectionately.

"We'll be back tomorrow for you two," I say softly, stroking Lady's mane. Aislin does the same for Belle, murmuring sweet words to her. We then remove their saddles and bridles, storing them neatly in a corner of the pen.

Once we're sure the horses are settled in for the night, we turn our attention to our bags. I sling my backpack and the saddlebags over my shoulder, and Aislin grabs her satchel. Shoulder to shoulder, we make our way back to the wooden walkway, our boots creating a rhythmic pattern on the wooden planks beneath us.

CHAPTER TEN

. THE TREEHOUSE .
AISLIN

s Nolan and I ascend the wooden walkway bordered with wood railings, even under the moon's incandescent glow, I make out the two-story treehouse. There are two windows to the right, then a balcony overlooking the valley. It's almost as if we are on top of the world. Coming up to the front door, we pass an outdoor gathering area to our right. It is situated at ground level with enough seating to fit a large party group comfortably. Nestled underneath the balcony, connected to the large party area, is an outdoor living room. It looks like a cozy spot to snuggle up and read a book.

"This is amazing," I say, marveling at the furnishings. "You don't think this is the old man's place, do you?" I ask Nolan.

"It could be, although I am betting it belongs to someone he knows."

Nolan and I stop at the front door, and I wait while he digs out the keys.

"Come on, hurry up. I want to see what the inside looks

like."

"Settle down." He chuckles under his breath.

As soon as Nolan opens the door, I slip past him and gaze around the open floor in amazement. A cute and quaint kitchen greets us to the left, and a cozy little area to play board games and watch movies to our right. Around the corner is a freestanding, winding wooden staircase and beyond the staircase, leads out onto the balcony that overlooks the valley.

"Wow..." Is all I can muster because I am blown away by all the bells and whistles and yet this is the most charming house I have seen in a long time.

"I know." Nolan replies, just as much in awe as I am.

We set our bags on the wooden floor and head for the balcony, enjoying the breeze as it combs through the branches and needles of the pine trees. The balcony is open on all sides, save for the fourth wall of windows, looking into the first floor of the treehouse. Black furniture is a sharp contrast against the light-colored wooden boards. I immediately sink into the sofa, positioned up against the windows, gazing at the beautiful night sky. Nolan joins me, sighing a huge breath of relief.

"We made it." He says, leaning his head back.

"We did, didn't we." I answer with a smile.

I watch as Nolan stretches his long legs outward, resting his boots on the coffee table in front of us. Dirt crumbles off his boots and onto the table, scattering everywhere. I picture my papa doing the same thing and my mum pointing her finger at him. Of course, I remember my papa protesting, but my mum wouldn't have any of it.

I chuckle softly; the memory bringing a warm feeling

to my chest. "You know, you remind me of my papa sometimes," I tell Nolan, nodding towards his boots. He raises an eyebrow, a smirk playing at the corners of his lips.

"Oh, yeah?" he asks, amused. "What did your papa do?"

"Exactly what you're doing right now," I reply, trying to keep my tone light but missing my papa fiercely. "He'd always come in from working outside and rest his boots on the coffee table, dirt and all."

Nolan looks down at the dirt-covered coffee table, and guilt briefly flashes across his face. He sits up, lacing his fingers together in his lap. "I'm sorry. I didn't mean to make a mess," he says sincerely.

I wave away his apology, leaning back into the couch cushions. "No, it's okay. If anything, it's oddly comforting," I admit, smiling softly. "My mum would always tell him off for it, though. But he'd just pretend not to hear her and carry on with his business."

Nolan laughs, his eyes crinkling at the corners, and I'm grateful for the shared moment of humor. "Well, I promise I'll clean it up as soon as my legs stop aching," he says, rubbing at his thigh.

I nod in understanding, sharing a conspiratorial grin with him. "I won't tell if you won't," I say playfully, acting as if I'm swearing a vow of secrecy. We share another laugh, and for a brief moment, it's like the weight of the world lifts from our shoulders.

"Well, I supposed we should head to bed. You go ahead and take the bed upstairs. I'll stay down here." Nolan offers with a smile.

"Really?" I am thrilled, but keep my face neutral. I don't want him thinking I am inconsiderate, because I'm not.

"Really. There is a sofa inside and outside. I may sleep out here, anyway. It's a great night to enjoy the stars and the fresh air, all the while sleeping on comfortable furniture." We both laugh light-heartedly.

"Okay. You want me to grab your things?" I offer as I stand up.

"Nah, it's okay. I'll see you in the morning."

"Okay, then. Well, goodnight." I smile before heading inside. I grab my satchel and climb the staircase. There is no question, tonight will be one of the best goodnight sleeps I will have had in quite a while. And boy am I looking forward to it.

As the sun's rays' peek through the bathroom window to my left, I groggily open my eyes. They flutter a couple times, adjusting to the morning light. Stretching, I sprawl out my arms and legs underneath the quilted comforter. I'm ready to fall back asleep when I remember where I am and my journey to find Aeneas in hopes of finding Destiny. Destiny's note to me lies in the open on the nightstand, and I reach over to grab it. I turn it over in my hands; the message committed already to memory.

> *If you want answers, come and find me.*
> *–Destiny*

Throwing my legs over the side of the bed, I slip the note back inside my satchel and stretch one last time before pushing myself out of bed. The bathroom is long and narrow, resting up against the left side of the bedroom wall. Two sinks sit beneath the east-facing window, looking out over the valley.

Dipping my hands under the faucet, I cup the cool liquid in my hands and splash it onto my tired face. The sudden burst of refreshment awakens my senses as the droplets trickle down my skin and drip back into the basin. Gradually, my fatigue dissipates, replaced by a renewed sense of energy and purpose, ready to face whatever challenges that may come my way. I reach for the hand towel that rests perfectly on the counter to the right of me and pad all the excess water off my face.

To my left are the toilet and the shower. Drawing back the white shower curtain, the clanking of the hooks against the metal rod startles me.

"Gah!" I hold back a scream, but jump backwards, bumping into the toilet. I land on the toilet and thankfully, not in the toilet.

"Is everything okay up there?" Nolan calls from the first floor.

"Yes," I respond, embarrassed. I have no reason to be. No one saw me. But the feeling is there.

I take a long shower, soaking in the calming effect of the water raining down on me from the suspended rain head above. All the built-up struggles and stresses of the journey slip down the drain. Stepping from the shower, I dry off, braid my hair, and slip on the clothes I have been wearing since the beginning of the trip.

"I should have really picked up another pair of traveling clothes yesterday." I grumble as I carefully descend the winding staircase. My stomach growls at the smell and sound of breakfast being prepared. I can't remember the last time I ate a decent breakfast.

As I step onto the wooden platform, I'm greeted by a warm breeze that sways the tree branches around me. The morning sun washes over everything, painting the valley and city with a golden glow. It's going to be a beautiful day.

"Good morning," Nolan calls out, cheerily flipping what appears to be a fluffy pancake. He looks effortlessly at home in the small, rustic outdoor kitchen, surrounded by an assortment of fresh pastries and colorful fruits. "I hope you're hungry!"

I smile and settle down at the small wooden table nestled in a corner of the platform. Pulling the chairs up, I can't help but feel grateful for this little haven from the world below. It's peaceful, secluded and has a certain enchanting quality to it. "I am," I reply, the corner of my mouth curling into a half smile. "Thank you for whipping up this breakfast, it looks amazing."

Nolan grins proudly and places a plate piled high with food in front of me. There are crispy croissants, steaming pancakes, and a vibrant fruit salad that looks like a work of art. My mouth waters at the sight of it all. "Dig in!" he encourages, taking a seat across from me.

As we eat, we chat about everything and nothing, our laughter melding with the sound of the leaves rustling in the breeze. I can't help but feel content, savoring each bite and the company of a new friend who's quickly becoming dear to me. The fresh air and delicious food seem to have a healing effect, and as I glance at Nolan through the dappled sunlight, I get the unexpected feeling that maybe, just maybe, everything will be okay.

"Well, we should pack up and get moving. It's going to be another long day of travel." Nolan says, getting up from his seat at the table and clearing away the breakfast plates.

"Sure," I nod, rising and heading inside. I pass by the small library nook under the winding wooden staircase and pause, admiring the map hung on the wall. I reach up and gently touch the map and catch a few titles of books; How to Run a One World Government, How to Strike Fear Into a Country, and The Secrets of Government.

"Nolan, I think you should come and look at this." A chill runs down my spine and suddenly I feel light-headed.

Nolan quickly steps over to see what I've found. His eyes widen as he sees the titles I point out. "We need to leave now." He whispers, scanning the shelves for even more unsettling titles.

I nod and head upstairs, quickly grabbing my things. By the time I return to the main level, Nolan has the saddlebags sitting next to the door. He is holding some papers and looks uneasy.

"This is not good news. This treehouse belongs to someone in a very powerful position."

"Well, it would explain the luxurious amenities during a time of depression and recession around the world." I say, with a new perspective as I look around. Suddenly, the room becomes cold and I rub my arms.

"Mm-hm. This place isn't safe for either of us. Not after what we have encountered over the past couple of weeks, since we met."

I nod. The unease hangs in the air as we double-check every room before leaving.

As we step outside and begin to saddle Lady and Belle, I can't help but look back at the treehouse, sensing something more sinister than we can imagine. With a deep breath and Nolan's reassuring nod, we begin our journey away from the mysterious residence, not knowing what danger may lie ahead.

. STIRRUP SCARE .
NOLAN

This morning definitely put a damper on things. Finding out we had slept in a place where possibly corrupt government planning took place sends chills up my spine. Now, for the next few days, Aislin and I will be traveling through heavy-traffic cities by horseback and I will need to keep an extra close eye on anything suspicious.

"How are you holding up?" I call over my shoulder.

"A little nervous. I haven't seen this much activity in a while." She admits, her voice wavering.

We continue riding along the busy streets, Lady's and Belle's hooves echoing against the cobblestones. I can feel the tension emanating from Aislin, and I'm sure she senses mine as well. We exchange nervous glances from time to time, both aware of the potential danger lurking in every corner.

As we pass through the city, I notice Aislin's grip on the reins tightening as her eyes dart around, taking in the bustling markets and weaving in and out of the swarm of people. She's always been cautious since the day I rescued her, but I can tell her concern has escalated.

"Hey," I say gently, riding up beside her. "We're going to be okay. I promise."

"How can you be so sure? Look where we are. In unfamiliar territory, surrounded by thousands of people. Any one of them could be following us."

"You just gotta trust me, okay?"

She nods, and I can see the fear still evident in her eyes, but her trust in me, to keep her safe, is unwavering.

We eventually clear the city and find ourselves on a more secluded path. I can sense Aislin's relief, and my own muscles unclench as we leave the busy streets behind. The ride is silent for a while and when I look back to check on Aislin, I notice her foot slip from the stirrup iron. Her cheeks turn pink and I half smile, relieved to see her maintain her balance.

"There must have been a dip I the road." The excuse is lame, and we both know it, but we let it go, each smirking to ourselves.

"Sure. Remember that when you actually come across one and then let me know, so I can avoid it." I reply, half chuckling to myself.

I watch her place her foot back in the stirrup iron, but it's like I pressed the slow-motion button. The popping sound of the leather stirrup snapping in half startles me. Bringing half the stirrup and iron along with her now dangling foot, it slowly slips off her boot and clatters to the gravel, echoing through the tunnel of trees lining the road. Having no support to regain her balance, Aislin starts to slide out of the saddle. Belle doesn't help matters, jumping to the side at the fall of the stirrup iron. The quick movement causes Aislin to slide from the saddle at a quicker rate.

My eyes grow wide with concern and astonishment, watching her fingers intertwine in Belle's mane, gripping chunks of Belle's coarse hair. Aislin sways with other worldly litheness, in sync with the gravitational pull. She slides out of the saddle, clinging from Belle's neck as the saddle rests against Belle's underside. I jump off of Lady and run over to calm Belle as Aislin slowly lowers herself to the ground. Her boots make a soft thud upon the ground.

I wrap my arm around her waist the second her feet touch the ground and feel her body tremble.

"Are you okay?" I ask.

She turns into me and rests her forehead against my chest. My heart beat races, pounding irregularly against my rib cage. I know Aislin can feel it, which only makes my blood pressure rise.

I want to stay like this, stroking her hair, letting her know I will always be here for her. But I pull back and lift her chin so our eyes meet. Funny, I am expecting her blue eyes to be somber and diluted from the fierce coldness they held, but even in this moment of weakness and vulnerability, her eyes still held that unwavering and unforgiving, piercing gaze.

"Are your eyes always this intense?" I inquire. I don't mean to ask, but then again, I didn't plan on seeing such intense, icy blue eyes either. What I wanted to ask was if she was sure she was okay.

She half laughs. I am not sure if she thinks I am joking or trying to lighten the mood, but I will take her laughing any day. Avoiding my eyes, she wiggles out of my grasp. Her pride is hurt and I back away to give her some space. There is no doubt she is mentally tough, but even superheroes have their breaking points.

"I think we should take a break here," I suggest, pointing

to a small clearing off the path that seems relatively hidden from passersby. Aislin nods gratefully, eager to rest after her spill.

We dismount and unpack for a quick break, allowing the horses to graze and rest as well. Sitting down on a nearby tree trunk, I look over at Aislin, who is tending to Belle.

"You know, when Greyson and I were younger, traveling with Aeneas, we didn't get to stay in any place too long, always moving around. And we mostly traveled by horseback, too. Lots of hard-learned lessons." I say, thinking back to all the spills I took.

Aislin chuckles and shakes her head. "Well, that explains why you're so good at riding. It took me forever just to learn how to properly sit in the saddle without feeling like I was going to fall off at any moment."

"Hey, you've improved a lot since then. You're pretty much a natural now." I give her a wink and she laughs, shaking her head again.

"Maybe, but I've still got a lot to learn."

We sit quietly for a moment, taking in the calming forest music, watching the sunlight stream through the branches, creating shifting patterns on the ground. It is a peaceful setting, and I can't help but feel content being out here with Aislin. Despite the seriousness of our situation, for a moment, it feels as if we are just two friends on a casual ride, enjoying each other's company and the beauty of nature.

I take the broken stirrup in my hand and grab my emergency sewing kit. Before Aislin and I start our journey again, the stirrup needs to be fixed.

Carefully, I thread the needle with thick, sturdy thread and begin to sew the broken leather strap back together. Aislin watches me intently, an odd mix of appreciation and concern in her eyes. As I work, she reaches into her saddlebag, pulling out a small flask of water and two apples. She hands one to me, and we snack as I repair the stirrup.

The sound of birdsong and rustling leaves is calming, and in this moment, I can glimpse the briefest memory of a simpler time, when our biggest worries were things like horses and riding lessons.

"Did Aeneas teach you how to sew a stirrup leather?" Aislin suddenly blurts out.

I glance up at her, surprised by the question. "Yes, actually," I admit, a slight smile forming on my lips. "He was always good with sewing, fixing anything we managed to break or tear. He taught me, just in case I ever needed it along my travels."

Aislin smiles softly, a nostalgic look in her eyes. "It's always good to have skills like that, especially on the road."

I nod in agreement, finishing the final stitches on the leather strap. I hold it up, inspecting my work to ensure it is secure and strong enough to last the remainder of our journey.

"Alright, I think it's ready," I announce, wiping the sweat from my brow. "We should be good to go now." I swing onto Lady's back and glance back to see Aislin hesitantly standing beside Belle.

"Would you like some help?" I ask and she nods.

I carefully dismount from Lady and walk over to Aislin, offering her a reassuring smile. "Don't worry, it's not as scary as it seems. I'll help you get on, then we'll ride together."

Aislin looks up at me, her eyes filled with uncertainty, but she takes my extended hand. I help her put her foot in the stirrup and then give her a boost as she lifts herself onto

Belle's back. Once she's settled, I climb back onto Lady.

"Ready?" I ask her, and she gives a small nod.

Aislin nods, her eyes still full of appreciation. "Thank you," she says, eyes full of appreciation. "I don't know what we would've done without you and your skills."

I grin, handing her the water flask back as we prepare to mount our horses. "What are friends for, right?"

With a final check to make sure everything is secure, we gently nudge our horses forward, starting our long-awaited journey side by side. Our brave smiles belie the thrilling mixture of excitement and fear that courses through us, but we're in this together, and somehow, that makes it all the more incredible.

CHAPTER ELEVEN

. THE BLACK ROSE .
NOLAN

The next morning, I wake up on the ground, with Aislin curled up beside me. I can't complain too much. Unfortunately, I need to stretch and move about to keep my muscles from cramping any more than what they already were. Carefully, I move her to rest against the tree that had kept my sleeping body propped up. Looking down at her, she looks so peaceful.

I walk around our little campsite deep in thought. The fire dwindled out overnight, and I know Aislin will be hungry once she wakes up. I need to get a fire going and then make breakfast.

Glancing over to where Lady and Belle are dozing, I think about hopping onto Lady's back and going for a morning ride, but two things cross my mind. First, I don't want to leave Aislin here all alone, especially after the last few days. And second, I know a morning ride will turn into a morning gallop.

As I watch her sleep, I can't help but feel responsible for her; feeling like she was put in my care for a reason. My hand wipes down my face as I come to realize the enormity of my situation. I sigh, needing to walk, think, and look for kindling for the fire.

Tears threaten, burning at the corners, as I head into the woods, collecting twigs as I go along. The forest seems to hold its breath, the air still and heavy with an unspoken weight. The sounds of snapping twigs and the rustling of leaves accompany me, as if the very trees themselves are urging me to continue, to protect her at all costs.

My thoughts are a maelstrom of emotions - fear, guilt, determination - intertwining and battling each other like a never-ending storm that rages inside my chest. As I grasp a handful of twigs, my knuckles turn white with tension, my heart beats frantically, and my breathing becomes more laborious. The enormity of the situation is a crushing weight upon my shoulders.

And still, amidst the internal chaos, there is a glimmer of hope, a fire that refuses to be extinguished - the feelings I have for her, I have found my reason to fight, to protect, and to face whatever challenges life may throw at us. With my arms full of an assortment of branches and twigs, I turn back toward our makeshift camp.

Rounding a bend in the path, my eyes land on a strangely beautiful anomaly; what looks to be a black rose. The deep crimson petals are stark against the vibrant apple green of the forest grass. Thin rays of morning shine softly upon it. I bend down and take a closer look, touching its delicate petals. A jolt of energy shocks me onto my butt, and my head suddenly feels fuzzy. I shake my head, rubbing my temples before opening my eyes. I don't know if my vision is blurry or if I am imagining Aeneas fading in and out of existence in front me.

"Nolan? Is that you?" Aeneas's voice sounds distant and

like he is standing in a cave.

"Aeneas? How…?"

"Shhh. I don't have much time. You need to listen carefully. Aislin is in danger…"

"Yeah, we know…" I respond, folding my arms over my chest.

"Quiet. Listen. Go to Varna. I will meet you there… they… don't… careful…"

"Aeneas, you are cutting out. What is going on?" But Aeneas vanishes before me.

I look down and see the black rose beckoning to me to pluck it. My hand reaches out to scoop it up softly, cupping it in my rough hands. Bringing the exquisite flower closer to me, it starts to wilt; and the petals begin to turn black. It starts from the core and the change in pigmentation creeps to the edges. Soon, the rose is no longer the deep crimson red I had laid my eyes on, but a velvet black rose.

When the camp comes into view, I catch sight of her still sleeping form, and relief washes over me. Gently, I stoke the fire with the collected kindling, watching the flames dance and grow, providing warmth and light to the quickly ascending morning light. I start preparing breakfast when I hear Aislin stir, waking up.

I rise to my feet and walk over to her. Kneeling down, I sweep the rose beneath her nose. I watch as her crisp blue eyes flutter open. She sucks in a sharp breath and covers her mouth with a slender hand as she gazes at the enchanting flower. Her expression is a mixture of awe and amusement.

"I came across this, this morning."

"Why is the rose black?" She asks, reaching out a delicate finger to stroke one of its petals. My eyes could have been playing tricks on me, but I swear I see the flower's petal reach towards Aislin's single finger. I shake my head in bewilderment. I don't know why. It's a baffling occurrence. I figure it has something to do with who she is, but I didn't want to burden Aislin with my suspicions.

"I don't know," I say truthfully, in the dark just as much as she is. I see the enchantment begin to fill her eyes as she continues to gaze upon it in wonder, but something is holding her back.

"What is it?" I ask, but she just shakes her head, declining in silence.

"Would you mind if I put it in your hair?" But I don't wait for her to answer, as I scoot closer to her, reaching up to slip the black rose into her swept-up hair. I am in shock at how stunning and exquisite it looks beside those cold icy blue eyes and pale blonde hair.

"Thank you." A shy smile lights up her face.

"You're welcome," I answer with a grin.

The sun's rays finally break over the horizon line, and the forest is erupting with song. We need to get going if we are going to make it to Varna.

"Come on, we need to eat some breakfast. Get some energy back in our system so we can get going. We have another long day of travel ahead of us." I stretch out my hand and help her to her feet.

We eat our meal in a comfortable silence, the sounds of the forest serving as a calming backdrop. Once we've eaten our fill, we pack up our belongings, making sure to leave no trace behind that can give away our presence to any unwanted pursuers.

I lead us to the first main road I can find, and we stay on

it for a while. It is still bright and early, so I'm not expecting to come across anyone just yet.

"So, where are we heading to now?" Aislin looks and sounds more alert than during breakfast and the pounding in my chest calms down a little.

"We are going to travel to Varna. It's a Bulgarian port on the Black Sea." I don't feel alerting her to my interaction with Aeneas this morning is a good idea.

"What's in Varna?" She asks. I try to take in a casual breath, not wanting to give anything away.

"A friend who I think may be able to help us." I answer, hoping she doesn't question further. But as we continue down the gravel road, she seems occupied with the scenery.

. THE COUPLE .

AISLIN

We skip lunch and try to cover as much ground as possible. Leaning forward, I scratch behind Belle's ears and her head pushes against my hand, making me smile. I continue to give Belle some attention, feeling Nolan's gaze on me. I shudder as a tingling sensation courses through my body. He keeps stirring up butterflies in my stomach and I don't know quite what to do about them. So, I ignore them.

I watch as Nolan picks up the pace, and I urge Belle to follow suit. Picking up her hooves, she moves into an easy trot as we catch up with Nolan and Lady. I'm not sure what the urgency is until we come to the top of the hill and a two-horse cart catches my attention. They are just at the bottom of the hill and Nolan is already halfway there.

Belle and I are only a few strides back when we reach Nolan and the horse-drawn cart. He is already asking questions by the time I move Belle on the inside of Nolan, next to the cart, and politely smile a hello. The couple in the driving seat are clean and well dressed. It's only been two days since our night at the treehouse, but subconsciously,

I am reminded of my dirty clothes and smelly hygiene. I nonchalantly bring my nose close to my left underarm and cough, gagging on my own body odor.

Nolan and the couple snap their attention to me as I try to contain my coughing. I weakly smile in their direction as I let another dry cough escape into the corner of my bent arm.

This is so embarrassing.

How despicably disgusting. I smell like rotten eggs. And that is putting it nicely and diplomatically at best.

"Are you okay?" Nolan asks me.

I nod, afraid if I open my mouth to talk, I will cough and expel my nasty, pungent breath on the couple, who are only an arm's length away. I am so embarrassed; all I want to do is crawl into a hermit's hole and never come back out. It must have shown, because the heat in my cheeks flare up.

"Would you like some water, dear?" The lady asks. She sits next to her husband and has to lean across him to hand me a jug that had been on the cart's floor.

I nod and smile as her husband takes the jug from this wife and hands it to me. I don't want to seem like a greedy little pig, but the water is so cool and crisp, it is refreshing. The sweetness of the liquid covers my taste buds before extinguishing the burning sensation in my throat. I gulp down a couple more generous swigs, forcing myself to stop. I wipe the excess from my lips with the back of my hand, and hand the jug back, saying thank you without sharing too much of my bad breath.

"Why don't you follow us back to our home? We are just down the road and around the bend. You can take a shower and I'll make a nice, hot meal for you." The lady is so kind, as she offers to help us out.

"Yeah, why don't you two come back with us?" The gentleman says, coaxing us.

I know we need to maintain our travel time, but I am so hungry. With all the running and hiding we've been doing; I am ready to eat a cow. The sun is already threatening to fall behind the horizon. I look at Nolan, because I know he must be starving as well. But by the look in his eyes, I already know his answer before he speaks.

"Thanks for the offer. It is really kind and generous of you, both. But we really must be getting on our way." He replies.

The gentleman nods in understanding, but the wife is just about to protest, when my stomach makes a loud gurgling sound, sending three pairs of eyes in my direction. My cheeks burn and all I want to do is find a hermit's hole and crawl in there.

"You really do not want to keep this poor girl from enjoying a homemade meal, do you?" The woman asks Nolan, directing a stern glare in his direction.

Nolan sighs, "No, I don't. But please understand that we are under tight time travel."

"Of course, we understand." The couple acknowledge, as a delighted smile crossed the wife's face.

I stare at Nolan, trying to keep my excitement from showing. My mouth waters thinking of a homemade meal and I don't know how much longer I can wait.

We follow the couple back to their home and listen as they tell us interesting facts about Bulgaria's culture and food. A few times, I catch the lady staring at my head and shrug it off the first two times, but the third time she turns to look, I scrunch my nose and huff.

"Do I have something on my head?" I ask.

The lady smiles and lightly laughs, "a matter of fact you do. That is a strange black rose. May I see it?" She asks, gesturing to the flower in my hair.

Feeling a bit embarrassed, I carefully untangle the black rose from my hair and pass it to her. As she inspects it, I watch the velvety black petals begin to wilt in her fair hands.

"What an unusual flower," she remarks, looking more intrigued than critical. "There is a Bulgarian legend about a black rose. It is said that black roses are a symbol of eternal love and commitment, as they withstand the test of time just as true love endures all challenges."

The lady gives me an encouraging smile as she hands the black rose back to me, unaware of it wilting. "Perhaps this rose is a sign for you, a symbol of love to remind you of your strength and the power of love to overcome all obstacles," she suggests gently.

But the moment I take the rose back, I watch in awe as the petals stop wilting and come back to life. I look up to see if the couple or Nolan noticed, but they have moved on to a new topic of discussion and I silently wonder if my new found powers have anything to do with the black rose conquering its fate with death.

There are too many questions filling my head as I stare at the rose. So, I slip it back into my hair and urge Belle to catch up with Nolan and the couple.

"I love driving the horses down this road." The wife mentions a wistful look on her face. "We planted these Magnolia trees when we had purchased the property years ago."

The trees line the road on either side, and are blooming white and pink flowers. Petals cover the gravel road as we continue to follow the couple, who seem to follow the sandy colored stonewall, bordering the road. Wrought iron bars emerge from the wall, giving the impression of wealth and sophistication. Nolan and I stare at each other with amazement.

We watch as the husband steers the horses to the left and through an iron gate. The woman turns around in her seat and waves her hand, "come on. Follow us. The stables are this way." We follow suit, guiding Belle and Lady down a cobblestone driveway. Passing through the iron gate brings a feeling of grandeur.

Exquisite flowers of every kind pristinely line the sandy colored stonewall, perfectly pruned and maintained. The driveway divides into two gravel paths, one leading to the left, the other went straight. We follow them to the left, and watch as the path opens up to a huge, green yard. There, next to the stonewall that surrounds the yard, grows a flourishing garden full of fruits, vegetables, herbs, and spices.

"We don't get much of a chance to head into the city, so we grow most of our food." The husband nods to the garden, noticing my prying eyes.

The aroma of the garden wafts up the driveway and fills my nose with sensuousness smells. My mouth waters as I realize exactly how hungry I am. In fact, I am so hungry, the aroma from the garden is enough that I can taste the sweetness and bitterness of each individual vegetable. All I want to do is eat everything in the garden.

The couple pull up to a barn made of the same sandy colored stones and pink climbing roses cover the building. Instead of stall doors, a piece of black nylon stretches across the opening, and two other horses greet us from their posts. Dark brown wooden beams make up the roof and provide some shelter from the blistering sun. There are a couple of extra empty stalls, I see, which means there is room for Belle and Lady. The spacious box stalls will give the girls some leg room to move around.

Just outside the stalls is a stone trough. The spigot is an old well spout, with an old-fashioned lever to pump water. As Nolan and I bring up Belle and Lady alongside the couple, the husband jumps down from the driving seat and holds up a hand for us to stay put, bellowing out a command that I can not understand.

"Berk will see to your lovely mares. He'll take excellent care of them and ready them for your continued trip." He says, rounding to the other side of the cart to help his lovely wife down.

The stable hand exits the barn and holds Belle and Lady while Nolan and I dismount. I am so sore; I almost collapse, trying to steady myself once my feet hit solid ground.

"Are you okay?" Nolan asks.

"Yeah, just sore. You would think I'd get used to this feeling." I attempt to smile but cringe as I take a step. Nolan chuckles a little and offers his arm.

"You do get accustomed to it. Here, let me help."

"Thanks," I smile, taking hold of his arm.

Berk, the stable hand, leads Belle and Lady to their temporary stalls, while Nolan helps me walk over to where our hosts are waiting for us. As we reach the couple, I don't recall ever exchanging introductions. Gazing upon the lady, now face-to-face with her, she reminds me a little of the Bulgarian actress, Yana Marinova. With her long reddish hair, hazel-green eyes, and rose ivory complexion, she is naturally beautiful. Very down to earth and easy to like.

"I don't believe I caught your name." I say politely to her.

It is hard for me to break out of my comfort zone and start a conversation, but I make an effort for the sake of being polite.

"Oh, my dear. I am so sorry. I don't believe we have properly introduced ourselves. I am Mariana and this is my husband, Nikola. And who might you two be?" Mariana asks. Her smile waivers a bit and a slight tension rises between us.

"I am Aislin and this is my traveling partner, Nolan." I smile, trying to assess why things just became a little more uncomfortable.

"Well, Aislin, you look worn from your travels. How about I show you one of our guest quarters and you can take a nice shower if you like?" The tension disappears with a smile that reaches her eyes, and I wonder if I'm just imagining things.

"Thanks. That would be amazing, actually." I answer her.

"Great, follow me. Let's get you two settled in, then."

Nolan and I follow Mariana and Nikola to their house, passing the lovely gardens to our left. Thinking no one is watching, I quickly reach over and snatch a couple of pea stalks.

"What do you think you're doing?" Nolan leans to whisper in my ear, making me jump sideways.

"Geez, don't scare me like that."

"Everything okay?" Mariana asks, glancing back and seeing the pea stalks in my hand. I blush, but she laughs and motions for me to try them.

"Do you like them?"

"These are crisp and sweet. They are delicious." I smile with praise.

"That makes me happy to hear you say that. There will be more during dinner."

I can't wait. Giddy inside, my stomach rumbles, a little softer this time.

CHAPTER TWELVE

. LION'S DEN .

AISLIN

*N*olan and I follow Mariana and Nikola through their lavishly decorated villa. The polished wooden floor, embellished with beautifully crafted marble designs, creaks gently beneath our footsteps as we make our way to the guest rooms.

"Here's your room, Aislin," Mariana gestures toward an elegant mahogany door on the left. Nikola gestures for Nolan to follow him down the hallway. "Follow me. Your room is at the other end of the hallway."

"Thank you, Mariana," I reply gratefully, entering my room. The room is inviting. A combination of modern minimalism and old charm with high ceilings, intricately carved moldings, and sleek, contemporary furniture. A gentle breeze whispers through the open balcony doors, revealing a stunning view of the sprawling property and lush gardens below.

"Well, I will leave you to it. Dinner is in an hour," Mariana excuses herself, leaving me to explore my room. My soft footsteps echo in the spacious room as I move to the bed, laying out my dress. I graze my fingers over it, remembering that the last time I wore it was back at the tavern for dinner with Nolan. I shudder, thinking about the stranger and how this whole journey started with that meeting. A shower sounds delightful, to help gain new perspective going forward.

I enter the luxurious bathroom. The marble tiles are cool beneath my bare feet, and I am immediately drawn to the gorgeous, glass-enclosed rain shower in the corner, lined with smooth river stones. There is also an elegant, clawfoot bathtub prominently placed beneath a massive, floor-to-ceiling window with an extravagant chandelier overhead.

For a moment, I consider indulging myself in a relaxing soak, but the anticipation of dinner and the desire for human connection decided otherwise. I opt for the invigorating rain shower instead.

Turning on the chrome faucets, a sudden cascade of water pours like a torrent over my body. I reach for the scented shower gel – a pleasant fragrant of lavender and honey – and lather my skin. The warm embrace of the water washes away more than just the travel grime; it soothes my tired muscles and calms my frazzled nerves.

It isn't until the rivulets turn cool, I realize I lingered longer than intended under the showerhead. Reluctantly, I turn off the water and, with a satisfied sigh, step onto a plush white rug. I wrap myself in a fluffy towel, feeling the weight of the fabric on my shoulders as I dry off.

I leave the comforting warmth of the bathroom and glance at the delicate, golden clock on the wall – just enough time to slip into my lace dress before dinner.

The bed is huge, covered in silk sheets and a down feather comforter. There is a fireplace across from the bed, with a beautiful landscape mural hanging above the stone mantle.

The room makes me think of royalty with the chosen color palette, accented with a variety of unique pieces, but all with one color in common; burgundy.

The area rug covers much of the room, matching the circular shape of the room, with skylight windows making up the ceiling. As I look at the bed again, before I exit the magnificent bedroom, I admire the sheer canopy that hangs above and drapes over solid mahogany wood bedposts. In its own right, the allure of the bed itself is very enticing and almost forbidding. I wonder whom Mariana and her husband give this room to when they have company over.

With a renewed sense of energy, I braid my damp hair and open the bedroom door, ready for dinner.

As I reach the bottom of the staircase, I head down the hall and enter into the main room. The grandeur of the room is breathtaking. It isn't huge like grand ballrooms, but someone masterfully decorated the room to make it feel and look larger than what it is. I am certain this is where everyone gathers and meets first on the social nights that are held here. Large, floor to ceiling windows face south.

As I stare out the windows, the beauty of the landscaped yard mesmerizes me. It is immaculate, blooming with exotic life, almost fairytale-like, and sways under the light touch of the wind, as the sun slowly begins to sink behind the horizon, setting the sky on fire.

"Isn't it gorgeous? I always find myself staring out these windows. It's almost magical some nights." I jump as Nikola's voice echoes behind me.

"I'm sorry. I didn't mean to frighten you." He replies, witnessing my immediate reaction to his unannounced entrance. "It is not usually so quiet in the house. And if it is, it is usually just my wife and I." He continues.

"Do you hold lots of parties?" I ask.

He chuckles softly and nods. "Yes, we enjoy hosting gatherings for friends, family, and acquaintances. We hold a lot of state dinners as well. It's a wonderful opportunity for people to come together and enjoy each other's company."

I nod, alarm bells ringing in my head at the mention of state dinners, and take a moment to look around the room more closely. Beautiful artwork adorns the walls, and the chandeliers above cast a warm, inviting glow. The furniture, though clearly elegant and of high quality, encourages mingling and conversation. I can almost hear the echoes of laughter and the clink of glasses from past events.

"It's really beautiful," I comment, trying to keep a pleasant face. All the while, my head is exploding with likely scenarios. My skin becomes prickly, and all I want to do is find Nolan and tell him.

"Thank you," he replies. "My wife and I put a lot of thought and effort into making our home welcoming and vibrant. We believe that a space such as this should be shared and enjoyed, not kept locked away and unused."

Just then, Nolan rounds the corner and smiles when he sees me.

"There you are. You look beautiful."

I blush at his compliment and am about to reply when Mariana appears in the doorway. Her face carries a warm and welcoming smile.

"Ah, there you are!" she exclaims, her eyes lighting up upon seeing her husband. "It's time to eat." She announces.

Dinner smells absolutely divine and is making my mouth water. It is becoming clear to me what a rarity homemade meals are when traveling. Funny how that never crossed my mind before we left. But here is the opportunity to have a nice homemade meal that Nolan and I will devour.

As Nolan and I enter the formal dining room, I can't help but ogle at the smorgasbord of food that is laid out on the table. The table itself is a piece of work; handcrafted no doubt. Completely carved out of one entire stone. I let my finger graze the smooth surface as I weigh out my food options.

"Please, go ahead and fill your plate. We will eat out on the verandah." Mariana gestures to the table and then directs our gaze toward the two glass doors leading out onto the terrace.

I raise a brow at Nolan and he shrugs, just as impressed as I am. But neither of us hesitates for a moment as we each grab a plate and start stacking the food as high as we dare. There is so much to choose from, I have to leave some things off my plate in hopes I will still have room for a second round. But just to be safe, I make sure to include three of the most decadent desserts displayed among the rest of the baked goodies. Reaching the end of the buffet table, I grab a fork and head through the double glass doors and onto the garden terrace.

Walking out onto the verandah, I make my way over to the three-sided horseshoe seating area. Huge climbing rose vines crawl along the wall and up the pergola. Little bottled tea lights are lit and hang delicately from the beams. Scattered about, they give off the ambiance of a firefly lit dinner. The center of the seating area is an old barn wood table with swirly black iron legs. The cushions match the taupe stones that make up not only the terrace floor but the seating bench as well. Matching the rest of the home.

Mariana pats the open spot next to her and makes room for me to sit down. I wonder if she and Nikola have any children. I take a seat next to her and sink into the plush cushions, like I am sitting on clouds.

"Everything looks delicious," I say, staring at my plate.

I don't wait for proper etiquette and just dive in, devouring the first thing my eyes see - a stuffed pepper. The flavors explode in my mouth: rice, minced meat, and a mixture of herbs and spices. I can't help but let out a satisfied "Mmm!"

Mariana grins proudly. "I'm glad you like it. Stuffed peppers are a Bulgarian classic. I can't have you leave Bulgaria without trying them."

As the sun sinks lower in the sky, bathing the gardens in a warm, golden light, Mariana and Nikola share stories about their life in Varna.

"Nikola and I love to go to the annual summer festivals. Last year, there is a wonderful jazz festival down by the harbor, and we danced the night away," Mariana tells us with a nostalgic smile. Nikola nods in agreement, adding, "There's something magical about the live music and the sea breeze mixing together, creating the perfect atmosphere for a fun and romantic evening."

Nikola pours us all another glass of raki, the traditional Bulgarian brandy, as the orange and purple hues of the sunset reflect on our faces. The gardens around us are filled with the beautiful colors of blooming flowers, and the gentle, balmy breeze of the Bulgarian spring evening sets a warm, tranquil atmosphere.

"You know," Mariana smiles, looking at Nolan and me, "we used to take our kids to the theater quite often," she tells us, her eyes sparkling with fond memories. "There's a fantastic children's theater here in Varna that puts on classic plays, and it was always a delight to watch the performers bring the stories to life."

Nikola nods in agreement, adding, "It was a great opportunity for our children to learn about our culture and expose them to the arts from an early age."

"How old are your children now?" I ask, taking another sip of my brandy.

"They are all grown now. Working for the government with different job positions." Mariana says proudly. "We will be expecting our first grandchild soon." She adds with a smile that reaches her eyes.

Nolan finishes a large helping of a rich, creamy moussaka and asks, "Mariana, this is exquisite. May I get the recipe? I would love to share this with my brother."

She laughs, "I would, but it's a family secret, passed down through generations. What does your brother do?"

"Him and I own a tavern. He is in charge of the food and drinks. I just help out where I am needed." Nolan shrugs and smiles, taking a swig of his drink.

"Dinner was excellent. Thank you, but Aislin and I should really get some sleep. We have to leave quite early tomorrow morning." Nolan nods and shakes Nikola's hand.

"It is our pleasure. Please, let us know if there is anything else we can do." Mariana rises from her seat to see us off.

"Yes, thank you, Mariana, for the wonderful evening." I say gratefully. She bends over and gives me a hug.

"You're welcome."

Nolan and I head back inside and, once out of earshot, I wait quietly for him to speak. The minutes tick by slowly, but when his shoulders slump forward slightly, I can feel the tension leave his body in a wave. It is almost suffocating, like a hot arid desert.

"Do they seem at all a little too friendly to you?" Nolan kept his voice down and avoided eye contact. I thought a moment before answering.

"Good, I'm not the only one thinking the same thing. And what do you make of their children's job, working for the government? It makes me all squirmy inside." I pay close attention to Nolan's unspoken body language, but he is good at hiding whatever it is that is bothering him.

"Me too." He says, shaking his head.

"Have you noticed anything with the help?" I ask, feeling like we are being watched.

He shakes his head as a maid rounds the hallway corner, only to duck her head and disappear down another hallway.

"Something strange is going on." I lower my voice to a whisper.

We near my room and suddenly I wish Nolan would stay with me. But that may raise suspicion; the last thing we need.

"Good night, Aislin. Be careful."

"You too," I say, trying to reassure him with a gentle smile that I will be fine.

I am just about to open the door when I hear quiet shuffling accompanied by some whispering. Silently, I peek around the door frame and witness Mariana snooping through my bag.

How did she get here so quickly? And why is she snooping through my things?

My first reaction is to storm into the room, but I hold back more out of curiosity. *What is she looking for?* I wonder.

She shoves my things back into my bag, frustrated. It's clear whatever she is looking for, she didn't find it. My heart recedes from my throat and settles back into my chest, though I am still unnerved. Moreso now than at dinner. With this new side to Mariana, I'm not sure if I want to stick around any longer. But if I tell Nolan, it will look a bit suspicious to Mariana and Nikola, I'm sure after we told them we would spend the night.

"Hey Mariana, I thought you went to bed." I decide to play innocent as I walk into the room. Caught off guard, she spins around like she had seen a ghost. That is until she sees me.

"Oh, Aislin. It's just you." Her smile wavers as she moves closer to me. She fidgets with her hands and I do my best not to step back away from her.

Of course, it's just me. Who else were you expecting?

"I was just dropping off your laundered clothes." She points to the neatly folded clothes on the chair in the corner. My hand wanders to my side, remembering the cave-like-hospital room I had escaped. Involuntarily, I shiver at the memory.

"Is something wrong, Aislin?"

I jerk my head to see she had inched closer, but she isn't looking at me. Her gaze is transfixed on my neck, where my mother's locket rests. I reach up to secure it within my hand. It occurs to me maybe she had been searching for my locket…

But why? What's special about my locket? My fingertips tighten around the locket.

"No, I'm fine. Just a little cold." I lie. I force the words a little too hard, but she doesn't seem to notice.

"I see. Nothing a few blankets can't fix. They're in the closet, dear. Now, I must get to bed." Mariana briskly exits the bedroom and suddenly the room feels like it has eyes everywhere, watching me.

Swallowing, I go over to my pile of clothes and slip on my traveling attire. This will have to do for pajamas. Not that I am not used to sleeping in them. But it is mentally hard to get past as I climb under the covers. Before shutting my eyes, I make sure my mother's locket is secure in my hand.

It feels like I just fell asleep when I am being shaken awake. It's Nolan.

. FIRTINA VALLEY .

NOLAN

I feel bad for abruptly leaving Aislin at her bedroom door. But this whole day just seemed planned. Like they had been waiting for us. As I continue down the hall, I rub my temples with moderate force in a slow, circular motion. Hoping to rid my headache. If I don't, it will be a long night of tossing and turning. I knew the moment I heard those ghosthounds the night I saved her; my life would be tossed upside down. I just didn't plan on becoming so paranoid about the smallest things. Like meeting a pleasant couple on the road, enjoying a wonderful homemade dinner, and now watching over my shoulder to make sure Mariana and Nikola don't try to double-cross us. Trusting anyone other than Aislin and Aeneas is near impossible now.

Rounding the corner, soft frustrated mumbles reach my ears. Quickly sliding behind a hallway statue, I watch as a flustered Nikola exits my bedroom and quietly continues down the hallway in the opposite direction.

What the...? I watch him pass me, heading down the hall.

I want to bull rush him and interrogate him about snooping around in my room. But I stop myself as he disappears. What good will it do me? This is his home. I am merely just a guest.

Am I being overly paranoid for no reason?

Emerging from my hiding spot, I cautiously look around to make sure no one has seen me. Satisfied, I enter my room and scour the place for anything unusual. I let out a hesitant sigh, not quite ready to let my guard down. Nothing seems out of the ordinary from when I had left it. But that meant nothing. Nikola could have planted a listening device. I will have to remain silent until morning. Just to be on the safe side.

Stripping down to my boxers, I step into the adjoining bathroom to brush my teeth, but the mirror above the sink reflects the mark on my chest that would forever remind me of who I truly am. I stare at it for a moment, unfeeling of emotion and wondering if I am interfering with Destiny's plan at all with Aislin. I will never hear the end of it if I am. Pulling myself back to reality, I hastily brush my teeth and climb into bed. I can only hope the morning comes quicker than I can fall asleep.

"Nolan..."

I open my eyes to find myself at the foot of an ancient stone bridge. I narrow my eyes, focusing on the blurry figure in the center of the bridge, looking downstream. The current rages beneath, crashing against the boulders. The sound is deafening. How did I heard my name?

Wait.

Where am I?

I take a moment to scan my surroundings. Forests cover the mountainsides, trapping me in the nook of its valley. The valley is lush with life. Wild and free, with flowers blooming everywhere.

"Nolan..."

My attention diverts back to the stranger on the bridge. He looks old and worn. I hesitate, but feel a familiar sense of peace. Moss covers the bridge and I am not sure how sturdy it is. I feel his eyes piercing me, prompting me forward. When I reach his side, for a brief moment I smile, finally recognizing Aeneas. But my smile fades as quickly as it appears.

"What am I doing here?" I ask. He stays silent for a moment and the weight he must have been carrying transfers to me.

"It took me a lot of effort to reach you." I know better than to speak out of turn with Aeneas. So, I wait patiently, watching the river carry on without a care.

"It's not safe where you are staying. You must leave immediately and come to me." His voice is but a whisper and I have to concentrate extra hard to catch what he says.

"But where am I? Where are we?" I can't help my curiosity.

"I can only protect you and Aislin for so long. My powers are draining quickly, and the force after Aislin is only growing stronger."

"But how are we supposed to find you?" I ask, a little peeved he is evading my question.

"Stick close to the Black Sea and head due East. Look for this bridge. Once you cross it, you will have complete protection." I am so sick and tired of his evasiveness. I turn to address him, but to my astonishment, he is fading fast.

"They are here. If you do not leave now, everything will be for naught." I glance in the direction Aeneas nods, back in the direction I had come, and feel my heart sink; ghosthounds. As they approach, darkness envelopes the valley and I watch as the flowers wilt. When I turn back to Aeneas, he is gone.

"But where can we find you?"

"Aeneas!"

But it is useless. As the ghosthounds draw nearer, I feel my body grow cold and being pulled backward. And then darkness.

"Firtina Valley."

I bolt upright, drenched in sweat. Aeneas had never come to me like that, ever. What scares me the most is how real it all felt. Was it a dream? Or had it actually taken place in the spiritual realm?

Firtina Valley.

It rings inside my head like a bell before it fades. The sense of urgency has me slipping into my riding clothes and throwing everything else into my knapsack. Quietly, I make my way down the hallway, precipitately making my way to Aislin's quarters. I am careful not to wake any of the help living within the house. I don't know who I can trust. All I know is I have to get Aislin out of this house as soon as I can. I quietly enter her bedroom and make my way to her bedside.

"Aislin...wake up." With a gentle but firm shake, I watch her groggily open her eyes. She looks around the dark room and then back at me with confusion.

"Nolan? What are you doing here? What time is it?"

"I'll explain later, but it's not safe here. We have to leave now." Dragging her out of bed, I head over to the door. "I'll keep watch. Pack up your things." The hallway remains calm and void of any activity, save for Aislin's shuffling about the room. Within a few minutes, she is ready. Grabbing her hand, I quickly but quietly lead us from the house down to the stable yard.

The gravel crunches loudly in the stillness of the night as we make our way to Belle and Lady's stall. The stable light shines brightly and I wonder if having the stable light on is normal practice around here. Perhaps one of the stable hands heard us approaching and turned on the light. But when we reach Belle and Lady's stall, they are empty. Panic sets in. *We are too late.*

"Looking for these two girls?" Aislin and I spin around to see the man who helped us earlier lead Belle and Lady over to us. As he nears, I gently push Aislin behind me.

"Do not worry. A familiar friend visited me and said you required help." His friendly smile looks forced. Although it may just be my paranoia, too. I keep Aislin behind me as I make a quick but thorough look over Belle and Lady for any abnormalities or devices that are not ours and might have been planted. Wasting precious time, I did a second check. We cannot afford to be followed. Though not completely satisfied with my look over, we don't have any more time. I will just need to trust him, against my better judgment.

As we follow him into the courtyard to mount, the house lights abruptly flood the darkness. I can make out two figures and hear them frantically shouting out commands. *Were we ever going to catch a break?* I wonder as I turn to help Aislin mount, but am surprised to see her already up in the saddle, waiting for me to mount Lady.

As I did so, I turn to the stable hand, "I don't know whether to thank you..." But I' not given time to finish. He slaps Belle's and Lady's rump hard, sending us off into the night.

"Whatever you do, do not look back. Got it, Aislin?" I yell over the sound of galloping hooves. I catch her nodding out of the corner of my eye, but it isn't enough to calm my nerves as the yelp of dogs is heard behind us and the start of a brawl. Heeding my own advice, I keep my eyes ahead, paying attention to where we are heading.

"Nolan!" Aislin's plea startles me. Glancing at her, I see her white, stricken face transfixed on something ahead.

"Watch out!" But it is already too late. As Lady comes to a sliding halt, everything runs in slow motion.

I watch helplessly as two burly men emerge from the trees, snatching hold of Belle's reins and grabbing hold of Aislin. I watch in horror as she struggles to free herself and I am completely useless. And without proper training, she isn't equipped to call upon her powers. They throw a burlap satchel over her head, tie her hands behind her back, and place her in the saddle with another man.

Then I see flashes of movement ahead of me. Whipping my head forward, I notice a line of mounted men with a tall, feminine silhouette standing center, guarded by two massive ghosthounds. But it doesn't matter as I sail through the air, over Lady's head, and towards the gravel road. Suddenly, I am transported back to my dream with Aeneas and the two ghosthounds closing in on me. Before I hit the ground, blacking out, all I can think about is how I have once again failed to keep Aislin safe.

CHAPTER THIRTEEN

. THE CHOSEN ONE .
AISLIN

Not again.... As I slowly come to. The sound of voices filter in from beyond the darkness of my confinement.

This time, it's different. Whatever I am laying on is cold and hard. Instinctively, I reach to grasp my locket, but something cold and heavy weighs my hand down. I shiver against the cold, damp air and hear the faint echo of voices above me. I'm not sure if I want to open my eyes, and my better judgement tells me not to. But my curiosity wins.

I blink repeatedly to adjust to the dim light in the room, while rust fills my nostrils and an engine's distant hum vibrates through the metal floor of which I lay. As I struggle to sit up, I look down and see metal shackles on my wrists and ankles anchored to the wall.

There are two people talking just outside my door. Their voices are low, but I make out a few words.

"Leaving Varna..." A rugged voice interrupts the silence.

"Ferry...Black Sea..." comes another voice.

"Georgia..." the first voice responds.

I strain to listen more closely, desperate for any information that might help me escape. But their conversation remains vague, filled with references I don't understand. I know we traveled to Varna and stayed with Mariana and Nikola at their villa. I remember Nolan also mentioning a friend who could help us in Varna.

A sudden howl whips through the vents and the entire room tosses back and forth. I can hear waves crash against the side and I feel panic set it. How can Nolan's friend help us if we're on a ferry? Then, realization hits me. Whoever took us hostage plans to take us by ferry to Georgia across the Black Sea. What's in Georgia?

Where is Nolan? I look around the room frantically but don't see him anywhere. *Am I by myself on this ferry? Please, no.* I beg silently.

Feeling helpless and frustrated, I try to pull at my restraints. The chains are tight and dig into my wrists and ankles. It's clear that whoever put me here knows what they are doing.

I'm not sure how long it's been when I hear footsteps outside the door. My heart races as the lock clicks and the door creaks open. The grinding metal of the door sounds like nails on a chalkboard, and I cringe, covering my ears with my hands.

"So, Aislin, we finally meet again."

A familiar voice rings through the room. Only the last time I heard it, it wasn't so...welcoming. If that is even possible, which I feel in my gut, it isn't. I can almost hear the smirk in her words. I keep my eyes shut, trying to keep my heart rate from racing. And that's when everything comes flooding back from...was it last night? Or this morning? I wonder. Nolan had come and woken me up, saying we had to leave. But we were ambushed.

But how?

"It's kind of you and your friend to decide to join us. I was beginning to think you were trying to avoid me." Her voice is like an intoxicating poison infiltrating my thoughts.

It is ill-fated that I only remember who she is because she is the one person I am trying to avoid at all costs. And now, here she stands, right in front of me. Every warning signal sounds off in my head. As I try to retreat from her impending presence, the clinking of metal resounds in the small, confined room, and I am reminded of the short leash I am given.

With no place to go, I finally dare to look upon the woman who I escaped from a little over two weeks ago and am taken aback by her beauty.

Long blonde hair, almost light brown, shines like liquid gold under the lights. Her eyes are steel, both in color and aura. I can't help but notice a slight metallic gleam to them. Tall and athletically toned, she wears a pencil skirt that lightly hugs her waist and a sophisticated blouse adorns her torso. Soft curls gracefully drape over her shoulders. Why is it the smart and pretty women are always the 'bad-girls'?

"The silent treatment? Really, Aislin? I thought you would have been more grateful to me for having saved you that night. Bringing you into my home and providing you with a warm and comfy place to sleep. Only to watch you wiggle out the window and run off. What were you running away from? Surely not me, were you?" Her voice is void of emotion but somehow resonates grief as her gaze pierces into me. I can feel her trying to pry into my thoughts and fight hard to turn my gaze away from hers. The terrifying thing is I can feel her mentally trying to control me and she almost succeeds.

Who is this woman? And how does she have the power to get inside my head?

Suddenly, I look down at my own hands, recalling the night I discovered my own powers. I feel sick. The world I grew up in is changing. Too fast for me to soak it all in. Everything I had known is a lie. It has to be. Could she have some weird powers that allow her to read my thoughts? Could she control my thoughts? This is all too much.

A silent lull takes over the room and I am too deep in thought when the firm intensity of a masculine grip on my jaw forces me to look straight into the eyes of a vaguely familiar face. But I can't remember where from? My heart flutters and rages against my chest. Something about him terrifies me.

"You look a lot like your mother. Do you know that, Aislin? Practically a spitting image." His eyes are dark and captivating, and his cologne is intensely invigorating. I watch his mouth contort into an evil grin as he turns to look at the woman. "Don't you think, Lavinia?" His sun-kissed complexion and dark features would be enticing if he didn't wear a smug look. Curious, I look at the woman known as Lavinia. I can't make out her reaction, but I swear her eyes glisten with sad pride.

If he is trying to cause turmoil in my already crowded brain, he is doing a mighty fine job. There is no hiding my surprise. How would he know what my mother looked like? His evil grin remains as his eyes light up with affirmation. Even the cloaked figure back at the tavern had mentioned both of my parents.

What is going on here? I want to ask, but keep quiet.

All this time, when I could have turned to these people for

solace, where had they been? Why did they decide to show up now? All at once. What is this journey to find Destiny really about? I wonder, wanting to ask someone, anyone, but afraid if I did, I would divulge information I shouldn't. Whatever information that may be, I have no clue.

I remain silent as I feel my expression already gives away too much. Smirking, he softly traces my jawline before stepping back. I would be surprised if he didn't bruise my jaw. His touch leaves an unsettling feeling in my stomach. Out of the corner of my eye, the woman also looks a bit unsettled by his caress.

I watch him casually retreat to the room's door. I am waiting for both of them to leave so that I can stretch and test my jaw for any potential damage. But as he opens the door, he turns back to me with his sinister smile, a gleam in his eyes. His leave of absence is more dreaded than a relief. The frigid tone of his voice feels like a thousand tiny ice needles pricking my skin.

"Be a good girl, Aislin. At least until we meet again."

As the two of them disappear behind the door, a disconcerting feeling stays behind and beds down in the pit of my stomach. Suddenly, I am alone in the room with no hope of escaping.

The creak of the door wakes me from a deep sleep. Glancing over to see who the intruder is, I am slightly surprised to see a young girl carrying a tray of food. I don't realize how hungry I am until the aroma of meat and fresh fruit wafts into my nose. To confirm my hunger, my stomach rumbles loudly, leaving a gratified smile on the girl's face.

"It's good to see you again. When you disappeared that

night, I wasn't sure I'd see you again." Her voice is familiar, and I search my memory to place where I had heard it.

"Clarice, is it?" I ask hesitantly, remembering her delicate voice from when she and the other girl, Amelia, argued outside my room, the night I had escaped from Lavinia.

"How do you know my name?" She asks, surprised.

"That night I escaped, I heard you and Amelia talking outside my door." I admit, sheepishly.

Her eyes grow big and she almost drops the tray of food. "You were awake!"

I nod my head and then clear my throat. "Clarice, do you know why I am here?" I ask, eyeing the food tray.

"Don't you know? You are the chosen one." Her smile doesn't falter, and her eyes glow with admiration. That is, until she sees my perplexed expression. "Oh, dear. I've said too much."

I watch a petrified Clarice make a mad dash to the door, leaving the tray of food on a table, just out of my reach. As she nears the door, it swings open, revealing a very determined man. The same man responsible for bruising my jaw earlier. He looks at Clarice with a slight scowl on his face.

"What are you doing here, Clarice?"

"Just doing your bidding. I brought her some food." She answers hastily, without making eye contact. His face softens ever so slightly.

"Good girl. Now, go. Lavinia needs you on the second floor." He opens the door slightly wider so she can get by.

"Yes, Master Kieran." She says, bowing before she disappeared through the door.

"Now, where were we?" He says, not hesitating as he

makes his way over to me.

Tall, dark, and handsome are a deadly combination, and I feel the butterflies return, fluttering nervously in my stomach. I have to breathe slowly so I don't suffocate from the evil aura that surrounds him.

"So, Aislin. What made you leave in such a hurry back in Croatia?" He stops inches from me, his cologne is intoxicating, and I begin to feel faint. The tension in my muscles starts to dissolve and I feel my resistance to him melt away. Whatever drug is in his cologne is quickly taking effect. But I have to stay strong. I can't let him win.

I remain silent. It's the only form of control I currently have. He wants something from me and whatever it is; he isn't getting it from me. As he silently stands there, patiently waiting like a predator ready to pounce, I suddenly feel his fingers gently run up my arm, slowly up my neck, and then behind my ear until he is at my nape. His forefinger and thumb easily wrap around my neck, over my pulsing veins. A possessed smile overtakes his features as he tilts my head up so our eyes locked on one another.

"Soon, you and I will rule this world. You will be mine, Aislin. Make no mistake. This is our destiny."

The butterflies in my stomach shoot up my throat and I suddenly can't control the fear that consumes me. Clarice had mentioned something about me being the chosen one. The chosen one for what? Whatever it is, I don't want any part of it. Where is Nolan? At least with Nolan, I feel safe. He doesn't know I am supposedly the chosen one, does he? No, that is a preposterous idea, and I quickly shake it from my thoughts.

Kieran's lips are suddenly closer. He has me pinned up against the wall with no way to escape. What is happening? Frozen with trepidation, I can't move or think. I wish Nolan was here. The thought runs across my mind.

"What could one harmless kiss do?" Kieran whispers, licking his lips as he stares desirably at mine.

"Kieran, the Boss would like to have a word with you."

Kieran swiftly withdraws from me, clearly peeved, but holds his composure. He looks toward the door to where Lavinia stands. I take this opportunity to breathe and calm my racing heart. That was way too close.

But before a resentful Kieran leaves the room, he turns to me. "This isn't over. I will be back and we will finish what we started."

Lavinia, for the first time, wears a sorrowful look before following him. I am left to stare at the tray of food, just out of my reach. My stomach growls in protest. But no one is there to help.

. FAMILY TIES .
NOLAN

 have been up for only a few minutes and already the spotlights glaring down on me are making me blind. Suspended in the air with my hands shackled over my head, I try to keep my breathing steady and my mind focused. The sound of waves hitting the hull of the ship makes me dizzy, and I close my eyes, hoping to find some inner calm.

As the ship rocks back and forth, I feel nauseous, but I force myself to focus. Suddenly, I hear voices getting closer. My heart races as I prepare for the worst. The sound of footsteps grows louder, and I brace myself for whoever is on the other side of the door.

"...I know..."

"...needs...done...plan..."

The groaning of the ship and the crashing waves against the haul make it difficult to hear their entire conversation. Curious to see who captured us, I hold my breath. Is it the people who are after Aislin? It is the only logical explanation

I can come up with. *What do they want with Aislin, anyway?*

"...better off alone." The male's voice is arrogant. He sounds preoccupied with something else. I can hear the heavier footsteps slow down. But the click of lighter footsteps quickens.

"...need you..." she speaks with a clipped tone. Probably irritated with the jerk for leaving her to do all the dirty work.

"Are you really going to be that pig-headed about the whole thing?" The woman asks. I hear their footsteps stop just outside the room's door. I can hear their conversation easily now, despite their hushed tones.

"You know precisely why I will not go with you. It will jeopardize everything. It is best he doesn't know. My personal life stays out of this." His words sound like a gavel. An attempt to lay down the law.

"We both know that is hogwash. What are you so fearful of? We both know I'm in the same predicament as you." The woman's response is stern and matter-of-fact. It doesn't leave much room for argument.

"The only difference is she doesn't know. He *knows* who I am." I can't quite pick up what the emotion is behind his frustrated whisper, but it seems like he is afraid. But afraid of what?

"And that might be just the leverage we need." There is a smugness in her voice and I can imagine her lips curving into a wicked smile.

Before I have the chance to pretend I hadn't been eavesdropping, the door swings open to reveal a beautiful woman in a tight-fitting skirt and befitting blouse. I try to keep my mouth shut, but I can feel my jaw go slack. I swallow the lump in my throat, trying to keep my mouth from going dry. But as she steps into the room, it is the man that follows her in, though, that surprises me the most. His presence leaves me speechless and light-headed. After all these years of avoiding him, he is here. I watch him fidget a little and wonder why. It isn't like he is incapable of physically hurting others. He already proved that.

"What are you doing here?" I finally find my voice, though raspy from the lack of moisture in my mouth. I try to break loose, although I already know it's impossible. My movement causes the echo of metal from my shackles to echo through the room.

"Ahhh, so he speaks. A better welcome than our last guest." She circles me, eyeing me thoroughly. "Well, at least she has good taste." I want to wring the woman's neck and struggle against my restraints.

"I could be asking you the same thing." His voice carries over the clinking metal, stopping my incessant thrashing. It isn't doing me any good, anyway. Although it seems he is baffled I am traveling with Aislin, he doesn't seem the least bit fazed by the rest of the plan. I find it disturbing and wonder what he is planning.

"I don't know. You tell me. You are the one who brought me here, right?" I inwardly chuckle, despite how I feel about seeing him again. I still manage to get under his skin. Although, this time, I don't know how smart it is, considering he has the upper hand this time, but I just can't help myself. "It's not like you have the guts to do anything, anyway."

"You little..." Face swollen red with animosity, he launches himself at me, landing a couple of swift blows. I feel blood trickle from my nose and possibly my eye. No doubt I will have a bruised face by the time he is done. Unfortunately, it's not something I can say I'm not familiar with.

"Come on. Is that the best you got? Gonna beat up a restrained hostage because you can't..."

Suddenly, his fist strikes my gut. And then again. I gasp desperately for air. If his female companion didn't step in, I don't know if I would make it out of here alive.

"Kieran, that's enough. We need him alive if our plan is to succeed." At that moment, her sharp tongue is music to my ears. I'm even luckier when he actually stops.

She pulls him away from me and scolds him. He huffs and puffs, still seething with anger. But he doesn't come at me again. Not yet, at least. I try my best to catch my breath, fighting back tears of pain and frustration. I didn't think he would take it this far. But maybe I'm wrong. Maybe he really is the monster I remember. Maybe I'm the one who needs to accept that reality before it's too late.

My vision is almost gone, save for the narrow slits between my eyelids. I watch him take a few steps back. No matter how much I despise him, I had to admit he is in great shape. But then again, he always had been.

"You've been warned, Nolan. Stay away. This is not your business. Don't end up like your mother." He is gone, out the door, before I can even get a word out. He knows as much as I do, staying away isn't an option. That's what makes his threat even more periling.

The last thing I see before everything goes black, is the woman exiting the room. Who is she, anyway? Why is she with *him*? And how did she manage such calm authority over my father?

CHAPTER FOURTEEN

. FOILED PLAN .
AISLIN

I don't know how long it's been since someone came to check-in on me, but the tray of food never left the table and I am becoming light-headed and a little cranky. Suddenly, the door flies open, nearly dislodging itself from its hinges. An exacerbated Kieran bolts through the door and closes it behind him. My heart pounds with sudden surprise, then shrinks in fear. At first, he just stares at me with lust-filled eyes. I watch his eyes soften a bit, but his body is tense like a tightly coiled spring, ready to release its pent-up energy at any given moment.

"My dear, Aislin. I think it's time we finished what we started."

I try to press myself flat against the wall, imagining I can disappear. It's different this time. His strides are deliberate and slow as he approaches. It only makes the anticipation of what is going to happen next that more unbearable.

"Please, don't," I beg. I know my words and begging mean nothing to him. But as he inches closer, I see his unwavering desire to have me, and it won't take him long to ruin me. A tear trickles down my cheek as he stops before me.

"You have such a melodic voice, Aislin. So, soft and sweet." His hand reaches out and his surprisingly soft fingers graze up and down my jaw. I feel my throat vibrate as a whimper escapes my lips.

"Do not be afraid. I would never hurt you." He murmurs in my ear, brushing aside a few stray strands of my hair. But before his lips can touch mine, I shy away, turning my head to the side. The touch of his lips on my cheek blaze with a burning sensation. I feel an evilness linger where his lips grazed my skin. If this is what I have to look forward to, I want to die.

With a soft hand, he reaches under my chin and forces me to look at him. He places his other hand on the wall next to my head and presses his physically fit body against mine. This time, I have no choice. My legs shake violently beneath me as he slowly leans in closer. His lips come close to brushing mine, but he stops for only just a moment.

"Please, I beg you, Kieran. Stop." Tears slowly slide down my face as I beg him one last time. I know once he starts there would be no turning back. I feel the evil aura leave him and wrap its talons around me, holding me in place. Oh, please stop. I scream inside my head. I choke a little as I try to swallow the abundance of saliva that had quickly accumulated in my mouth.

"Hush." He whispers, resting a single finger against my quivering lips. "Everything will be just fine. You'll see."

I am about to pass out from sheer terror, but there is a sudden loud clang of metal on metal as the door swings open and slams into the wall. I glance sideways to see who it is and choke with happiness.

"Nolan, help!" I scream. With new strength and free

from Kieran's spell, I fight to loosen his grip on me. But I am no longer the focus of his attention as Nolan bull-rushes him, sending him skidding across the floor.

Nolan doesn't waste any time. Unlocking the shackles that bind me to the wall, he pulls me towards the door. We race down the ship's corridor and I am trusting Nolan has a plan to escape.

"This way." He whispers, tugging me to the left.

We weave our way through the corridors, hiding behind containers and machinery. As I follow Nolan, I'm not even sure he knows which way he is going. The next corridor looks no different from the last. But I would rather be with him, getting lost on this massive ship, then alone trying to escape myself.

"Hold up, Nolan. I need to catch my breath." I pull hard on his hand, stopping to catch my breath. My heart is racing and my anxiety and adrenaline are about to burst. This is too much hysteria to take in such a short amount of time. My body quivers with exhaustion and it's hard to ignore the jelly-like feeling in my legs. As bad as I want to stay where we are and let my racing heart calm down, I know we have to keep moving. I nudge Nolan to let him know we can move again, but he holds up his hand, signaling me to stop.

"Hold on. I think I hear the horses." He says, standing still.

"What good are they going to do us, Nolan?" I ask. "We are on a ship in the middle of the Black Sea."

He sighs, rubbing his hand over his face. "Back this way. Follow me." He pulls me and without much resistance, I follow but stop shy as he turns back down the hallway we had just come from.

"Are you crazy?" But before I can continue with my

rant, he cuts me off.

"Trust me. Otherwise, we won't ever get out of here." He counters. I look skeptically at him and down the corridor before letting out a resistant huff but follow him anyway.

"Alright. Lead the way." I don't want to argue and waste valuable time.

"There they are!" Echoes a guard's voice.

Nolan and I both freeze, looking up ahead to see some of the guards. *Kill me now. I knew this was going to happen. How come I didn't insist we stay on the course we were taking? We would have been just fine. Now look at what we are up against. The crazy and insane part of it all is, Nolan is still dragging me towards everyone we are trying to avoid. Can he not see or hear them? The closer we come, the more I feel my stomach in my throat.*

We are almost on top of them when I am suddenly yanked into a hidden narrow corridor with room for only one person at a time. Nolan pushes me in front of him and forces me to pick up my pace.

"Do you even know where you are going?" I ask breathlessly.

"No, but I am positive this will lead us to the upper deck."

"How can you be so sure?"

Nolan doesn't respond, but pushes me forward. We are both ready to faint from exhaustion, and then I hear a loud commotion above us. By the sounds of thrashing metal and men yelling at each other, it sounds like a storm has hit. I cover my ears and cringe as a loud bolt of thunder shakes the entire ship. I reach out to grip Nolan, and he wraps his arms around me.

"We'll be okay. I promise." I nod against his chest, too

scared to look up. "Come on, we need to get above deck and find a safe place to hide for the night."

"How do you know it's night?"

Nolan lets a half smile creep onto his face, and my heart melts. I missed seeing his smile, and it gives me encouragement to keep going.

"I have an internal clock." He admits.

Nodding, I turn back and start down the narrow corridor again. It doesn't take long to reach the end when we are met with a spiral staircase leading us to the upper deck. I can hear the howling wind incessantly pounding the door at the top of the stairs. Just the thought of having to climb up the stairs is a daunting task. But with Nolan behind me, encouraging and pushing me forward, I make it up the stairs.

The echo of boots clambering up the stairs is deafening, as the sound has nowhere to go but up. Each step is a pounding beat against my chest. I feel my blood vessels in my head beat with each pump of my heart. The metal grate stairs are steep, narrow, and go on for what seems like forever. I am beginning to wonder if I am ever going to reach the upper deck. And then there it is; the door leading to the deck; freedom.

But as soon as Nolan cracks the door open, the sheer force of the wind hits us like a brick wall. I have to shield my face with my hand to protect it from the driving rain. I can barely make out the outlines of the cargo containers and the creaking of the ship as it pitching through the waves making me feel sick to my stomach.

The wind whips my hair around and the rain soaks through my clothes instantly. I cling to Nolan's arm as we carefully make our way across the slippery deck, searching for somewhere safe to lie low until morning.

The cargo containers loom around us, their metal sides rattling and creaking in the gusts of wind. Finally, Nolan pulls me towards a corner of the deck. He pushes open a door and we enter a small room, barely big enough for the two of us. It's dark, but as our eyes adjust, we can just make out an empty room, except for some old rope and a shredded tarp.

"We're safe here," he says, reassuring me. "No one will find us."

I nod, my teeth chattering from the cold. Nolan takes off his jacket and wraps it around me, trying to keep me warm.

"Let's get some rest," he says, taking the tarp and folding it to create a barrier from the cold, damp floor before settling down on it. "We can plan our next move in the morning."

"Nolan?" I ask half asleep.

"Yes?" His voice is soft and warm. New feelings stir in my stomach as my head rests in the crook of his neck.

"How did you escape?" I hadn't time to think about it until now. But it seemed awfully strange the perfect timing of his rescue.

"Honestly, I'm not sure. It all happened so fast. I just remember hearing the lady and the man arguing about you outside my door. I don't recall how I escaped, but when I got out of the room, I grabbed the guard's keys to free you."

"Thank you." I yawn, snuggling in for a long night.

"Good night, Aislin."

I curl up next to him, grateful for the warmth. The storm rages on outside, but I feel safe in Nolan's arms. As I drift off to sleep, I can't help but wonder what will happen next. Will we be able to escape? Or will our captors find us before we have the chance? Only time will tell.

. GIRL OVERBOARD .
AISLIN

 orning comes too quick, and before I know it, I am waking up to Nolan's warm body next to mine. The sound of the raging storm outside seems to have calmed down, but I know our situation hasn't.

"Good morning." His breath tickles my ear and sends a jolt of feelings coursing through my body.

I smile and look up from where my head is resting on his chest. "Morning."

The tiny space is overloaded with hormones as we look at each other, our eyes completely adjusted to the darkness. Somehow, the distance between us becomes shorter and shorter until…

As if on cue, the door to our compartment closet unlocks and swings open with a screech. Nolan's grip on my hand tightens as we brace ourselves for what's coming, and the bright light outside momentarily blinds us.

I squint my eyes and try to make out the figures standing in front of us. A swarm of guards surrounds us, with the lady and her male companion in the middle, looking down at us with amused expressions. It takes me a moment to recognize the guard who pulls me from the closet and restrains me; Adrian.

"Did you miss me?" He chuckles arrogantly. I wince in pain, feeling the bruises forming on my skin.

"You wish." I spit out, fighting against his hold.

"I would watch what you say here."

"Is that a threat?"

"Yes, and a promise of things to come if you're not careful." He whispers in my ear. I grind my teeth and make one last struggle against his grip, but at this point, it's useless.

I watch as they yank Nolan up by his shirt collar and two burly men take over, restraining him. I see fear in his eyes, but it's not fear for himself as he looks at me, refusing to back down. "What do you want from us?" he demands boldly.

"Tsk, tsk. What makes you think you're important?" She says, smirking at Nolan before turning her attention to me.

I watch Nolan's face turn fire engine red, but refrain from lunging at the woman. The muscles in his arm flex though as his gaze drifts over to Kieran. I avoid his gaze, remembering the close call the night before.

If only she and Kieran would disappear for a minute, then I could escape. But where would I go? My eyes wander out to the open waters. They are calmer compared to the raging waves last night, but the sudden memory of drowning at the watermill floods my thoughts and I baulk at the idea of jumping overboard. But did I really have a choice if I escaped? There is nowhere to hide on this ship without being found.

Shivering, I turn my attention from the water, avoiding the lady's gaze and find Nolan's. A cloth wraps around Nolan's head to keep him from talking and I can feel anger building inside me.

"Aislin, dear. Don't test me again. Escaping me is not an option and you will fail." She turns to leave and the crowd of guards parts, but she stops and turns back to look at me. "You can run all you want. But you will never be able to hide from me."

I stumble back into Adrian at her words. For they are not just words or a promise. I feel her emotion as if it is my own, and the words spoken as if I spoke them. I can feel her inside my head, messing with my emotions and my thoughts. Adrian tightens his hold on me as I try to squirm out of his grip, but I can't fight her anymore and I feel myself lose the internal battle as I no longer have control over my body. I fall limp against Adrian, fully conscious of my situation.

"Good girl. Behave." She smiles before leaving the group with Kieran on her heels.

I need to escape.

I focus on turning a possible escape into a successful one. The night I faced Adrian and Marko in the forest comes flooding back. I need to save Nolan again. I can't find Aeneas without him. I need him. There is no possible way Nolan will escape and save me again. So, however I escape, I have to make sure I can save Nolan. But if I don't act quickly, I won't get another chance at ever escaping again. Gazing at Nolan, he looks so defeated.

With Lavinia gone, I start to feel her spell wear off on me. Adrian's grip loosens and although it's subtle, it's noticeable. Snatching the chance, I grind my heel into the top of his foot.

"Gah!!" He yelps, into my ear.

Wrenching free from his grip, the only escape I have is jumping overboard. With all the chaos ensuing quickly, my gaze rests on the port side railing, just beyond the line of guards in front of me.

I catch Nolan's pleading gaze and ignore it. My legs make a mad dash toward the railing. I'm not giving Nolan a chance to react. I convince myself this is the only way, my only chance, to save Nolan.

"Get her! What are you all standing around for?" I hear Adrian yell and smile to myself. I wonder what Lavinia will do to him, letting me escape twice.

Adrenaline races through me. Any sense of reasoning has vanished. In front of me, bright milky blue waters crash against the ship as I hurdle over the side and to my fate.

CHAPTER FIFTEEN

. CONSQUENCES .
NOLAN

Time stops as I watch Aislin jump ship into the Black Sea. Chaos ensues with all the deckhands and guards running around like chickens with their heads cut off.

"Man overboard!" Some idiot yells.

Lavinia reappears out of thin air, beside herself with fury.

"Well get her back! Don't just stand there, you fools!" She squeals.

"Yes, Lavinia." They all reply in unison.

I watch as the crew moves to the port side to look over the railing and into the waters that spread out before them. I have to give them credit for not running into each other, as they all flood together over to the railing, looking for Aislin. Watching these guy's level of competency raises a few questions. Like are these guys really that dull, or is Lavinia dumb enough to hire these guys on to help her? If she is really as powerful as she looks and acts, then having smart help would have been to her advantage, right?

"She's nowhere, Lavinia." One of them calls out.

"Yeah, she's vanished." Another one chimes in.

"Adrian!" She calls out.

I smirk on the sidelines and hold back a chuckle. *This outta be good.*

Adrian emerges from a group of men on the far left. "Yes, Lavinia."

I snort, not able to contain myself any longer. They both glare at me, but Lavinia's gaze penetrates mine and I can feel her thoughts inside my head. I try to look away, but am transfixed. My head feels like it will explode at any moment. I am about to pass out when she breaks eye contact and focuses back on Adrian.

"I am not even going to bother asking how she escaped." I can feel her eyes narrow, piercing through him, but I can't see his reaction. Goosebumps cover my arms as I listen to her frigid voice. "All I need you to do is promise me you will find her by this afternoon. No excuses." Lavinia digs her fingers into her temples and releases an exasperated sigh. She then turns to address everyone else on the deck.

"She'll be back." She says, bringing her hands back down to rest tensely against her sides.

"Keep an eye out for her. In the meantime, back to your stations and bring the prisoner below." She pivots to face the door that leads below deck, but then stops.

"I do not want another fiasco like this again. Do you understand?" By her tone, she is not asking but silently threatening anyone who undermines her authority.

"Yes, Lavinia." The chorus of men sing.

With each step of resistance from me, the men assigned to escort me below shove me forward. Every once in a while, they find it amusing, even necessary to stun me with their tasers, leaving me vulnerable long enough for them to control my next few steps, as I stumble forward.

"Get moving." One of them says, shoving me forward as we descend the metal staircase. My boots clatter against the stairs, echoing like a cave. With my hands tied, I work hard, keeping my balance as we descend the stairs.

I need to get out of here alive, for Aislin's sake. As I move to take the last step, I catch my foot on the edge of the stair and lose my footing, stumbling into the guard ahead of me.

"Enough of that child's play, Sam." The guard in front of me barks, turning around to glare at the younger crew member, assuming he tasered me, causing me to stumble forward. Sam doesn't look a day older than me. Probably in his late twenties.

The only good that comes from my stumble, as I understand, is no more being tasered, or at least until we reach the interrogation room.

"It wasn't me, Eddie!" Sam protests.

"Yeah, I bet it wasn't. In any case, no more. From anyone. Got it? We need him coherent for Lavinia." Eddie orders.

For the rest of the trek, through the maze of the under workings of the ship, the party escorting me remains quiet.

It's annoying. Really annoying. If she is trying to break me, she is right on track as she taps her manicured nails against the metal interrogation table. The spotlight glares down directly on my, making me half-blind while continuing to ask stupid questions that she already knows the answers to. Does she really, honestly, expect me to answer them? Probably not. My guess is, she's trying to buy time, to see if Aislin will show up to rescue me. If I know Aislin, the way I think I do, she is smarter than this.

"Do you truly think keeping me here will bring Aislin to you?" I inquire, speaking for the first time since the removal of the gag. My voice feels hoarse. I am tempted to take a sip of the glass of water sitting on the table, but don't.

"Yes, actually, I do. Let me tell you why. It's quite simple, really. She can either die trying to swim for her life, face the creatures of the deep who are always looking for their next meal, or come on board the ship to save her handsomely gorgeous beau and that pathetic thing of a horse. Now, you tell me, what sounds more appealing to you?"

The temptation to spit on her perfect hand, the one doing the clickity-click, is overwhelming. Despite she is probably correct about Aislin's slim options for survival, I'm not giving into her mind games.

Lavinia is about to continue with her worthless and time-consuming questions, when Eddie opens the door positioned behind me. I know it's Eddie because of the blocked-out glass window doubling as a mirror, reflecting Eddie on its surface. Why would anyone think that wasn't inconspicuous? The allure of intimidation didn't work for me.

"What is it Eddie? Can't you see we are busy?" Lavinia looks at me pointedly, before turning her steely gaze on Eddie.

"Sorry Lavinia. But one of the men above deck thinks they spotted her. Said it looks like she is hiding inside one of our lifeboats."

Now that I can picture her doing. The mental visual of Aislin hiding out on a lifeboat is quite amusing. But I don't want to give anything away, so I subtly swallow and nonchalantly look away, avoiding both their gazes. The scary part is, Eddie and the gang above were probably telling the truth, and that is the last thing I need.

Too many thoughts flash across her eyes, and an uneasiness settles over me with tension growing quickly. Standing, she brushes herself off while her eyes penetrate mine.

"Bring him with us. He may prove to be of use to us." Her voice is already halfway out the door when I feel myself being hoisted up out of my chair.

Shoving me forward, Eddie stays behind me while I trail Lavinia. Everything between the day I rescued Aislin from those ghosthounds until now is starting to come together. But one question remains unanswered: why? Why is Lavinia so intent on getting Aislin back? Is Aislin dangerous? Shivering, the thought is nerve-racking, since I never bothered to think of whether Aislin is really who she said she is.

I know who you are, Aislin Camille Burd...

The stranger's voice from the tavern weasels its way into my head. Goosebumps surface all over my arms and the tiny hairs on my neck stiffen. I take a deep breath. *Okay, what am I missing here?*

"Keep it moving, half-wit." Eddie says, shoving me forward again. I didn't realize, until now, how much I'm slacking. Even Lavinia is now tapping her heel against the metal grated walkway, making the unbearable ringing in my head. I already have a headache, but what's a headache without a full-fledged migraine? I want to scream 'stop the ringing' but have a feeling it won't do me any good.

"Keep him moving Eddie. I don't have all day." She turns to head above deck, and I can hear her grumble, but can't make out any of it. I certainly don't want to catch up with her just to eavesdrop, making it look suspicious. But it doesn't seem to matter, as I am pushed forward.

"Yes, Lavinia." Eddie replies.

As we near the door leading to the upper deck, I notice Lavinia's slender hand grip a pair of sunglasses and it doesn't take me long to figure out why. As soon as she throws open the door, the sunlight floods in through the doorway, blinding me. I try my best to shield my eyes with no luck.

"Ahh!" I exclaim under my breath. Even just an hour below deck and my eyes feel like they're on fire. I try to block out the discomfort by turning my head away, but the white dots flickering behind my tightly pinched eyelids make it nearly impossible to find relief.

Stumbling forward and out onto the open, sunny deck, Eddie is right behind me, making sure my feet keep moving. I am so distracted by the sun's penetrating glare and Eddie trying to feel important by throwing commands at me, everything else around me drowns out. I'm trying to pay attention and figure out where Aislin is hiding, but Lavinia is distracting me on purpose, I am sure of it.

"Where is she?" Her voice cuts through all the commotion.

The frustration and annoyance in her voice is a ticking time bomb. It feels like a brewing thunderstorm is about to unleash its fury and I am right in the center of it all. I watch as Lavinia stalks her way over to a guy who looks to be in charge of the deckhands. Her back is straight and her shoulders square; she means business. Everything about her is intimidating.

"We think we saw her on the port side, in one of the lifeboats." The man answers Lavinia coolly, but I can see the beads of sweat glistening off his forehead.

Lavinia raises an eyebrow. I'm not sure if she is going to blow her top with all that steam radiating off her, but her ability to restrain her temper is impressive. With all those embers inside her waiting to ignite, I shiver at how dangerous this woman really is. Suddenly, I am overwhelmed at the high stakes Aislin is up against and I feel my hope start to drain.

"Which one? Do you not know there is more than just one lifeboat on the port side? Do you take me for an idiot? Do you think I am not knowledgeable and informed enough to know everything about this ship and everyone on it?"

If I were a dog, my tail would be between my legs. As it is, I am already looking for cover. Some place to hide. I don't want to be anywhere near her when her last reserves run out and her internal ticking time bomb explodes.

"No Lavinia. Of course not." The guy gulps down his fear. It's like hearing a pin needle drop. "She would be on the second one from the front." He continues.

"Have you sent anyone to confirm she is even in there?" Lavinia narrows her eyes at the guy and I can feel the surrounding air become thin. I am having a difficult time breathing, but watch as the guy wraps his hands around his neck, indicting he can't breathe.

"It's a yes or no question, Perry. What is it?" The tapping of her heel reminds me of a Jack-in-the-box, and I brace myself for the witch to pop out, but the heel keeps on tapping.

"...No..." Perry strains to answer.

The tapping of her heel stops, and everyone holds their breath. The surrounding thin atmosphere doesn't let up as Lavinia continues to stare at Perry.

"Oh, I see." Lavinia calmly says, nodding as if she understands. Then points to the lifeboat and says, "Perry, go and check to see if she's there, will you?"

The tension in the air is unyielding and I find I am still holding my breath. Something doesn't feel right. I have no doubt Aislin is nearby, probably watching this whole thing. But as Perry cautiously and slowly works his way over to the lifeboat, my instinct screams for him to stop and come back.

Unclasping the cover, he peels it back, revealing nothing. The boat is empty. Lavinia doesn't waste any time as she raises her right hand, suspending Perry in midair. I watch, terrified, as he flails his arms like a crazy man over the blue water.

"Wait, Lavinia, no! Please, put me down. I have a wife and children." He pleads.

"As you wish, Perry." She shrugs, dropping her hand.

"No!" Perry screams as Lavinia releases her hold on him. We all watch the blue waters engulf him, but no one rushes to rescue him.

Her composure doesn't even falter a millimeter. The possibility of her heart being made of steel, to match her soulless gaze, would not be a surprise to me at this point.

Desperately, I scan the forward, hoping, searching for Aislin's familiar gaze and choke with relief when our eyes meet. Her familiar icy blue eyes fill with fear and send chills down my spine. Within seconds, rough hands grip my arms and pull me farther away from where Aislin hides on the starboard side.

I don't have to look where I am being drug to, I already know. But that doesn't stop me from fighting my way free, or at least trying to. Jerking and pulling my shoulders away from their grasp is the best I can do, seeing as my hands are still tied. For a moment, Greyson flashes through my head. Thinking of his ability to free himself from impossible situations. I wish and plead with the gods for his help.

Suddenly, the guys stop dragging me and, without warning, hoist me up and throw me overboard. For a split second, I feel the sweet release of rough hands relinquishing me, and I am airborne long enough to watch Aislin disappear back onto the ship. A gust of wind rushes past my face as I plummet towards the choppy waves of the Black Sea. The shock of the cold water hits me like a ton of bricks as I struggle to hold my breath. With no way of fighting back, the sea swallows me and my last thoughts are; will Aislin save me?

. THE LOCKET .
AISLIN

"**A**s you wish, Perry." Her voice carries over the wind and I can't watch as I hear the splash of Perry's body hit the water and his cries for help that are ignored.

Her name and facial features begin to register with me. Lavinia. The woman hunting me down since my escape from that dreadfully damp and isolated stone room. I recognized her face before recalling her name.

My chest rises and falls as I try to regain my strength. I am exhausted from treading water, trying to stay above the water's surface. My saving grace is the ship's hidden ladder on the side of the haul. Probably used for performing maintenance checks on the ship. I can still feel the strain in my arms and a pinched nerve in my neck from pulling myself out of the water to reach the ladder's lower platform. As I breathe in, I feel my lungs burn from the salt water and shiver against the wind.

"Let's check over here. She may be hiding on the ship already." Two men come up from my left and I sink lower into the shadows.

"I don't understand what is so special about this girl and why Lavinia has to keep everything so secret." Their footsteps are heavy and I feel the deck floor vibrate beneath me.

"Over time, you get used to it. Soon, it doesn't even bother you."

"Easy for you to say. You've been with Lavinia since she started this crazy hunt thirteen years ago."

Thirteen years ago? I shake my head. That seems impossible. Searching for someone that long and never giving up hope.

As the men continue down the deck, I cautiously move from my hiding spot and witness two burly men move Nolan over to the side of the ship. I try to get his attention, but he is too lost in thought to see me. I silently mouth 'no', slowly shaking my head, trying to force the men to stop telepathically. But it isn't working. Of course, it isn't working, why would it? Seeing Nolan's expression morph from relief to confusion only frustrates me more, as I try to hold back my scream. Getting caught is not going to help either of us.

I try to swallow the lump in my throat, but it is pointless. Nothing is going according to my plan. And after pulling and dragging myself up out of the water, which was a daunting enough task, now I am about to face it all over again.

I have one objective; to save Nolan.

Nolan's body disrupts the water with a popping splash. In an instant, I clear the ship's railing, before plunging beneath the water's surface.

My eyes burn as I frantically search the clear water for Nolan. I finally see him and he is sinking fast. Focusing on reaching him, my head pounds with anxiousness as I propel myself forward. I don't know how long he has before passing out, but I can't jeopardize any chance I have at reaching him.

It feels like forever before I reach Nolan. His legs are tiring fast, as he tries to keep himself from sinking any further. It's hard not to notice the sea life actively swimming around us. Especially sharks. Though, the serenity and tranquility of it all is soothing on a terrifying and intimidating level.

I wrap my fingers around my locket and suddenly realize I have a bigger problem to solve. How am I going to show Nolan the true purpose of my locket?

Locking eyes with Nolan, I lift my locket to my mouth and put part of it between my lips. Exhaling through my nose, I watch as Nolan starts to panic, but I remain calm. Then, for demonstration purposes, I exaggerate, sucking on my locket, breathing in through my mouth a fresh supply of oxygen. Nolan's bewildered expression morphs as his eyes widen in astonishment. Treading closer to Nolan, I extend my locket for him to put between his lips, but he points to the discoloration of my locket from rose pink to charcoal. I smile, as the depleted oxygen from the locket is minimal, hoping he understands it's not a big deal.

Our faces are so close.... I feel an electric spark jolt through my heart as butterflies swarm my insides. I can trace every marble streak in those hazel eyes of his. It is terrifyingly comforting. The bubbles of carbon dioxide tickle my neck as I watch Nolan exhale. And as he inhales, my locket pulses a glowing pink, as Nolan almost completely drains it empty. He releases my locket from his lips, it is time to untie Nolan's hands.

It's Nolan who surprises me this time, as his smile lights up his face. With twinkling eyes, he brings his legs up against his chest. At first, I am confused. Then something metal glistens in the sunlit waters, and I smile knowingly. Swiping the blade from its sheath, I'm careful as I saw through the coated rope used to bind Nolan's hands together. In unison, as I work to free his hands, we make our way to the surface. I do the best I can, pushing towards the sun's rays, as does Nolan, trying not to sink and drag me along with him.

Reaching the water's surface, we both break through and gasp for air. With Nolan's hands free, we both tread water for a silent moment. Looking out to where the cargo ship is, I groan. All that time spent beneath the water's surface had allotted the ship time to gain some distance. I don't know if I have it in me to swim the distance to reach the ship. The ladder on the side of the cargo ship I climbed up earlier today now he laughs hauntingly in my face.

"I hope you have the energy to swim and catch that ship, because I sure in tarnation do not." My ragged breathing only confirms my exhaustion as I struggle to tread water.

"Come on, Aislin, you can't believe that. I'll race you there. If you win, I will buy you lunch or dinner wherever you like." The proposal is sweet and kind. But sadly, I know the psychology behind what he is trying to do, and it isn't working. I am so tired, my body begs, no, is screaming at me to stop. I have used everything and now I feel like a floating corpse.

Whatever it is, it is hard. But I continue to lie still. If this is what the tortures of the fiery lake feel like, I repent. I want plush, cushy, soft. "Oomph." The exertion comes with little effort from my lips as I push myself upright. Eyes still closed, I tuck my legs, folding them Indian style. My forehead rests in my hands and my elbows in the crease between my knees.

My lungs feel like they are collapsing, and my rib cage feels like it is poking through my organs every time I breathe. I don't know what I did to deserve such agony throughout my entire body. I can't even open my eyes. All I want to do is just lay back down and sleep eternity away.

Then I remember…. Nolan being tossed overboard.

I try to jump up, but a pair of hands are suddenly restraining me from standing. Blinking a few times, I am perplexed by my surroundings until my eyes rest on Nolan. A sigh of relief exits my lungs with such force I become lightheaded immediately. Leaning over my folded legs and counting to ten, I take slow and deep breaths, trying to gain my composure before doing something rash that I will later regret.

"Ash, everything is okay. We are in one of the lifeboats. You would have collided into the yellow tarp if I didn't stop you from standing." He whispers.

The dripping sound of water distracts me. It is a stark reminder of my drenching wet clothes and water-logged boots. Sighing, I pull off my boots, half expecting to find sea life plop down right in front of me. Thank goodness, nothing of the sort happens. I steal a look over at Nolan, and am sure we both look how we feel. Only, he looks more awake than I feel.

"How did…?" I begin, but it feels like I swallowed sandpaper, and lots of it. So, I stop, hoping Nolan would finish my thought and answer my question.

"Well, it wasn't too difficult, as you were just floating. The trouble was getting you onto the ladder's lower platform." He shrugs, but there is relief in his eyes.

He started chuckling as I felt my eyes ogle in disbelief. He had drug me across the water, to the ship, lifted me onto the ladder, and now here we sit, in the safety and comfort of the lifeboat. No wonder why my body aches all over the place. I feel like I have been tossed around like a rag doll. Who knew, maybe I had. But one thing is for certain; Nolan had saved my life. Again.

CHAPTER SIXTEEN

. HUNGRY .
AISLIN

The next morning, I wake up sore and groggy eyed. Nolan and I fell asleep on the lifeboat, and that was a far cry from being comfortable. The waft of food makes my stomach gurgle. I feel my cheeks grow warm with embarrassment, trying to avoid eye contact. The ship's upper deck is quiet, but after the last couple of days, I am a bit hesitant to get out of our hiding spot. Stealing a glance at Nolan, it looks like he sup to anything to get some food as well.

"Are you hungry?" Keeping my voice low, I smile at Nolan and his vigorously shaking head.

"I thought you would never ask. That swim has made me hungrier than a starving caveman." Raising a quizzical eyebrow at him, he quickly clarifies, "an inside joke between Greyson and I."

"Do you miss him?" I ask, even though it is none of my business.

"Yes. I would be lying if I didn't say I am homesick. This is as far and as long as I have ever been away from the tavern or without Greyson and traveling together."

Nodding understandingly, I swivel onto my knees and peek out over the side of the lifeboat. The coast is clear.

"You ready? It looks clear to me." I say, glancing back to get an okay from Nolan.

"More ready than I will ever be. Let's do this." He answers.

"Great. Me first. You follow." I say, getting ready to exit the lifeboat, but Nolan pulls me back in. "What the..." And then he covers my mouth. Glaring at him, I follow his finger, pointing in the direction of a security guard.

"I will go first." He argues in hushed tones.

"No way. I do not plan on saving your tush again. Plus, you're big and bulky." I answer, matter of fact.

"Not like you're any better, miss I-don't-plan-ahead." Nolan shoots back.

Flushing a deep crimson, my icy blue eyes feel cold as I glare at him. "Pardon me for saving your hide twice already, Mr. I-am-better-than-you." I know he can throw back that he has saved my life as well, but as far as that situation went, we were on an even playing field.

"Fine, ladies first." His teeth grit together, and it's the first time I have seen him openly resist.

But instead of making a big deal of it, I reply, "thank you," closely double checking the perimeter around the lifeboat, before slipping over the side and gently landing on all fours, like a cat, before standing.

Nolan follows suit, and I hold back a comment when I hear his boots meet the deck. Out of the safety of the lifeboat, there is no time for arguing. Following Nolan, he directs our path, as he seems to know exactly where the food is.

Do they even have a lunchroom on these things? I wonder.

If they do, what are they like? Clean? Dirty? Old looking? Modernized? The questions overload my thoughts.

It doesn't take long for our noses to direct our hungry stomachs in the right direction. Of course, I should have been paying close attention to where Nolan is heading, with all the winding staircases.

Smashing abruptly into Nolan's back, he turns to look at me with his finger to his lips. It's then I see where we are. In front of me is a door halfway ajar. Mounted on the wall, next to the door, is a sign informing Nolan and I we have reached the cafeteria. I smile back at him. That is, until I hear a loud commotion coming from the other side. My smile quickly turns into a frown. But it makes perfect sense why we smell food. Because everyone is eating. Phooey. And I feel a big stomach gurgle coming on too.

"Now what do we do?" I whine, but Nolan holds a finger to his lips and turns back the way we came.

I am glad to see he is just as determined to get food into his stomach as I am. Heading to the right; it seems Nolan is trying to find a way into the kitchen. The only way this new idea will work is if no one is in the kitchen. Cringing, my stomach suddenly grumbles and I think the entire ship will hear. Nolan sure hears it, turning to look back at me, mouthing 'really?' in a sarcastic way. I shrug helplessly. What am I supposed to do? I can't exactly tell my stomach to quit complaining.

The door labeled 'kitchen' fills me with such joy, I think I am going to burst. Finally, I am going to eat and my stomach will be satisfied and silent. I don't have a clue what to expect when I pull the door open, but anything at this moment sounds good. Well, okay, not octopus or shark and definitely not clams, oysters or fish eggs.

"I want you to find her. Track her down. Do whatever you have to do. I need that girl before we dock in one hour." The voice is faint, but Nolan and I know exactly who the voice belongs to. *So much for breakfast*, I scowl. Would I ever catch a break on this ship? I remember someone mentioning the ferry would take three days. And this is the third day. Despite our situation, hope begins to stir within me and I find it hard to accept the possibility of not eating.

"I understand the urgency of your situation, and my men are doing everything in their power to accommodate you." A man's voice answers. "You already threw one of my best men overboard, with little thought."

"Is that a threat, Captain? Because let me remind you who you work for." Lavinia's voice easily overpowers the captain.

With the kitchen door closed, Nolan or I can't pick up any more of the mumbling. But I know the conversation isn't over. I'm tempted to open the door, but Nolan places his hand on mine, which already finds its resting place on the doorknob. Looking up at him, he shakes his head sternly. Scowling, I withdraw my hand. Why did he have to squelch my curiosity? And then the doorknob rattles. Nolan and I watch it slowly turn. It feels like someone is twisting my gut. And then the door slowly opens as voices escape through the opening in the doorway.

. BAD LUCK .
NOLAN

Split-second reflexes have me grabbing Aislin's hand and running back down the hallway, away from the kitchen door. I have no idea where we are going. Just anywhere away from everyone who is after us.

"Do you remember where we heard the horses yesterday?" I quietly ask, tugging Aislin to the left without hesitation.

"No, why? Do you?" She pants as she tries to keep up with my long strides.

As bad as I want to stay and catch my breath, I know we have to keep moving. Looking over my shoulder, there isn't much choice. Suddenly, we come to a "T", leaving us only two options and seeing as we are not going back the way we came, that leaves us one option.

"Let's go this way. We need to keep moving. Come on, Aislin." Pulling her toward me, I catch her off balance, but keep my pace. I won't let her become comfortable with our current pace.

"Wait, this looks familiar." It is her turn to catch me off guard, as she forces her body weight to rein me in. I oblige and stop.

"What is…?" I start to ask.

"Shhh… Wait and listen." She interrupts me.

Then we both hear it. Lady and Belle's whinny echoes through the metal hallways.

"Come on, this way."

As we wind our way through the cramped and musty corridors of the cargo ship, I feel the pounding of my heart in my chest. The urgency of our mission is ever-present. The fear of what can happen if we don't get to the horses before the ship docks weighs heavily on my mind.

I follow close behind her, her footsteps quiet in the dimly lit passageway, as my eyes scan the twisted maze of hallways for any sign of the horse stalls.

Suddenly, the soft whicker of Lady and Belle drifts through the air. She turns to me, her eyes wide with excitement.

"It's them!" She whispers urgently, beckoning me to follow her. We hurry along the corridor, drawing closer and closer to the sound. Maybe we will make it after all.

It is subtle, but immediately noticeable, as the narrow walkway begins to widen. I see the staircase leading to the bottom level, where Lady and Belle must be. I am expecting Aislin to slow down going down the stairs, but that isn't what she is thinking. I cuss under my breath as her pace quickens, and then she is sliding down the railing with precision and perfect balance. It's a great way to conserve energy and time efficient. So, I follow her example without delay. The stairs are steep and long. And I am beginning to wonder if I am ever going to reach the bottom level. And then I land, both feet beneath me, right behind Aislin, but we don't stop there.

I don't know exactly how Aislin plans to hide or not get caught, but I know I can't keep this pace up forever. The lower level is packed tightly with cargo containers. And with the flood lights overhead, the shadows and tight spaces will be our only saving grace. The twisting and winding between the containers definitely is not as easy as Aislin makes it out to be. At least for me anyway. The maze seems to be a fluid dance routine to her, and I am finding it difficult to keep up. Finally, breaking down, I grab Aislin's arm just before it slips out of reach.

"You have to knock it down a couple of notches. I am not as flexible and lithe as you are." I whisper. I had whacked my funny bone on the last corner of a container, and now I stand in front of Aislin, rubbing the bejeezus out of it. But all Aislin does is nod and then pull me into a tight, dark corner. I can hear the horse's nervous snorts, but it doesn't take long before I see other shadows patrolling near our hideout and wonder how long we can stay here before getting caught.

"All hands-on deck. Docking will begin shortly." The voice over the P.A. system is crisp and clear. It sounds like the captain.

"Can you believe it? We are so close!" The guy standing in front of our hideout complains.

"Where did they run off to?" Another asks.

"Beats me. But two of us should stay behind and keep a lookout." A third guard voices.

"I agree. They will want to use the horses as an escape." And then a fourth voice pipes in. It makes me hesitate to think how many deckhands have really followed us down here.

"Adrian, you head up with the rest of the guys. Lavinia isn't too pleased you let those two escape your grasp in the forest, and then again with the girl yesterday. And Bart, why don't you head up with Adrian?" A familiar voice says, but I can't put a name to the voice. "Sam and I will stay behind. Keep your eyes and ears open. They may have escaped back up the stairs. We don't want to rule out any possibilities."

"Yes, Eddie." Adrian and Bart reply in unison.

Eddie! No wonder why Sam and Eddie's voice sound so familiar. That dimwit, Sam, is the little punk who tasered me. I'm going to punch his lights out once Adrian and Bart leave. But I feel Aislin's icy stare on me. Her frosty glare keeps me frozen in place. But her touch is soft and gentle, sucking the anger from me and leaving my muscles relaxed. It won't last long, but for now, the calming sedative of her touch on my arm is enough to keep me quiet. I am not sure what kind of trick or mind game she is playing, but it reminds me of Lavinia's capabilities, making me shudder at the thought.

I panic for a second, thinking something strange is happening to Aislin, as I only hear myself breathing. So, I hold my breath, and listen for her breathing, only to realize our breathing synced together. I try to offset my breathing, but with her hand still on my arm, I find it impossible. It's like her touch is regulating my heartbeat and breathing.

Focusing intently on Aislin and my breathing, I miss the clamoring of boots on the stairs. But Aislin's touch changes. I don't know how I notice, as her grip is the same placid and lucid touch. But I feel her heartbeat quicken because my heartbeat is mimicking her heartbeat. I'm not sure if I should be scared, but I am definitely curious to know how she is doing it.

Catching my attention, Aislin motions for us to slowly stand from our crouched positions. I know she has the right idea. If we don't make our move soon, we will never escape. We start heading toward Lady and Belle, when she pulls my arm to the right, sharply, I might add. I grind my teeth in protest and to keep myself quiet. I have to keep reminding myself that she is stronger than she looks.

"I am pretty psyched you chose me to stay over Bart. He's pretty airheaded, ain't he?" Sam's voice is just on the other side of the container Aislin and I are hiding behind.

"Actually, Lavinia asked me to keep an eye on you." Eddie says. I can hear the silent weight of every word he speaks, as the two of them pace back and forth, guarding the horses.

"Why would she ask you to do something like that?" Sam argues.

"Because apparently you get taser happy and, according to everyone else on the ship, are unpredictable. You are still the youngest with a bigger ego than all of us put together. That sends red flags to Lavinia. She's smart and you would do well to learn fast and to listen to orders, or you won't last long." The warning goes unanswered and the two continue their pacing.

There is a sudden jolt as the ship docks, launching me into Aislin. Our noses almost touch and our breath entwine together. In the heat of the moment, our eyes lock on each other, searching for something we both know is there.

Then, with a sudden surge of courage, I lean in and press my lips to hers. It's soft at first, tentative, as if we're both afraid of what might happen if we let go.

But then something shifts, and the kiss becomes something more. Our bodies press together, our mouths moving in perfect unison as everything else fades away.

For a moment, I forget where we are, forget that we're on a cargo ship surrounded by danger. It's just me and Aislin, lost in the euphoria of our first kiss.

And as we finally break apart, gasping for breath, I see her cheeks flush and her face softens with a slight smile in the corner of her mouth. I know that this is just the beginning. There's so much more to explore, so many more moments to share together. And I can't wait to see where this journey takes us next.

"Do you think they are still down here?" Sam asks, breaking the silence between Aislin and me and bringing me back down to earth.

I can see his shadow as I inch my way over to where he stands until I feel Aislin stop me with her arm. With a sparkle in her eye, she reinforces her block with a severe shake of her head. Believe me, I want to argue the point, but keep my mouth shut. If it was up to me, we would be caught by now. That is a fact.

"Yes. I know they are. This is their only logical way out because of the cargo door." Eddie answers beginning to pace again.

"What is so special about this girl, anyway? I mean, why does Lavinia make it out to be a life-or-death situation whether or not we catch her?" Sam asks, with more questions I am sure clouding his brain.

There is a long sigh from Eddie, as he stops his pacing.

"You still haven't heard the story?" Eddie sounds perplexed. Like he didn't know how to process Sam's naivety of the situation.

"What story?"

I have to hold back my own snort. He sounds like a side-tracked little kid, ready for story-time.

There is a long pause, and I find myself getting antsy with anticipation. I don't want to admit it, but I am pretty certain I'm not the only other person interested in knowing this supposed story. Especially if it deals with the connection between Lavinia and Aislin. Which is hard to believe, but I don't want to shut out the possibility.

"The story of Lavinia, of course. Geez." Eddie states matter-of-fact, like Sam's question had been blasphemy against Lavinia.

"What does that have anything to do with the girl?" Sam asks, but is interrupted by Eddie's loud, bold and hearty laugh before he can ask any more of his naïve questions.

"What does Lavinia's story have to do with the girl? Everything! The reason that girl exists is because of Lavinia. Man, where have you been? It's legend. One of the greatest stories ever told. I can't believe you have never heard Lavinia's story. It's probably just myth, but even so, it explains a lot." Eddie babbles on.

Turning my attention to Aislin, I notice she has stopped breathing, frozen in place. Reaching over, I pinch her arm. Maybe a little harder than I intended, but it works. She withdraws her arm swiftly out of my reach, rubbing it persistently. But her focus is laser, and she doesn't budge from her spot.

I hope to hear more from Eddie, about Lavinia's story, but am blinded by the sunlight that peeks its way under the cargo door. The rattling sound of steel on steel is loud enough to wake a person from a coma. Covering my ears has no effect on preserving my hearing. The oversized garage door continues to screech, letting in more and more sunlight. So this is our way out, huh?

Maybe it wouldn't be such an appalling task if I knew where Lady's stall is located. I know there isn't much of an open opportunity to escape, and that timing would be everything. Suddenly, I begin to wonder why I am always the one to get caught. What if it happens again? Is it something I am doing wrong? I hunt and track for a living... I should be stealthier than I am. Maybe it's something I am not doing.

I keep a close eye on Aislin. Who knows, maybe it is her quick impulses that kept her from getting caught. Like Greyson. The negative thoughts keep working their way into my head.

"Earth to Nolan!" The soft demand of Aislin's voice tickles my ear.

She jabs her elbow into my side, startling me.

I gently rub my left side and raise my eyebrows. With an expectant and exasperated look, I mouth 'yes?'

Scowling, Aislin points to the horses. Turning my gaze to Lady and Belle; something is different. What is it? It is awfully quiet. Quiet! Where are Eddie and Sam? They must have been called away while I was off in 'la-la' land. Now is our chance. Looking back to confirm with Aislin our plan, she is gone.

I sneak a peek around the cargo container to see Aislin in Belle's stall.

How?

Aislin waves frantically for me to get a move on it. I grit my teeth; this is becoming old. I am either a step ahead, too soon, or a step behind, too late. Within five seconds, I am in Lady's stall and vaulting onto her bare back. With one swift kick, I entwine my fingers through Lady's mane and take off after Aislin and Belle.

Aislin firmly but gently guides Belle toward the opening cargo door. The door is not completely open, and I don't know if we are going to make it in time to squeeze under or if we will have to wait.

"Hey! Stop them!" Lavinia's voice rings from the walkway overhead. I don't have to, but I glance up to see her stationed, glaring down at us, and she is furious. Urging Lady faster and closer to the door's opening, I'm not going to be caught again. Not if I have anything to say about it.

Finally, able to taste freedom after three days, I can't wait to get off this ferry. A few strides behind Aislin and Belle, and I feel the warm sunlight on my face. Distracted by thoughts of meeting with Aeneas, Lady's head flings back and the crest of her neck slams into my face, causing my nose to sear in pain.

A few men lasso Lady and fight to keep her grounded as she kicks and bucks out at the men. I hold on tight, not much else I can do now. Then suddenly another lasso falls over me, wrapping me in a snug hug.

"I got him!" A crewman yells.

I can't hold on, as I am pulled from Lady's back and land hard on the floor. When I glance up to see where Aislin and Belle are, I catch the last few seconds of Aislin becoming one with Belle's neck, as they narrowly graze the bottom of the cargo door and into freedom.

"Get off me!" I yell, kicking out at one of the crewmen who snuck up on me. My boot lands just under his chin and knocks him to the ground.

Quickly, glancing back in Aislin's direction, I watch the duo pivot to see Lady and I restrained. Belle is hyper and excited as Lady whinnies for help. And I watch Aislin's face fall. Shaking my head, I can't live with myself if she and Belle come back to rescue Lady and I. My eyes adjust to the sunlight, which is now pouring in full force into the cargo ship. But all I see is Aislin and Belle's silhouette. It is majestic, with the golden rays engulfing them from behind.

"Run and don't look back! I'll catch up. Find him!" I am so transfixed with Aislin; I overlook the crewmen that now surrounds Lady and I. I have done everything I can do to keep Lavinia in the dark about where we are heading. Now it is up to Aislin until I can meet up with her.

I can't be sure if she hears me or not, but I watch her turn Belle around and dash off. The sun will be setting soon and I hope she finds safety and shelter before then. Otherwise, I fear what might be out there, waiting to grab her.

CHAPTER SEVENTEEN

. FREEDOM .

AISLIN

I'm not sure if the sting of salty tears is me crying or from the brittle wind of the sea coming ashore. This is so unfair! If only Nolan had made it, this would be a lot easier. Instead, now I face making decisions about what direction and what street I need to turn down to get out of this stupid town. The clang of metal on the cobblestone rings in my ears, making me deaf to everything else but the ringing of horseshoes against stone.

I rein back Belle, trying to acclimate myself to the new surroundings. It is a bustling town with people moving about in every direction. I have no choice but to blend in and move along with the traffic.

I urge Belle forward, weaving in and out of the crowd, trying to stay unnoticed. My eyes dart around, scanning for any signs of danger. I know I have to get out of town as fast as possible, and so I push through, trying to make my way out of the city and back to the forest.

The sound of Belle's hoofbeats echo through the trees. The leaves rustle softly, and I take in the serene surroundings, finally able to breathe and relax. We stay off of the main roads and avoid towns, trying to keep a low profile. The idea of being spotted by anyone associated with Lavinia and having them report me to her sends shivers down my spine.

We press on, navigating the twists and turns of the woodland paths. Every now and then, I catch a glimpse of wildlife; deer, squirrels, and even a fox once. The journey is longer than I thought it would be, and Belle is getting tired. The terrain is rough, and the path is narrow, so I slow Belle down and we take our time. I hear my heart pounding in my chest as we trudge along and watch Belle's ear swivel, listening for any danger that might try to sneak up on us.

It is nerve-racking, navigating without Nolan. I should have been involved more. Especially because, for the most part, I am guessing which way to head, based on the sun. And what little knowledge I am able to recall from my childhood, having studied my father's globes and maps, I am using now. But directional application is not something I am even remotely good at.

Traveling by myself, I am beginning to have Nolan withdrawals. But I won't let him know that. It may be I am just lonely for company. His company.... Oh, shut up. I tell myself, remembering those thirteen years I spent alone after my parents disappeared after the war and I got along just fine by myself. But it makes it that much harder for me to even admit to myself that I miss Nolan. I told Nolan and tried to convince myself that this journey is just business. And yet, I can't get the kiss we shared out of my head.

Nolan suddenly is thrown against me as the ship comes to a halt at the dock. He is so close; I can feel his warm breath on me.

As our eyes lock on each other, my heart leaps into my throat. All I can think about is, don't do this, Nolan. Don't do this. But as he leans in and presses his lips against mine, everything fades away and I am lost in his kiss.

I never expected to feel this way. My heart races, my nerves tingle, and I can hardly breathe. Nolan's lips on mine are sending shockwaves through every part of my body, and I can't believe how good it feels.

At first, his kiss is gentle. But then Nolan's body presses against mine, and our mouths move together in perfect harmony. I can feel his hands on my waist, his fingers gripping me tightly.

As our kiss deepens, I find myself responding to him. My hands are on his shoulders, anchoring him to me as I let myself get lost in the moment. This passion, this connection, it's unlike anything I've ever experienced before.

When we finally pull apart, gasping for breath, I can hardly believe what's just happened. But as I look into Nolan's eyes, mixed feelings stir within me. What will happen now?

Belle whinnies for my attention, and I lean over to scratch between her ears. The scary part is that without him, I am just all-around lost.

Pathetic, I sigh as Belle continues to pick her way through the forest.

It has been a nice and quiet day, with a throng of songbirds to fill the empty space that would have surely drowned me in my own loneliness. For the most part, I sit quietly, but interject every once in a while. At this point, I'm not even sure if I will make it to meet Aeneas. How is Nolan going to find us if I am lost?

Our path is slowly becoming lost with night approaching. The thick forest canopy is making it harder and harder to continue with travel, let alone find a decently safe place to bed down for the night. The hooting of owls startles Belle and me, bringing me to the cognizance that we are not the only living things lurking at this time of night.

Finally, after hours of traveling, we arrive at the entrance to the national park. I'm relieved to see the welcome sign for the national park. I push Belle forward, excited, as we make our way towards the entrance. But just as we are entering the park, I hear a voice calling out to me.

"Hey, there!"

I turn Belle around and see a kind-looking old man beckoning me over. I hesitate for a moment, then make my way towards him.

"Are you lost?" he asks, concern etched across his face.

I nod my head, unable to speak. I am so relieved to find someone who will help me.

"Well, I have a bed-and-breakfast not too far from here. You are more than welcome to rest for the night. It's not safe to be out here on your own," he says, his voice gentle and soothing.

I feel the weight of the world lifting off my shoulders. I know I have taken a huge risk getting here, but now I feel like I have made it.

"Thank you. Thank you so much," I manage to say, as tears stream down my face, the events of the day finally catching up to me.

He smiles at me kindly before leading me towards his home. Finally, I can rest and gather my strength before continuing my journey to find Aeneas.

. GWENORE & THE WHITE STAG .
AISLIN

"**A**islin, my dear. Wake up."

"Just a little bit longer mom. It's too early." I moan, rolling over to my other side, not even bothering to open my eyes.

"Aislin, it's time to wake up. You have a long journey ahead of you and you are going in the wrong direction. Come on, get up."

Gentle fingers caress my jaw and lift my head so our eyes would meet. Fluttering them open, slowly, I look upon a golden, bronzed face. Definitely not my mom. The beholder's eyes are the color of rich, earthy soil. Her glossy hair mimics the color of her eyes, but is neatly piled high atop her head. Not a strand of hair is out of place. Her facial features are strong but feminine. High cheek bones, narrow jaw, slender nose, and a short-forehead.

Taken aback, my feet quickly find solid ground beneath them. I'm not even near the height of her shoulder. The exquisite form of a lady who stands before should not even exist. I have to look away for a moment to readjust my eyes. Too beautiful to even glance at, I work hard not to gape at her. Where had she come from? I glance about, expecting to see the room I fell asleep in, but I am surrounded by soft, fluffy clouds.

"Who are you and where I am?" I demand, glaring at the bronzed goddess.

"And how do you know my name and about my journey?" I add, terrified that she holds such powerful information.

Her slender smile is soft and gentle. Normally, I would have expected some wrinkles to form next to her eyes, but they never appeared. That is strange.

"I am Gwenore, a friend of Destiny's. And currently you are still asleep in your bed in the inn. I have come to help redirect your path. As you are heading in the wrong direction." Her slender smile is gentle, matching her smooth voice.

"Yeah, you mentioned that earlier.... Are you even real?" I ask, raising a brow, more skeptical than interested in the answer.

A songbird laugh escapes her earthy lips. "Yes, dear. I am real."

"Then how come I am dreaming?" My inquiry is more spoken to myself, but somehow manages to slip from my parted lips.

"Technically, we are in your subconscious. I am not close enough to visit you in person, Aislin. This is the best I can do." She answers me.

Hmph. Crossing my arms, I pout like a little toddler.

Wait a second. Did she mention she's a friend of

Destiny's? I feel my eyes widen in hope and disbelief. Maybe I don't need to find Aeneas any more. Maybe I never had to! If she is Destiny's friend, maybe she can help. Maybe she can answer my questions. I eye her suspiciously for a moment, trying to figure her out before going all haywire on her.

"A friend of Destiny's? Where is she? Who is she? Why does she need me to find her? Why can't she come and find me? How do you know her? Why are you here? ..." Before I can say anything more, I am silenced by her hand. I try to continue rambling off my questions, but nothing comes out.

This time her gentle laugh is irritating, as I am sure she must have found my explosion of insecurities cute. Not so much. I want answers and I want them now. Not tomorrow, or in a few months. I have been through enough traumatic events these past few weeks to last me the rest of my life. I don't need any more.

"Yes, I am a friend of Destiny's. But I am sorry I cannot answer your questions..." I stop her, interjecting as I find she has let her guard down.

"Why not?" Even to me, my tone is more forceful than I intend it to be.

"Because time is precious and sparse, with no time to be telling stories..."

"They aren't stories I am asking. They are questions with simple answers." I interrupt her again. She is frustrating. And a pain in my butt.

Pausing for a moment, she smiles at me, while glancing over me, before continuing on. "Destiny will answer all your questions. I am not in the position to do so, my dear." She tries searching out my eyes, the windows to my soul, but I look away, more focused at jabbing the toe of my boot into the ground.

"Why not?" I ask again.

"Because it is not as simple as answering just questions without context and explanation." She answers in a hushed tone. Almost like the answer itself is heavier than the weight of the world.

"Well, you got the time thing right, anyway. But I don't know how much time I have left before my time runs out. Do you even know what I have been through?" I ask her, finally glancing up to look at her, only to catch her still staring at me. She shakes her head. "Enough life-threatening events to last me to my grave. And even maybe into the next life, if there is even such a thing." Her eyes darken to a depthless, dark abyss.

"Now is not the time for this or answering your questions, Aislin. Like I said, that is Destiny's area of expertise, not mine." She is stern with me and I sigh, disappointed. Somehow, I knew she wouldn't answer my questions.

"You have a task, Aislin Camille Burd. And that task is to find Aeneas. He is the only one who can tell you where and how to find Destiny. And your time is running thin." Her eyes become sunken with sadness. Like she is beginning to lose hope.

"Well, how do you expect me to find this old, mystery man, when my navigator and travel companion has been abducted?" I am a little frustrated, but mostly worried. For the past three weeks I have been haunted with trying to find Destiny and now I am running out of time. Rubbing my forehead in contemplation, I don't realize I am tapping my foot.

"Excuse me, companion?"

Looking up, I see her confusion.

"Nolan." I answer her. But when I see the confusion

on her face, I sigh. "He saved my life three weeks ago from a couple of ghosthounds when I escaped from some confinement center, after finding the note left in my satchel to find Destiny." I explain in one big breath.

She tsk-tsked and shook her head. Mumbling, she begins to pace in circles, flailing her arms in hysterics.

"Is there something I should know?" I don't dare move from my spot; afraid I will be hit by her unpredictably flailing hands.

Stopping suddenly, she looks at me, like she is lost. But her eyes quickly clear as she walks over to me.

"Just be careful. Something is not right." She cups my cheeks between her slender, bronzed hands and digs her gaze into mine.

Shuddering, I remember the creepy, shadowy figure and wonder if I should mention that encounter. It had been the one who had mentioned that Nolan is the only person who can even find Aeneas, in order to find Destiny. That it is Nolan who should guide me. Or at least, now that I look back on the weird encounter, that was exactly the intended implication. Sneaky.

"Well, the shadowy figure at the tavern is the one who mentioned Nolan is the only one who knows how to find this old man, Aeneas." I interject. I watch as her eyes are no longer the rich, dark earthy color they had once been, but now they are as dark as storm clouds and just as dangerous to look at.

"I must go. Watch out, Aislin. This is no place for the future..." She stops herself quite abruptly and replaces the silence with a half-hearted attempt at a smile. "This is no place for a young lady, such as yourself, with such a big task ahead of you. Keep a close eye on Nolan. If he is who

I think he is, the fates have dealt you a mighty twisty and complicated hand, my dear one. One they should have never meddled with to begin with."

"Wait! How do I get to Aeneas?" Reaching to grab her arm, our figures both began to shimmer. At my attempt to touch her, she must feel, because she stops.

"In the morning, follow the white stag. He will lead you in the right direction." And then she is gone.

I open my eyes slowly, still feeling a bit groggy from the long ride on Belle the previous day. As I sit up and look around the room, I try to remember how I ended up here. Then it came to me - the gentle old man I met at Mtirala National Park entrance invited me to stay at his quaint bed and breakfast.

I swing my legs over the side of the bed and rub my eyes, trying to rid myself of the last remnants of sleep. I can't help but feel a twinge of sadness as I remember I'm still alone on this journey. Nolan's capture weighs heavily on my mind, but I can't let it distract me from my mission. With a deep breath, I stand up and make my way to the window, taking in the stunning view of the rolling hills and serene countryside.

The old man's kindness has given me a sense of comfort I haven't felt in weeks, and I'm grateful for the momentary respite. But I know I must leave soon and continue on my journey to find Aeneas. I gather my things and head downstairs.

As I step into the kitchen, the sweet aroma of freshly brewed coffee fills my nostrils. The old man is already awake, sipping his coffee at the table.

"Good morning," he greets me warmly. "Did you sleep well?"

"I did," I reply, feeling grateful for his kindness. "Thank you so much for letting me stay here."

"It's no trouble at all," he says with a smile. "But now, enough talk - you must be starving!"

He leads me to the table where a generous spread of pastries, fruits, and eggs awaits me. I can't help but feel spoiled by his hospitality. We chat amiably as I eat, and I find myself cautiously sharing my travels with him.

The old man listens intently, and when I finish, he places a comforting hand on mine. "My dear, you have already shown great strength and bravery," his voice is full of kindness. "But do be careful. The road ahead is treacherous, and there are many dangers lurking in the shadows."

With his words in mind, I pack up my things and head out to the stables to ready Belle for our journey. Grateful for his kindness and emboldened by his encouragement, I ride out into the morning light, feeling more determined than ever to find Aeneas.

As the sun begins to rise, casting a warm golden glow over the landscape, I can feel a sense of hope blooming within me. The old man's words echo in my mind as I ride through the forest.

Suddenly, a flash of movement catches my eye, and I pull Belle to a stop. There, in the distance, I can see a white stag gracefully making its way through the trees. Then I remember my encounter with Gwenore and everything comes flooding back. I push her comment about Nolan to the back and focus on the white stag. Without hesitation, I urge Belle forward, following the stag deeper into the forest.

He is very gentle, but his pace is ground eating. Never

faulting for even a second as we travel through the windy, unmarked forest trails. The snap of twigs stung my legs, penetrating my clothes. Keeping up with him is not easy, leaving me to trust Belle with loose reins. Not my first choice. But I am not about to risk taking a wrong turn. Though the fact that I have the grandest creature in all the forest as my guide, makes things pretty good. Or at least compared to the last couple of days.

As we ride deeper into the woods, the trees begin to grow denser, the shadows darker. The air is thick with the scent of pine and earth, and I can feel my heart racing with fear. Tightening my grip on the reins, Belle tenses in response. It is pointless to try to calm her down when I'm not even calm. Coaxing her, telling her it is going to be alright, is a waste of my breath.

Jerking to a stop, Belle suddenly stops all forward motion. I don't blame her, but would have at least liked a warning. The forest is no longer navigable. Darkness has fallen and before us, strewn about, is a barren forest of dead trees. Frantically looking around, I don't see the white stag anymore. Where has he gone to?! He can't have just disappeared like that! Or could he? And even if he can, why has he deserted us? Swallowing hard, I glance back cautiously into the dead forest and try to outweigh my options.

Suddenly, a howl echoes through the trees and a cold breeze wraps itself around me. I know that howl. The howl of ghosthounds. I can faintly hear branches snapping behind me and as they close in, the earth rumbles more violently with each second that passes. I look back into the forest with its dark shadows and swallow.

I am beyond scared. And terrified doesn't even cover the half of it. More like paralyzed. Circling Belle once, in front of the foreboding forest, I find my thoughts fighting each other. What am I supposed to do?!

"Aislin! Run!!!" Gwenore's voice rings inside my head.

CHAPTER EIGHTEEN

. GHOSTHOUNDS .

AISLIN

*B*elle gallops as fast as she can through the dense forest full of upended roots and dead trees. My heart pounds in my chest as I hear the terrifying howls of ghosthounds behind me.

Their piercing silver eyes glow in the dark as they run after us, their jaws snapping and teeth gnashing. I can feel their hot breath on the back of my neck as Belle dodges and weaves through the trees, trying to lose them.

I know that if we don't get away soon, it will be too late. I remember Nolan mentioning ghosthounds are known for their incredible speed and strength, and I doubt we can outrun them for long. But Belle is a fighter, and she is determined to keep us alive. With every stride, she pushes herself harder, her strong legs carrying us deeper into the forest. The moon shines cold and bright through the trees, casting long shadows on the forest floor.

My thoughts are quickly interrupted as a ghosthound leaps over a fallen log, its sharp claws just missing Belle's hind leg, but manages to slice open mine. Sliding off from

Belle's back, I crumple to the ground.

The pain explodes through my body like wildfire, spreading from my leg to every nerve and muscle. I gasp in agony, clutching my leg. The ghosthound is still snapping and snarling, ready to pounce again, but Belle stands protectively over me. She flattens her ears against her head and bares her teeth in warning.

"Get away!" I try to shout, but my voice comes out weak and strained. I can feel blood pouring from the deep gash on my thigh, soaking through my jeans and seeping into the dirt.

The ghosthound circles us, testing our defenses, and I feel a wave of dizziness and nausea wash over me. The pain is too much to bear, and I'm losing blood fast. I can't even stand, let alone fight. I'm helpless, vulnerable, and terrified.

But then, something inside me burns and I look down at my hands as they become hotter. My telekinesis powers that had lay dormant from my last interaction with a ghosthound are igniting within me. My thoughts become clear, and I feel the energy coursing through me, ready to be unleashed.

I lift my hand, lifting the ghosthound that is circling us off its feet. It howls in anger and surprise, but I don't relent. With a flick of my wrist, the creature is thrown across the small clearing, slamming into a tree with a sickening thud. I grin triumphantly.

But there's no time to celebrate. Belle and I are still in danger, as the other ghosthounds close in fast. I turn my attention to the next one, and before it can attack, I push it back with a burst of telekinetic energy. It stumbles back, snarling, but I don't give it a chance to recover. With another flick of my wrist, it's lifted into the air and tossed away.

I'm stronger than I remember, and as the ghosthounds close in around me, I feel no fear. Lifting and throwing each one with ease, I defend myself and Belle. Finally, the last ghosthound falls to the ground, whimpering in defeat. I am just about to stand up when a familiar chuckle reaches my ears.

"Well, well, well. You have grown in power since the last time we fought. But I'm ready for you this time, Aislin."

I look up to see Adrian and freeze. I would have gladly fought off a dozen more ghosthounds than face him. My body starts to shake with fear, but I can't let Adrian win and take me back to Lavinia. I focus my thoughts on him and will my telekinetic powers to come forth.

At first, my powers seem to be failing me, but then I feel a surge of strength as I lift Adrian off the ground and throw him across the small open forest expanse. He lands with a thud, but I see him getting back up. I close my eyes and concentrate harder, willing my powers to grow stronger.

"Come on, Aislin. Is that the best you got?"

As Adrian charges towards me, I feel a sudden burst of energy and I raise my hands in front of me. A gust of wind sweeps towards him and I watch as he struggles to stay on his feet, but I keep pushing the wind towards him, hoping to knock him off balance.

Finally, he falls to the ground, but I know he's not done yet. I glance at Belle, reassuring myself that she's safe. Then, I turn to face Adrian once more. My arms start to glow with a shimmering light as I sense my powers growing stronger.

With a fierce determination, I raise my arms and push my telekinetic powers towards him with all my might. Adrian struggles against the invisible force, but I keep pushing until I see him fall to the ground.

As I stand there, panting and exhausted, I realize that my telekinetic powers have been completely depleted. But I won't let that stop me from fighting back. I know I have to protect Belle and myself. I keep my eyes fixed on Adrian as he slowly gets up, his eyes fixed on me with a triumphant glint.

He charges me, fists raised, and I quickly dodge to the side. I manage to land a hit on his shoulder, but he barely flinches. I know I can't take him on with brute force alone. So, I dodge and weave, my movements quick and fluid as I try to tire him out. When he swings, I duck and spin, landing a kick to his stomach. He staggers back, but doesn't fall.

"Just make this easier on yourself and come back with me to see Lavinia."

"I don't think so."

I have to end this quickly. I dart forward and grab a fallen branch, gripping it tightly in my hands. Adrian rushes forward, but I swing the branch with all my might, connecting with his side.

He grunts in pain, and I take the opportunity to strike again, hitting him across the back. He falls to the ground, groaning. I stand over him, breathing heavily.

That's when I see his eyes change, a fierce determination taking hold. I know I have to finish this now and raise the branch again, ready to strike the final blow. But before I can, I feel a sudden jolt of pain shoot through my body and everything goes black.

. UNLIKELY HELP .
NOLAN

I groan as I slowly come to consciousness. My head throbs from the blow that knocked me out, and my whole-body aches from being hauled around like a sack of potatoes. I gingerly raise my hand to my head and feel a lump forming.

I open my eyes, taking a moment to adjust to the dim light. My heart sinks at the realization of being locked in a dungeon cell. My hands are bound tightly behind my back as I lay on the damp stone floor. I try to sit up, but my head spins and I sink back down, feeling helpless.

Immediately, my thoughts turn to Aislin and Belle. Where are they? Were they okay? Had Lavinia caught them, too? My heart races with fear and worry for Aislin's safety. I know she's strong and capable, but she is also alone without me to help her.

I wriggle my wrists, trying to get free of the ropes that bind me. But they are too tight. I take a deep breath and close my eyes. I have to stay strong and focused. Aislin is out there somewhere, and I have to trust that she will make her way to safety, while I do everything in my power to protect her, even if it means sacrificing myself.

As I lay there, my mind racing with thoughts of Aislin and Belle, I silently vow to never give up hope and never stop searching for a way out of this dungeon.

It's just a waiting game now. Whenever they decide to come and get me. It isn't like I have a choice in the matter. And then I hear it; the clicking of shoes. Or at least I think so. The sound drifts down the stone hallway, the clicks getting closer, until they stopped.

No, don't stop! Come back! My thoughts almost turn to tears. I want out of this hellhole.

Then I see it from the corner of the room. Or a tiny ray of it; light. A very faint, and soft glow. That's probably all my eyes can handle at this point, anyway. Though the clicking of shoes has stopped, I know at least one person is on the other side of this wall. Because I didn't find a doorknob on any of the surrounding walls, I'm not sure how I even got here, let alone how I am supposed to get out.

As the glow of light grows slowly brighter, I resort to shielding my eyes. Though I want to see who is coming, the light is proving to be too blinding for my eyes to handle. Silence fills my cell. There is no creaking of a door opening, and no sound of footfalls.

It's a strange feeling, though, sensing the light fading back to black again. And the feeling I am no longer alone sends chills down my spine. They stand on the other side of the room, unmoving. Unfortunately, the way the room is designed, I can't even make out a silhouette of the body that occupies the room with me. But I don't need a silhouette to know it is her.

"How did you get in here? Aren't you afraid of not being

able to get out?" I ask, startling myself with how unprepared my voice sounded. Weak and hoarse.

"What? Not even a hi?" She mocks. I ignore her.

"Where are we?" I ask, more concerned with other matters than becoming her friend.

"It doesn't matter. I got here through the door, didn't you see...Oh sorry, that isn't very thoughtful of me." I hear the amusement in her voice.

"How do you plan on getting out of here?" I ask again. With each spoken word, I feel my voice strengthening.

"I have a guard outside waiting for my command." She answers. Her voice is smooth. Too smooth.

"Why are you here, Lavinia? What do you want from me?" My voice betrays me. I am already fed up with her being here.

"I thought you would like to know more about your dear Aislin. But if you're not interested, I can come back at another time." She coos.

The offer of her leaving me is too tempting, almost overpowering. But my curiosity and how Lavinia can possibly know anything about Aislin wins me over.

"I'm listening." I comply.

"You know, Aislin and I were..." She pauses, like she is trying to find the right words, "once best friends. Inseparable, really. We did everything together." I hear Lavinia's voice change, but I'm not sure in what way.

My lips tighten into a straight line, undecided if she is even remotely telling an inkling of truth. To say something like that, claiming to have once been the best friend of someone you now track and hunt down...something just isn't right with the story. I am about to question Lavinia when she continues with her explanation.

"That is until I learned the truth. Aislin escaped before they could question her. And I was held prisoner." Lavinia pauses, probably more for suspense or drama, and it's working.

The wheels inside my head are churning like a rusty car needing to be oiled. When I rescued Aislin from the ghosthounds that night in the field, it was a little suspicious. But knowing what I know now, things are slowly starting to come together, one piece at a time.

"Learning the truth, they trained me to track her down. I spent years tracking and hunting her. She is good, Nolan. If she doesn't want to be found, she won't be. That is, until three weeks ago, when one of my men happened to cross paths with her at a bar."

Again, Lavinia pauses. But this time, it's different. It isn't a pause for effect. I can actually feel her reliving a moment.

"Nolan, you have to know, all those years, in training, I changed. Knowing the truth about her, I can't pretend that I didn't know things. Plus, they had me go under reconstruction. I look nothing like I once did. But when Adrian came back with her, feelings for her I thought I lost came flooding back..."

I mumble under my breath. Something about Lavinia's story doesn't add up, but I can't tell which part.

"Are you questioning my story?" Lavinia snaps and I back off. I want to know what happened to Aislin, and making Lavinia defensive isn't going to help me.

"Go on." My voice is submissive and shaky, which in turn seems to make Lavinia settle down a little.

"That night was unplanned. The chance of crossing paths with her was slim to none in the years I had been tracking her down. And all my men know that. So, when Adrian saw his one chance, he took it." She falls silent for a moment, and I take the time to process everything, but it's not enough. "A few days later, she escaped. But I'm sure you know that already."

I feel hot and faint with an overload of information that I can't process or know how to, even if I tried. What is true and what is missing? But my head hurts too much to think anymore.

"Get out, Lavinia. Now!" I charge her. Suddenly, my emotions rage with uncertainty. My entire world is coming to an end, collapsing before me. Upside down, everything is spinning out of control. Who do I trust?

"So be it, Nolan. Just remember, I'm not the bad guy." And with that, she disappears before I can get my hands around her fragile neck and choke the life out of her. Instead, I run clear, straight into the wall ahead of me. I pound my fists ferociously on the wall.

In the comfort of the blackness that surrounds me, I collapse to the floor and tremble with confusion and mixed feelings before passing out into a deep sleep.

I sit alone in my cell, my mind racing with what Lavinia said about Aislin. Lost in thought, I barely notice someone creeping into my cell. But it's hard to ignore a looming presence.

"Who's there?" I demand, jumping to my feet and straining my eyes to catch a glimpse of the intruder.

"It's just me," a haggard voice whispers in the shadows.

I frown, rubbing my eyes to try to make out a figure in the darkness. "Who are you? What do you want?"

"The name's Bart," the voice replies, drawing closer. "I'm a guard here, but I don't agree with what Lavinia's doing. I saw how you helped Aislin and her horse escape, and I want to help."

I glance in his direction suspiciously. I can't see his facial expression, or see anything for that matter. All I have to rely on is the tone of his voice and my instincts. "How do I know I can trust you?" I ask, trying to keep my voice low so as not to alert any other guards nearby.

Bart lets out a sigh. "I don't blame you for being cautious, but you don't have many options right now. You're stuck in this cell and Lavinia won't let anyone else near you."

He pauses for a moment before continuing. "Look, I don't have much time. I can get you out of here, but you need to act fast. I can give you a key to your cell," Bart offers, "and if you can get free, I can sneak you out of the castle and show you where Lady and your things are being kept. From there, you can sneak out of the castle, find Aislin, and make a run for it. What do you say?"

I can feel my heart pounding against my chest as I weigh my options. Do I trust this guard who has suddenly appeared out of nowhere? Or do I stay put and hope for another opportunity to escape?

"But won't you get caught and punished?" I ask, suddenly feeling guilty about putting this stranger in danger.

"I'm willing to take that risk," he says resolutely. "I can't stand by and watch innocent people suffer at the hands of tyranny. Let's get you out of here."

My heart speeds up with anticipation as he slips a key into my hand, barely visible in the dimness. "Thank you," I whisper, feeling a sense of hope and determination that I hadn't felt in a long time. "Let's do this."

Bart nods back, his voice relieved. "Good. I'll have to wait a bit for the other guards to change shifts, but once they do, I'll come back and get you out of here." He turns to leave, but then stops. "One more thing you should probably know."

"What's that?" I ask, wondering if I should be concerned or not.

"I overheard Lavinia mention that she had a tracking device implanted into Aislin."

"BART!" Came Lavinia's voice down the dungeon corridor.

"Coming!" He quickly replies heading out the door.

"Bart, wait!" I try to stop him, but he's too fast. I rub my temples at this new information. Aislin having a tracking device implanted would explain a lot.

But where... And then it hits me.

Her wound I healed.

CHAPTER NINETEEN

. A DREAM .
AISLIN

It hurts to move. The muscles in my legs are useless, incapacitated from something I can't remember. My head throbs. The agonizing pounding in my head is my poor blood vessels threatening to erupt.

I am so exhausted; I feel like I'm not even part of my body. Like I am looking down on myself. But only darkness surrounds me. I'm not even going to bother opening my eyes. What's the point? It's too painful. Everything aches as I start to feel myself blackout again.

"Aislin, I need you to go to your room, please. Hurry up."

I head upstairs with my mum right behind me. She's been acting strange lately. The past couple of days have been weird, but Papa keeps telling me she is okay. But I don't believe him. He doesn't know mum and I share this special connection. It's kind of strange. I suppose he suspects something because we all know he isn't my real father. Mum won't tell me who my real Papa is because she says it's complicated.

Today, when I woke up, the sun wasn't shining like it always did. Every morning, since I can remember, the sun would peek through my window and warm my face. It would light up my entire bedroom in its magical golden glow.

But, instead, I woke up to dark clouds and heavy, thick smoke outside my window. Mum doesn't even try to make me feel better.

"It's just a huge forest fire, sweetie. That's why the sun is not shining today."

But we both know she is lying.

"It will clear up, baby. You'll see. Then, we can go outside and play. Promise." Her eyes are sad, but she tries to smile as she brushes my hair back.

"But what if it doesn't, mummy?" I ask, searching for any reassurance that I am wrong and she is right. But the gloom that paints her face does not wash off. And for the first time, I am scared.

"Then you stay in your room until I come to get you. Okay, baby girl?" She cups my face with her soft, gentle hands. She stares long and hard at me and she knows that I know she isn't telling me something. But I don't pester her, because I am a good little girl. Even though I just turned ten today. September twenty-first.

I nodded in acknowledgment. But before I can give her a kiss or a hug, I hear the downstairs doorbell, then someone knocking on it. I watch my mum's face go pale as her gaze travels from the hallway, back to me. Quickly pulling me close, she kisses my forehead and then the top of my head. Butterflies swarm my insides.

"I'm scared mummy. What's going on?" I ask.

"Stay here, baby girl. Remember what we practiced. I love you, baby girl. I'm so sorry." And then she shuts the door and locks it.

I stay still, staring at my door, waiting for her to come back and get me. Just like she promised. But the seconds pass by, feeling like hours. I listen as I hear Mum and Papa talk, then the door opens.

Though the door is new, there is still a faint creak as it opens.

Sitting down on my bedroom floor, I remain silent. Whoever is knocking on the door is quiet. All I can hear is the mumbling of a conversation. It doesn't matter how quiet I am being.

So intrigued by what is being discussed downstairs, I don't feel the change in my room, or the breeze that rattles my window open. The commotion downstairs is now an uproar. They are mad and angry at something.

"Where is she, Georgina? We had a deal. Remember?" The voice is low and deep. Demanding. It makes me scoot back until I am resting up against my bed. Bringing my knees to my chest, it's clear they are looking for me.

"She's visiting her grandparents," Mum replies. If I were able to see Mum's face, I know it would have been very believable. Then I hear a loud clap and Mum moans.

"Keep your hands off her, you filthy, political tyrant." Papa's voice is different. I don't recognize it, but I feel the hatred and dislike of each word he speaks. It makes me shiver.

"Her grandparents are dead, Georgina. We burned their house down after a thorough inspection. Now, I am going to ask again, where is she?" The voice completely ignores Papa.

I hear Mum's cry of disbelief. I know she is crying because I feel it and taste my own tears wash down my cheeks. A couple of them even stop on my lips. It takes everything to keep quiet and not sob. I want to, though. I want to run to Mum and hug her and cry with her.

"She's not here," Mum replies again. Mum is brave. I always looked up to her. I want to be like her when I grow up. Fearless.

"We'll see about that. Take her with, leave him here. You two stay with him and don't let him out of your sight." The demanding voice says, giving orders, as he must have been the one in charge.

"You're coming with me and we are going to play hide-and-seek."

I can hear lots of footsteps on the stairs, and I begin to panic. What had Mum said? 'When I mention your grandparents, you go and hide in your secret place in the closet. Okay, pretty girl?"

Scrambling to my knees, I crawl as softly and as quickly as I can to my closet. I can't believe I missed Mum's warning. Reaching my closet, I try to open the door with my fingers, but it's stuck. Taking a quick break, I look back at my bedroom door. It is on the opposite wall of my closet door. The doorknob starts to jiggle, and I remember Mum had locked me in my bedroom.

"You are smarter than I remember, Georgina. Where is the key?" The voice asks, becoming impatient. But I don't wait for Mum's response.

Focusing hard on opening my closet door, I finally succeed. Crawling inside, I leave the door open a crack, so I can see who this mean man is. The man who is threatening my mum and who wants me.

What's going to happen to me?

Mum made it quite clear that I am not supposed to come out for any reason. So, I stay put and wait, swallowing my heart back into chest a million times in the moments that pass by.

"Don't tell me you swallowed the key, Georgina." Came the scary voice.

Mum swallowed the keys? How am I supposed to get out of my room!?

"Fine, Georgina. You've left me no choice." He threatens.

I hear gunshots and then cracking of splintered wood from my bedroom door. Covering my mouth to keep from screaming, I can't hold back the tears. Blinded by my tears, I quickly scoot back until my back is up against my closet wall. I am so scared, but I want to *see this man and my mum one more time.*

He is very tall and has dark hair and a dark beard. I can't see his eyes because of his sunglasses, but he is wearing black slacks, or at least that is what Mum calls them, and they cover the top of his black boots. His black shirt is tight. Mum would have told me he would rip it if it were anymore tighter. But if there are two things I will always remember, one is his tattoo on his neck and the second is his leather jacket that hides half of his tattoo.

Squinting my eyes, I try desperately to make out his tattoo. Whoever he is, he is going to pay when I get older. I swear it. No one messes with my mum. I can't quite make out the full tattoo, but what I do see is three jagged lines. There is writing under it, but it is tiny.

Frustration and anger set in and I can feel my body heat up, but I stay put. I need to see Mum one more time, knowing they were going to take her away from me. I'm not dumb, but it still hurts knowing what is about to come.

"Well, where is she, Georgina? We are on a strict time frame." He chides. I watch him shove Mum forward and quickly cover my mouth. Her right cheek is completely black and blue. But there is something brave and strong in her eyes.

Mum isn't easily fooled, either. She spots me like a black dot on a white sheet of paper. She knows me and I knew it. Her gaze quickly finds mine through the tiny crack in my closet door. She glares at me. I feel her eyes burn inside me and I can feel her say 'GO!' Before I move toward my secret place, I mouth, 'I love you.' And for a short moment, I feel her eyes smile at me.

"She's not here. I told you that, Kieran. You'll never find her so long as I live." Mum is jerked out of my sight. It all happens too quickly. There's a loud crack before I watch my mum fall to the floor. Blood oozes from her eye onto the carpet.

"MUM!"

I can't help it and I don't regret it as the word comes flying out of my mouth. I'm not prepared for the bad man who reaches his mean fingers around my door and throws it open, tearing a hole into the wall.

"Ahhhhhhh!"

As I scream, the bad guy cringes and covers his ears. Not wasting any time, I quickly crawl over to the closet wall and swing open the secret door. I crawl inside and turn around to shut the door, only to see him knock his head on the edge of the door, cursing under his breath. The impact of the man's head against the door sends it flying back as it shuts itself. I watch as the light filtering into my closet fades fast.

Hitting the lock switch fast, I hear the bolt latch into place. I sit there, silent. Thankful that Mum and Papa had me do these drills once a week.

I can't move. Mum and Papa told me I would be safe here. That nothing could get me. But I hear him pounding. He is beating on the walls and it sounds like my heart pounding against my chest. They are pounding together; His fists and my heart.

A moment of silence fills my ears. The deafening silence is killing me. Then, I hear it. The gunshots. But I can't be sure if Mum is still alive or.... The thought leaves me numb. My scream gets caught in my throat and I'm frozen in place. Stunned, but I am safe.

I wake up in a cold sweat as I jostle to and fro on a creaking floor. The soft thud of hooves rings in my ears. I can't remember a time since that awful day when my dreams were so vivid. It's as if I relived the whole nightmare. I shake violently at the memory, and try to convince myself that it's just a dream, and it's over now. But it's impossible to shake off the feeling of terror that grips me. I feel like I'm drowning in them as panic rises in my chest and tears stream down my face. Taking a deep breath, I try to calm down, but it's not working.

I'm not sure how long I've been out. It still seems like it is dark out, or maybe I am just in a dark room. My eyes are still too heavy to open, so I try using my other senses to determine my surroundings. Though it is quite difficult to focus with all that humming and mumbling flooding my ears.

"Thank you, Aeneas. I don't know how you found us, but your timing was impeccable." The voice is soft and gentle, but I know that voice belongs to Nolan.

Aeneas? First, relief floods me. But it leaves with me with more questions.

"No worries, Nolan. Fate has a funny way of handing out surprises." Aeneas's voice is a little grouchy, but I feel a sense of calm from him.

I finally find the strength to stir, but something is restraining me. I try prying my eyes open. Forget my other senses. I want to know where I am and I want answers. Opening my mouth proves useless, as no sound escapes my lips. One last attempt at trying to get Nolan's attention, and I bump my leg into something hard.

"Gah!!!!" I squeal as my leg throbs with excruciating pain.

"She's awake!" Nolan's voice breaks through my screaming. It sounds like it is coming from behind me.

"Well, it's about time. Be careful with her. Just remove the blindfold. Let her come to and calm down first." He says, as if I am a wild horse that needs taming. I try to snort but end up coughing a lung full of mucus instead.

Gentle hands lift my head and I feel fingers untying something. The cloth that was tied around my head, slips away. So that's why I can't see…. Slowly, I try opening my eyes again and am immediately blinded by the bright sun's rays.

After adjusting to the daylight, my eyes make out the back of a wagon and I hear a couple of horses snort. I barely make out the silhouette of Lady and Belle trailing the wagon with the sun high above in the sky. Being in the back of a wagon explains all the jostling about. There is one blanket beneath me and sadly, it's not enough of a cushion against the hardwood.

"Where am I?" Comes my raspy voice.

. AENEAS .

NOLAN

The wagon creaks and jostles over tree roots and fights against the potholes covering the forest path. The sun peeks through the leaves and songbirds fill the silence. But no matter the distractions, my gaze remains on Aislin. I don't know how to answer her or where to even begin. So many things have happened since I last saw her, and everything blends together.

"We are about an hour from Aeneas's home, and then I can answer your questions. But you should really rest right now." I gently advise.

"More like a little place of heaven, if you ask me." Aeneas remarks under his breath.

I roll my eyes at the old man's comment and half-heartedly smile at Aislin and ask, "how are you doing? Are you okay?" They are simple questions, with heavy answers. Even I know that.

"My leg hurts... What happened?" She looks up at me from her position on the wagon floor.

"You were attacked by a group of ghosthounds and…"

"…Adrian." She interrupts, seeming to remember.

"Yeah. I was able to find you before he brought you back to Lavinia."

"But how?" She scrunches her nose and slight wrinkles form on her forehead.

I sigh and comb my fingers through my hair. How do I tell her a tracking device had been implanted where her wound was?

"What?" She persists.

"Lavinia had a tracking device implanted in your side."

Aislin reaches for her side where a fresh bandage wraps around her ribcage. I can see she wants to say something, but nothing leaves her lips.

"I'm not dreaming, am I?" She asks instead.

Perplexed by her question, I shake my head, not quite understanding the question.

"No. You are not dreaming." I answer, raising an eyebrow.

"Then what are you doing here?" She questions me. Her voice is soft and weak.

"That is a long story. One I would be happy to tell you, just not right now." I say, trying to avoid this conversation.

"Why?"

"Oh, just tell her, Nolan. We have a ways yet before we reach my humble abode." Aeneas butts in, and I clench my teeth tight, but give in.

"I escaped with some help from Bart. He is also the

one who helped me locate you using your tracker." I smile, hoping to avoid the longer version of the story for when she is feeling better. I have a lot of questions I would like to ask Aislin myself.

She nods thoughtfully before holding up her hands. "Why are my hands tied together?"

I let out a soft whistle and comb my fingers through my hair. She stares at me, hesitancy in her eyes. Keeping my head low and averting my gaze, I focus on untying her hands. There is a lack of trust I feel from her.

"It was a precaution," I answer, referring to her hands being tied.

"Why?" She asks softly. Something is bothering her, and I wish I knew how to ask her what is wrong without making it look like I am prying.

I stop what I am doing and look up to face her. Her crystallizing blue eyes send a sharp tingling sensation down my spine. I don't believe I will ever become accustomed to those eyes.

"You must have been dreaming because you were thrashing around. Pretty violently, I might add." I answer her.

"Oh." Her eyes flicker only for a second. But I see it; fear.

Fear of what? I wonder.

"I didn't say anything, did I?" It takes her a moment to gather the words. Whatever she is trying to hide, I hope it's nothing I should be concerned about.

"No, you didn't. Just a lot of whimpering, some tears, and an abundance of thrashing." My tone is soft as I am still uncertain how to determine what is going on inside that head of hers.

"You're sure?" It is more confirmation to herself. I can hear it in her voice. But it's still directed as a question.

"Aislin, you didn't say anything. Is there something you would like to tell me?" I ask, finally able to get the question out. But all the hoping and wishing in the world wouldn't have changed her answer....

"No."

"Okay," I said. There is a short pause as the wagon falls into a large pothole, unseating us all.

"Are you sure?" I question, watching her begin to tremble and start to fidget with her hands.

"Yes. Now please stop asking." She avoids eye contact, and I stop asking her questions.

Not another word is spoken as we continue down the pothole covered path. There is a heaviness that settles above us all, and it feels like time is just standing still. I am so exhausted by our travels and wonder how Aislin is hanging in there.

"Are we there yet? I don't know how much longer I can go on sitting in this wagon." There is too much tension, making the wagon feel overcrowded.

With a sudden, jarring halt, the wagon comes to a stop.

"Go on, get out." He motions to me. I look at him like he's insane.

"You want me to walk the rest of the way? I don't even know where you live." I reply, dumbfounded.

Aeneas smirks behind his long, grey beard as he hops down from his perch and unties the horses.

I glance around, taking in our surroundings. The only concern I have, is what lays before us; nothing but thousand-year-old trees, covered in thick layers of moss. But nowhere do I see any sign of human residence. I can feel my nerves begin to twitch.

Glancing back at Aislin, the confusion on her face sums up how I feel; lost and hopeless.

"Is this some kind of joke?" I ask, a little agitated.

Aeneas eyes me for a moment, before he answers, "when do I ever joke, Nolan?"

I feel myself balk at the question and just about to comment back when he treads over to a tree.

"Come on, we have work and things to discuss before your departure. And don't worry about the horses. They are safe and free to roam these parts of the woods." Aeneas pushes a knot in the tree and a hidden door swings open.

Aislin and I are awestruck.

"Come on, you two, we don't have all the time in the world. Not if you are to meet with Destiny." He waves us to follow him as he disappears inside the tree.

Aislin and I hesitantly walk toward the tree, our strides in sync. I am silent for a moment, before leaning over to whisper, "have you ever seen an underground home before?"

She snorts, leaving me with a mixed message. Unsure how to process what her snort means; I proceed with my next question with caution.

"Is that a yes you have, or a no, you have not?" I keep my tone neutral.

"Of course, I have. I just didn't expect it out of him." She says, directing a pointed finger in Aeneas's direction.

"Well, that makes two of us..." I say, thinking of all the times living with him, not once did my brother and I live in an underground home with Aeneas.

"Where did you see an underground home?" I ask, genuinely curious. I avoid meeting her gaze, still shy from her last response, and keep my eyes straight ahead.

"I lived in one." Her matter-of-fact tone stops me in my tracks, but she keeps moving towards the tree, undisturbed. But it kind of makes sense now, looking back on how she reacted back at the tavern. I don't know why, but in the weeks we have traveled together, I never pegged her for someone to live in an underground home. But it makes sense now.

We stop at the wooden door where Aeneas entered the tree, and peek our heads inside. Suddenly, I feel like Alice in Wonderland. Had he really disappeared down inside the tree?

"Aren't you going to go?" Aislin asks, looking at me.

"Ladies first." I counter, looking at her. I am met with a shrug.

"Okay." She says, taking the first step inside the trunk.

It only takes me a moment to realize what a jerk I am being. Rubbing my temples, I grab Aislin's arm before she takes another step inside the tree.

"Wait, I will go first." I say, moving in front of her. I feel the tension around her relax. Her lips firmly press together as she nods, but that is the extent of her reply. Taking hold of her hand, I attempt to do my best leading her down the root entwined staircase.

The tree's roots are thick and gnarly, twisting and turning to form intricate steps spiraling down underground. Tiny green budding leaves peek out from between the roots and sway gently in the breeze, making the staircase a living, breathing organism. As we descend, the roots gradually grow thicker, creating a cozy and cocoon-like atmosphere, while sunlight penetrates the trunk and filters down from above, dappling the staircase with patches of light.

All I can think about is how thankful I am to have some assurance of solidness beneath me, instead of tumbling down some dark hole and not knowing where I am going to end up.

"I feel like Alice in Wonderland." Aislin's voice echoes in the stairwell.

"Funny you say that. That's what I was thinking." I know we are coming to the bottom of the staircase because of the soft glowing light that lights the rest of our path.

"Really?" The suspicion in her voice tells me she is expecting my answer to be some kind of joke.

"Yeah. No joke. I thought it the moment I saw the hole in the trunk." I answer.

"Watch your step," I add, as we reach solid ground.

"Thank you," Aislin says, quickly turning her head to avoid looking at me, but I see a little flushing in her cheeks.

"You're welcome," I reply.

At the bottom of the staircase, we enter a small underground home, filled with the soft glow of lamps made from tree bark. The walls are made of smooth tree roots, creating a rustic and natural feeling, and the space is filled with comfortable furniture made from natural elements. The room is spellbinding, and in the middle of the room stands Aeneas.

"Come on, you two. We are wasting precious time." Aeneas's voice echoes, as he sits on a moss-covered pedestal made from a boulder.

CHAPTER TWENTY

. UNANSWERED QUESTIONS .
NOLAN

*A*eneas is surrounded by floating lights. They are lights…. *Right?*

Wait.

Are those fireflies?

Yes! Aeneas had fireflies in his home. Not believing it, I reach out my hand and watch as one lands on my finger. I am in awe.

Aislin's breath is warm against my forearm as I watch her lean over to study the firefly more closely. The firefly remains glowing on my finger, undisturbed by Aislin and her curiosity. So intrigued by the one on my finger, she is unaware of one that lands on her hair, followed by a few more adorning her hair.

"They're sure fond of you, Aislin." Comes Aeneas's voice as he moves closer to the entrance, where Aislin and I stand.

"What?" She looks at me, before catching sight of a soft glow in her hair, out of the corner of her eye.

"The fireflies. Some have found a resting place in your hair. Take a look." Aeneas says stepping aside to reveal a full-length mirror.

"Oh!" The soft-spoken word is only a whisper, as Aislin carefully straightens, captivated by the reflection of her glowing hair.

"It suits you." The words tumble from my mouth with little resistance.

Aeneas raises a grey, bushy brow in my direction, but there is no way I can deny what I had just said out loud. My only saving grace is Aislin's absorption with her reflection, much to my ego's sake, to notice my flaming cheeks of embarrassment.

"Why are they nesting in my hair?" Aislin's sweet voice is captivating, just like she is.

"Because you are special, Aislin, and don't forget that. Now, come, we have much to discuss." Aeneas turns around and heads down another tunnel. Or is it still considered a hallway being an underground home and all?

It takes a moment for Aislin to break away from the mirror, intrigued by the glowing fireflies in her hair. I don't blame her, as I am still staring at them myself. The fireflies make Aislin's presence seem like royalty. But royalty went the way of the dinosaurs, along with the English monarchy when the war started.

We follow Aeneas through the tunnel where the walls are alive with the gentle glow of pulsing lichen, lighting the way for us. I take a deep breath of the clean and sweet air, smelling strongly of earth and sap.

We finally enter the main room, lit by candles and a few moss cushions resting on the dirt floor. In the center of the room, a fireplace made of gathered stones glows with warmth. I didn't realize how much cooler it is underground until now.

I walk past a moss cushion that looks extremely comfortable and watch as Aislin sits gracefully. I pick a cushion of ferns and sit, watching Aeneas as he picks the last cushion and joins us. He is somber, which makes me wonder what this is truly about.

"Nolan, I think Aislin needs to hear your experience while being held captive. It may help her make some connections, so she may better explain to us her experiences these past couple of days. It will also be a refresher for me, which I may need as well." Aeneas's voice is steady but heavy. The graveness in his voice is not something that makes me feel safe.

I glance at Aislin, and she eyes me. I can't read her thoughts or her emotions, which makes me uncomfortable to the point of fidgeting in my seat. Not sure where to start, I'm not even sure she is ready to hear about my experience or what I learned from Lavinia.

"Well, after you escaped, they covered my head and where they kept me in a dungeon cell, in her castle, for a couple of days..."

"...And that's when Bart showed up and helped me escape."

I finally finish sharing my experience of the last couple of days being held captive in Lavinia's dungeon. I watch Aislin take it all in, but I see it in her eyes, the rejection.

"But why would she say that? Manipulate you into thinking her and I were once best friends. That doesn't even make any sense." Tears stream down her face and all I want to do is hug her.

"I don't know, Aislin. I'm just telling you about my experience." My shoulders sag as I release a heavy sigh.

She nods, trying to control her sobbing. "So, how did you and Aeneas find me, then?" She asks, still trying to catch her breath.

"Well, I found you first, with the help of Bart locating your tracking device." I mention, hesitantly, not sure how she is going to respond.

"And you got it out? The tracking device?"

I nod my head.

"And that's what my wound was all about in the first place?"

"I believe so."

She looks down at the ground, silent. Suddenly the room feels void. Like the three of us were physically in the room, but mentally and spiritually someplace else. Aeneas has been quiet for some time, and I glance over to see if he is still with us. He seems off in another world too, contemplating things.

"Aeneas?" I say boldly.

"Hmmm?" He startles from his trance and looks at me.

"What happened to my leg?" She interrupts, looks down at her leg, heavily bandaged.

"It looks like one of the ghosthounds chasing you sliced open your leg pretty good. I didn't have time to look at it because I was fighting off Adrian."

Suddenly her eyes grow wide, realization setting in. "Adrian? I remember now. I was using my powers, Nolan, to fight them off. And then I got so weak, I must have passed out."

"Yeah. When I arrived, Adrian was getting ready to leave with you over his shoulders. And then, Aeneas appeared out of the blue. Said he could sense we were near."

"Wait, powers?" Aeneas sits upright, dislodging the burgundy hood from his head. "What powers?"

"She has telekinesis powers. They are strong, but she hasn't learned to harness them yet." I explain, not sure if Aislin even knew what her powers were.

I can almost see the gears turning in Aeneas's head as he processes the information. "This is very interesting. Something I didn't foresee."

"What do you mean, you didn't foresee it?" It's Aislin's turn to sit up straight, suddenly interested in what Aeneas has to say.

Aeneas sighs and rubs his temples. "That is another conversation for another time."

"Why? I am sick and tired of people not answering my questions!" Aislin bolts upright, and I can almost see steam billowing from her ears.

"SILENCE!" Suddenly, Aeneas's voice shakes the entire room and his crystal blue eyes blaze. Dirt from the ceiling starts to crumble away, hitting the floor. Aislin is shaking, but sits down and scoots closer to me.

"Aislin, I know you have a lot of questions. But some questions cannot just merely be answered. They need context. And some context I cannot give you, so therefore, some questions I cannot answer for you right now."

"It's getting late. Let's head to bed and talk some more tomorrow morning. Nolan, take a right out of the room and follow the tunnel to the end. Your room is on the left. Aislin, follow me."

I give Aislin's shoulders a light squeeze before getting up and heading to my bedroom. It's going to a be a long night of no sleep as I ponder the last couple of day's events. I wonder what Aeneas has in store for us tomorrow.

. A BEDTIME STORY .

AISLIN

*G*lowing crystal formations that adorn the walls light the path for us as the rich burgundy fabric of his cloak sways majestically as he walks, leading me through the tunnel towards my bedroom I can't help but marvel at the intricacy of his underground treehouse. Woven vines form the tunnel walls and a sweet fragrance fills the air from the flowers the grow on the walls.

He walks silently beside me; his footsteps barely audible on the soft earth beneath us. He carries a lantern in his hand, casting a warm glow over our surroundings. I feel safe with him beside me, his calm presence reassuring me in this time of uncertainty.

"Have you ever heard the tale of Psyche and Eros?" he asks, his voice melodic.

I glance over to see his age-weathered face light up. I shake my head, but am fascinated already by the eagerness in his voice.

"Psyche was the most beautiful woman in the world,

but unfortunately, she was also very lonely. One day, her beauty attracted the attention of Aphrodite, the goddess of love and beauty. Aphrodite became jealous of Psyche and asked her son Eros, the god of love, to make Psyche fall in love with the ugliest man in the world."

I shudder at the thought of such a terrible fate.

"However, when Eros saw Psyche, he was enchanted by her beauty and instead of shooting her with the arrow of love to make her fall in love with someone else, he accidentally hurt himself with his own bow and fell deeply in love with her."

Aeneas' story sends shivers down my spine, imagining the young girl's beautiful figure and the magical love of Eros.

"Psyche, on the other hand, was afraid of never finding love and decided to take matters into her own hands. She went to a temple to pray for a lover, and Aphrodite appeared before her, promising to give her the love she sought if she completed a series of tasks.

The tasks were nearly impossible, including sorting a mountain of mixed grains and fetching golden fleece from a dangerous river. Psyche received help from various sources, including ants, a reed, and an eagle, and eventually completed all the tasks.

However, after Psyche completed her last task, Aphrodite was still angry with her and instead of fulfilling her promise, sent her to the underworld to bring back a box of beauty cream from Persephone, the wife of Hades. Psyche was able to retrieve the cream, but became curious about what was in the box and opened it. As soon as she did, she was overcome by a deep sleep."

I can't help but feel my heart ache for Psyche. To be so

close to love and yet so far away from it must have been torture.

"Eros, who had been searching for Psyche, found her asleep and used his powers to wake her up. When they were finally reunited, Eros pleaded with Zeus to grant Psyche immortality so that they could spend eternity together. Zeus agreed, and Psyche became a goddess, living happily ever after with Eros."

I smile at the happy ending but can't help but feel a twinge of sadness. Would I ever find such a happy ending as Psyche? I don't know, but I hold on to hope that it's possible.

"Thank you for the story. But I am not sure why you chose this story."

"I am telling you the story because there is a lesson to be learned. Although Psyche and Eros were able to be together forever, it only made Aphrodite's jealously worse. Now, Aphrodite had to look upon Psyche for an eternity. Always reminded she was second to Psyche, even though she was the goddess of love and beauty."

"Okay, so what's the lesson? Am I missing something?"

Aeneas chuckles softly. "There is a prophesy that Psyche had a child with Eros and that one day, Aphrodite would align with Ares, the god of war, and wage war on humanity. And the only one who can stop this war, is the child of Psyche and Eros.

Be careful, Aislin, on your journey to find Destiny. Not everything is as it seems. Be smart and trust your instincts. Don't let your heart make the decisions for you."

Okay.... if that isn't a bit ominous.

He stops and turns to me, handing me an old, ornate key. "If you should ever find yourself in need of help, this key will direct your path to Destiny."

I nod and take the key.

As Aeneas shows me to my bed and bids me goodnight, I can't help but feel grateful for his hospitality and his tale. It gives me hope that even the most impossible love stories can have happy endings.

As we approach my temporary quarters, Aeneas stopps outside a wooden door and turns to me. "Here we are," he says, his voice low and gentle. "I hope you find everything to your liking."

I nod, smiling up at him. "It's perfect, thank you," I reply.

Aeneas gestures for me to enter the room first, holding the lantern high to illuminate the space. As I enter the room, I am instantly surrounded by nature. The walls are a mix of tree roots, vines, and dirt. A musty smell fills the air, which evokes the earthy scent of the surrounding forest. The ceiling is low, adding to the cozy atmosphere of the room.

The bedroom is sparsely furnished, with only a small bedside table and a hand-carved wooden chair in one corner. A woven basket hangs from a rogue root stretching across the ceiling, filled with wildflowers and other forest treasures.

In the center of the room, a moss and fern bed rests on a thick wooden plank. I run my hand over the soft, lush greenery and enjoy the feel of tiny fern leaves tickling my fingertips.

Taking a deep breath, I inhale the earthy scent that emanates from the bed. It smells fresh and pure, like a forest after a rainstorm. As I lay down on the bed, I feel the texture of the moss slightly compressing under my weight, yet it still remains plush and welcoming.

"I hope you will be comfortable here," Aeneas says, his voice tinged with a hint of concern.

"I'm sure I will be," I assure him, feeling grateful for his hospitality. "Thank you, Aeneas. You've been so kind to us."

He smiles at me warmly. "It's my pleasure. Now get some rest, and I'll see you in the morning."

I nod, feeling a sense of peace settle over me as Aeneas closes the door behind me. This is exactly where we need to be to find Destiny, and I am grateful for the opportunity to rest before the journey ahead.

CHAPTER TWENTY ONE

. HOPELESS .
AISLIN

When I wake, a soft, golden light bathes the room. I sit up groggily and rub my eyes, suddenly remembering where I am. As I get out of bed and stretch, I can't help but feel a sense of wonder at the magical abode that surrounds me.

I step out of the room and find Aeneas in the living area, brewing a pot of tea. "Good morning, Aislin," he says with a smile.

"Good morning, Aeneas," I reply, still feeling a bit disoriented. "What a vivid dream I had last night."

Aeneas raises an eyebrow. "Oh?"

"I dreamt of Psyche and Eros, the story you were telling me last night. It seemed so vivid, like I was actually there watching their love unfold."

Aeneas nods, pouring me a cup of tea. "Some say that the stories of the gods and goddesses are simply myths, but I believe that they are much more than that. They are tales of love, betrayal, and redemption, timeless reminders of the power of the human heart."

I take a sip of the fragrant tea, savoring the warmth that spreads through my body. As I gaze around the room, I feel more lost now than I did when I started this little escapade to find Destiny. There is one question, however, that matters more than anything to me right now. And if I don't ask it, my journey to find Destiny may have been a big, fat lie.

I trace the rim of my teacup with my finger in thought, debating on how to ask Aeneas the question. But I can't think of a graceful way to put it, so I decide to just ask. No beating around the bush. I look up to lock eyes with Aeneas. "Does Destiny even exist? A human being I can go to and talk to and see with my own two eyes?" I ask. I thought maybe he would try to trick me or draw out the answer, but he simply smiles.

"Well, I wouldn't go as far as to call her a human being. But yes, you will be able to see, touch, and talk to her. Though I can't guarantee she will be very agreeable." Aeneas answers.

"What's that supposed to mean?" Alarmed, I wonder what I just gotten myself into.

"She's peculiar and doesn't always make sense when she talks." He is thoughtful as he answers my questions.

"Is she coherent?" I ask, more skeptical now than before.

"She's more coherent than anyone I know. I would not and do not underestimate her. She will have you circling a maze if you let her." I do not take Aeneas's warning lightly and make a mental note of it. At least I know now that Destiny can answer my questions in-person. My only fear is, will she?

I am just taking a sip of my tea when the sound of footsteps catches my attention. I look up to see Nolan walking into the main living area, where Aeneas and I are sitting. It looks like he just woke up as he rubs his eyes, making his way over to us.

"Morning," he yawns, still half asleep.

"Good morning," Aeneas replies, a smile on his face. "Sleep well?"

"Yeah, I did," Nolan smiles. "What are you guys up to?"

"Just having some tea," I say, motioning to the cups on the table.

"Mind if I join you?" He asks, already reaching for a cup.

"Not at all," Aeneas says, pouring him some tea.

Nolan sits down next to me on one of the fern cushions, blowing on his tea before taking a careful sip. I can tell he is still waking up by his slow and deliberate movements. But as the warmth of the tea spreads through his body, he seems to come to life.

"You know, Nolan," I start, turning to face him. "There is one question I have been meaning to ask since yesterday, after telling me what happened to you."

Nolan raises a brow. "What's that?"

"Why would she tell you everything she did? What was her motivation in doing so? What does she have to gain from telling you all that?"

After Aeneas's story of Psyche and Eros and telling me things aren't as they always appear, it got me thinking about what Lavinia had told Nolan while being held prisoner.

"I don't know, Aislin. I wish I could tell you an answer."

"Well, you would be the first." I grumble.

"I don't know, maybe she wants someone to sympathize

with her? If what she says is true, then maybe…"

"What? Go back to her and let her interrogate me. If she truly was my best friend, she wouldn't do that."

"But she said they told her the truth…"

"About me? Yeah, what truth, Nolan? That I'm an orphan? That I was separated from my parents on the day I turned ten? Or maybe it's…." But the tears are flooding from my eyes and I can't even see anymore. Everything blurs together. One big brown blob all around me.

Like a bullet, I shoot to my feet. This is becoming too much and too painful. So much, I don't think I can handle staying in the room any longer. I feel like I am going to be sick and before either of them can stop me; I flee out of the room and make a dash for the rooted stairwell to get some much-needed fresh air. Above ground.

Like a torrential downpour, tears stream down my face. It feels like the weight of a boulder is crushing my chest. Hyperventilating, I lean over, gripping the tree's trunk while I puke up the tea I had been sipping. How can I tell them the only best friend I ever had was my mum? And *they killed* her. I hurl more acidic liquids as the picture of my mother fills my head and then the ringing of the gunshot resounds clear as a bell in my head.

Wrapping my arms around my body, I try to comfort myself. The bark from the tree is rough, as I lean against it and slide down to rest on the ground. Rocking back and forth, I continue to cry, inhaling and exhaling shaky breaths. If only I had my teddy bear to squeeze and my mum to comfort me, then everything would be okay.

I still can feel the acid gurgle in my stomach. As I stand, I can still feel the acid gurgle in my stomach, threatening to come back up. For just a few minutes, I needed to be by myself. It's almost been a year since I had an emotional break down like this and I don't want the guy's to see me so vulnerable. It is embarrassing. Humiliating.

Deciding it's probably best to rejoin the guys back underground, I make my way slowly back down the winding, rooted stairs. Tight spaces never really did agree with me, and I can feel my body constricting in protest as I continue to descend underground. Skipping a few steps to reach solid ground faster, I reappear in the main room, where Nolan and Aeneas are waiting for me, with lunch ready.

The main room has the same plush cushions as the room with the firepit, only there is no table to eat at. For how closed off Aeneas's home feels from the world above ground, it is relatively bare of any large furniture, making it seem bigger than it is and quite cozy, actually. I find myself quickly sitting comfortably, eating a bowl of porridge that Aeneas hands me.

The porridge warms and soothes me and I feel my heart beat and breathing come down. I can't quite enjoy it as flashbacks of the last day I saw my mum keeps running over and over in my head. I have to force myself to swallow the last bite before setting it down and releasing a heavy sigh. It is time to share with Nolan and Aeneas the day I lost my parents.

After reliving the worst day of my life, I feel worse, not better. In fact, vocalizing the day that has haunted me for over a decade feels like I am standing in the room, watching everything play out all over again, and not being able to do a darn thing about it. It makes me feel helpless.

I am void. It feels like when your arm or leg loses feeling, but then it comes back. Well, that dead weight sensation didn't leave. It consumes me physically, emotionally, mentally, and spiritually. I no longer feel... I feel like a zombie with nothing to offer, nothing to give, and completely and utterly useless.

"Aislin...?" A soft voice speaks up across from me, pulling me out of my trance. Looking up, I find myself gazing into soothing honey-brown eyes. They belong to Aeneas. He wears a gentle expression.

"You are special, Aislin. You have quite a gift. But only Destiny can answer all of your questions. All I know is one thing; don't lose hope or sight of who you are and you will never be alone." His words are welcomed, but I have to force a smile of thanks.

"Thanks, Aeneas, but I'm afraid that would mean much more coming from my parents," I answer him, trying to be gentle with my words, but it's the truth. My body aches so much, I feel sick. All I want to do is fall asleep and die.

"I understand. But know that your parents are very proud of you, Aislin, and they love you very much. I can't imagine what it's like losing both parents..." I cut him off, for many reasons. Two main reasons ring clear.

"How do you know anything about my parents? And no doubt you can't comprehend what it's like to lose your parents. But I can tell you the emptiness you will always feel is unbearable and haunting." I am almost on the verge of tears, but I suddenly feel rage at Aeneas for trying to show me empathy when he is failing miserably at it.

My vision is becoming cloudy as the threat of tears burn at the corners of my eyes. I watch a very blurry Aeneas get up from where he sat across the room and make his way over to me. Kneeling in front of me, the old man cups my face in one of his worn and wrinkled hands. His rough looking hand is surprisingly soft and as gentle as a newborn baby's skin. I try to look away, but he holds my gaze firmly.

"But I do know what it's like to lose a daughter..." He says those words so softly that I have a hard time focusing on what he said.

"Are you..." My face contorts, but I don't have to finish my question, as he knows what I am going to ask. He shakes his head.

"No, I am not your grandfather, Aislin. But I did take your mother under my protection when she, too, had lost her way and was pregnant with you. But that is a story for another time."

I am too mentally exhausted to argue with him now. I really want to hear the story, but I just nod.

"I'm tired. I'm going to go lay down." Getting up, I wander back to my bedroom.

"Nolan, sit and stay. Give her time." I hear Aeneas speak to Nolan and silently thank him.

I enter my room, shut the door, and fall onto the bed. Closing my eyes, I drift off to sleep.

. REVELATION .
AISLIN

"*A*islin, wake up." Says a soft voice.

Not again.

I groggily rub my eyes. I don't know how many more of these dreams I can take. But when I open my eyes, I am terrified to find myself shackled to a wall.

Oh no, oh no, oh no. How did this happen? I panic and pull hard on the chains, but they don't budge. Only clink against each other, ringing in the emptiness of the room. I glance around and see Clarice moving some things around, avoiding my gaze.

Then the door flies open, and Kieran stands in the doorway. I feel my pulse jump and my heart leap into my throat.

"Thank you, Clarice. You can go now." He says, but his

gaze rests on me. Clarice nods and quickly exits the room.

As he moves closer, nothing comes out of his mouth. I don't know what terrifies me more, his silence or the intoxicating, lustful look he is giving me. I writhe beneath the hold of the shackles as he draws closer and closer. Though he doesn't speak, I feel another spiritual presence with him.

"Come to me, Aislin. We are meant to be together." The words are not spoken but form inside my mind.

"No! Get out!" I scream, shaking my head, trying and get rid of the voice. It sends chills up and down my spine. But I feel it laugh as it lingers.

"You are mine, Aislin. No one can save you. Not your mother, not even Destiny herself."

I scream louder, pulling hard against my restraints, and feel them cut into my wrists. Looking down, I see drops of blood fall to the floor in quick succession. My screaming doesn't stop Kieran from advancing and he is soon standing in front of me. Quiet, with those lust-filled, possessed eyes. I try to look away, but his hand gently but firmly grips my face. Staring into his eyes, this is too real to be a dream.

The heat from his body radiates off of him and envelopes me. I feel like I have been mummified alive. His breath is surprisingly sweet and makes me light-headed. I can feel myself drifting off as he leans in closer and closer.

I finally give in and close my eyes. *Where is Nolan?*

Without warning, there is a sudden crack of splintering wood followed by a large crash. My eyes fly open just in time to see Kieran's lips almost connect with mine. Whipping my head in the direction of the deafening sound, I see the door splintered across the floor and Nolan standing there. His eyes are blazing in fury, fists clenched as he spots Kieran.

But it is too late. His lips graze my soft cheek, sending a burning sensation coursing through my entire body.

"Ahhh!" I fight hard, pushing against Kieran with all my strength, but it is no use. He is physically overpowering and holds me easily in place. The burning smell of skin reaches my nose and I feel tears race down my face.

"Nolan, help me!" I plead. I hear his boots echo off the stone floor as he closes in on Kieran and I. But suddenly everything is in slow motion. I watch as Nolan makes contact with Kieran's shoulder. And that's when I see it. The tattoo on Kieran's neck as it snaps to the side. Even this close up, I still can't read the text beneath the three jagged line symbol. It looks to be written in an ancient text. Now, why would he have a tattoo in an ancient dialect? I wonder as I watch the two grown men hit the floor.

Then a blinding white flash of light lights up the room and time stands still. My shackles disintegrate, but my wrists still drip blood. Scared, but too intrigued, I walk over to where Nolan and Kieran are frozen in time. Nolan is in the middle of delivering a series of blows and Kieran wears a devilish smirk, not fazed at all by Nolan's reaction.

"How…" I speak, reaching out to touch Nolan, but then think better of it and retract my hand.

"I stopped time." Comes an enchanting female voice.

"Who's there?" I spin around but see nothing.

"Don't be frightened, Aislin. You are safe now."

"I would feel safer knowing who I am talking to," I respond curtly.

"I am Destiny." I stop going around in circles like a dog chasing its tail.

"Then why not show yourself?" There is a light laugh as

I wait for an answer. I'm skeptical that this is even Destiny.

"It would be a waste of energy on my part."

"Then why are you here?" I ask.

"Saving you."

"But Nolan came and saved me. So, why are you here?"

"Ah, yes. Nolan is here because of me. And you are here because Kieran summoned you. So, here I am saving you."

"Then why stay and not leave?" Still having a difficult time accepting the voice as Destiny's, she has piqued my curiosity.

"Because I want you to know something about Nolan and Kieran." I scoff. If it is the same warning Gwenore has already shared with me, Destiny is wasting her time.

"And what's that?" I quip, a bit agitated. There is silence, and I suddenly feel a little guilty. I sigh and bite my lip before offering an apology. "I'm sorry."

"As you should be." The silence comes again and lasts a moment before I feel the room take a breath.

That's strange.

"Do you see the tattoo on Kieran's neck?"

I nod, afraid to speak, but I don't know if Destiny can see my response. Whether or not she can, she continues, "the Greek text beneath the symbol reads 'Greyson and Nolan'." And suddenly the presence of Destiny vanishes along with the room around me.

Waking up drenched in sweat, I immediately feel my cheek and am petrified to feel a massive burn mark where

Kieran had kissed me. That hadn't happened the last time I had been with him in person. I almost can't bring myself to examine my wrist, but I am too curious. Before I look down, I bring my fingers to my wrist and feel for a cut. And sure enough, there is dried blood on my wrist. I shudder at the realization that what I had just experienced was very real.

Then the realization of Kieran's tattoo floods my thoughts. *Greyson and Nolan.* Somehow, the three of them are bonded together. I hadn't seen a tattoo on Nolan, but then again, I hadn't seen him naked either. At the thought, despite my hatred for him currently, I can't stop my cheeks from flushing hot with embarrassment.

With Gwenore's warning about Nolan and Destiny's revelation of Kieran's tattoo, that left me with only one choice.

CHAPTER TWENTY TWO

. GONE .
NOLAN

"**A**ISLIN!"

Bolting upright in bed, I pat myself all over, feeling for anything unusual. But I am still in one piece.

For the love of Zeus... I rub my temples and comb my finger through my hair. That was one horrific nightmare. I stare at the wall for a minute, debating if I should go check on Aislin.

Swinging my legs over the side of the bed, I get up and quickly lean against the wall so I don't pass out. Feeling light-headed, I shut my eyes, breathe in and out, and count to ten. Feeling better, I stumble my way through the dark to Aislin's room. I raise my hand to knock on her door, but stop. It's quite on the other side. Do I really want to wake her? Sighing softly, I reassure myself that Aislin is fine. No one can reach her here. She is safe.

I turn around and head back to my room. I would talk to Aislin in the morning to see if she was okay.

Waking up without sunlight is strange and disorienting. I lay awake awhile, thinking about yesterday and last night. I could have probably handled things differently. Maybe a little more sympathetic towards Aislin instead of forcing the subject matter on her when she clearly wasn't ready.

"Nolan, breakfast is ready." Aeneas's voice carries down the hallway and filters into my room. Sighing, I slip on a new pair of pants, courtesy of Aeneas, before meeting up with him in the main room.

"I've decided to let her sleep in a little." Aeneas mentions, noting my confusion when I don't see Aislin in the room. I nod, walking over to the counter and grabbing a plate of meat, cheese, and fruit. We eat in silence for a few minutes, enjoying the solace.

"I'm going to pack and then go and get Lady and Belle ready."

Aeneas nods, as he sips thoughtfully on his morning tea. The aroma is potent, giving me a headache. Whatever he is drinking, he didn't offer any to me. I would have respectfully declined the offer. He probably knows that and doesn't bother to ask.

As I enter my room, I head to the closet and look through the clothes Aeneas had provided. There is a new bag leaning up against the wall and next to it is a new bow and a quiver full of arrows. A large smile spreads across my face.

"You shouldn't have," I say under my breath, thanking Aeneas silently.

After packing a few things, I lay back down on the bed and sort out my thoughts. My head hurts too much with everything that has happened, and I just need to think things through. This morning is no doubt going to be tension-filled between Aislin and I. Especially after sharing how she lost her parents. I guess what is really bothering me is what Aislin admitted seeing Kieran do to her mum. She hadn't mentioned anything about her dad, but one can only guess.

Getting up off the bed, it is time to get the horses ready. I grab my bag of new clothes and my new bow and quiver and head out into the tunnel. I stop by Aislin's closed door, and raise my hand to knock, but stop midway through the air. Lowering my hand, I lean my forehead against the door and softly exhale, closing my eyes.

"I'm sorry, Aislin. For yesterday. I should have been more sympathetic toward your feelings and sensitive to the situation." I wait patiently for a few minutes, in the hope that she might answer the door and accept my apology. I plan on wrapping her in a hug and telling her everything will be alright. But she never even answers me. I pinch the bridge of my nose, taking a few deep breaths, trying to buy some time. But when it is clear she isn't going to come out or even speak to me, I leave her door and slowly make my way to Aeneas's backyard.

The sunlight illuminates the forest, highlighting the vibrant greens and the few reds, golds, and blues of flowers sporadically blooming among the foliage. Birds sing merrily and fly from branch to branch, energizing the day with their presence. It doesn't take long to find Lady chowing down on the thick vegetation, enjoying the company of Aeneas's two horses. I scratch behind her ears and down her neck as I look around for Belle. But it becomes clear Belle is nowhere in sight. I start to panic.

Leaving Lady to her breakfast, I make a perimeter check. The forest is dense and Belle can't have gone too far. As I narrow down the search area, I begin to wonder what happened to her. Surely it wasn't a ghosthound.

Though rogue ghosthounds were solitary monsters and hunted alone, Lady and her companions would have alerted Aeneas and I. It is possible that Lavinia and Kieran had sent someone to retrieve Belle, but it just didn't seem likely.

The only other explanation is Belle had wandered off. *Great.* Aislin and I are supposed to leave this morning and Belle is nowhere to be found. Maybe Aeneas would allow Aislin to borrow one of his horses.

I head back underground to inform Aeneas of the slight change in plans. When I reach the main room, he is no longer there. But the humming of an old man reaches my ears, and I follow it to the room with the fire pit. He is sitting cross-legged, meditating. Silently, I join him, waiting for him to finish. I am half expecting to find Aislin here as well, but the absence of her presence leaves me wondering if she ever plans on coming out of her room.

"You will have a long journey ahead of you. It will not be easy finding Destiny." His gravelly voice is absorbed by the walls.

"I figure as much," I admit, rubbing my temples. *What luck.*

"Are the horses ready?"

I contemplate how to tell him Belle is missing. How I looked thoroughly and had still come up empty-handed. Nothing like telling it how it is, I suppose.

"Belle's gone."

There is a moment of silence. I almost think he doesn't hear me. Then, a slight sigh, followed by a dry cough, has me turning to look at him.

"I thought so." He doesn't even look at me.

"You *thought* so?" My eyes bore into him with disbelief.

What is this? Is everyone keeping secrets from me? "What's *that* supposed to mean?"

"Exactly what I said." He stands, handing me a piece of paper. "You might want to read this." Then he leaves the room. I don't recognize the handwriting until I notice Aislin's signature at the bottom.

Dear Nolan and Aeneas,

Thank you for your time trying to help me find Destiny. These past few days have given me time to think and to reevaluate the next part of my journey, which I must continue alone. Nolan, please don't follow me. Also, you are probably wondering where Belle is. I hope it's okay if I borrowed her for the rest of my journey. I know you both must have a lot of questions and someday I hope to answer them. Until then, take care.

All the best,

Aislin

P.S. I'll miss your companionship, Nolan, but I must do this alone.

I stare at the note for a while. There are too many questions running through my head. I don't know where to start. How? Why? Is it something I did or said? Is it because of yesterday? So frazzled with confusion, my head throbs.

Standing, I walk down the hallway, stopping outside of Aislin's closed door. When had she left? I wonder, pushing the door open.

"I wouldn't go in there if I were you." Echoes Aeneas's voice, but it is already too late as I step inside.

The bedsheets are strewn across the floor like a whirlwind had blown through. Walking over to the bed, being sure not to trip, I brush my fingers along where there had clearly been a lot of tossing. Did she have another nightmare? My eyebrows crease with concern. I move around to the other side and catch sight of little red blotches on the bed; blood.

My knees hit the floor hard, and I can feel them bruise. With my arms outstretched, I rest my head against the bed. My chest heaves as I breathe. I don't want to admit I feel dejected. I can't deny over the past three weeks, I hadn't developed some deep attachment to her. The sound of approaching footsteps stops outside the doorway. I look up to see Aeneas's solemn expression.

"She's gone."

. AUTHOR'S NOTE .

Please leave a review!

If you enjoyed reading *The Chronicle Keeper*, you can help spread the word and leave a review. Every review helps, no matter how big or small. Even if it is just a star rating. Your review matters.

Amazon | BookBub | Goodreads

ALSO…If you would like to stay in the loop and get updates on free new short stories, or when the next book in the Earth's Guardian series is available, please visit my website or my linktr.ee page.

authorwrenkingsley.com
linktr.ee/authorwrenkingsley

. COMING SOON .

Aislin and Nolan continue their journey to find Destiny, but when Aislin crosses paths with the stranger from the tavern, things seem to get a little more complicated. The bigger question is this: Is Aislin ready to hear what Destiny has to tell her, about what lies ahead and the truth about Nolan?

Find out in the next installment of the
Earth's Guardian Series, Book 2
The Path to Destiny

Be sure to subscribe to my newsletter for updates!

. ALSO BY WREN KINGSLEY .

EARTH'S GUARDIAN SERIES

The Chronicle Keeper ~ Book 1 (Available Now)
The Path to Destiny ~ Book 2 (*Coming Soon!*)
The Last Oracle ~ Book 3 (*TBA*)
The Queen's Amulet ~ Book 4 (*TBA*)
The Hidden Truth ~ Book 5 (*TBA*)
The Family Affair ~ Book 6 (*TBA*)
The Chosen One ~ Book 7 (*TBA*)

STANDALONE SHORT STORIES

Cinderella and the Nutcracker
(*Subscribe to Wren's Newsletter*)

. ABOUT WREN KINGSLEY .

Wren is an emerging author of the Earth's Guardian series. A mix of adventure, a little fantasy, some mythology, and a slow kindling romance. She is a single mom of two wonderful and talented children, and a dog named Dali. She loves reading, writing, watching movies, and sitting by the fire drinking hot chocolate. When she isn't busy with family affairs, she is working on writing the Earth's Guardian.

The Chronicle Keeper is Wren's first book in the Earth's Guardian series and will contain seven books.

The easiest way to follow her is to visit her linktr.ee profile where all her social links are in one place or you can visit her author website.

authorwrenkingsley.com
linktr.ee/authorwrenkingsley

www.ingramcontent.com/pod-product-compliance
Lightning Source LLC
Chambersburg PA
CBHW030918300726
48970CB00001B/220